The Ru

The Rulers of the Lakes

by Joseph A. Altsheler

Copyright © 7/16/2015
Jefferson Publication

ISBN-13: 978-1515108078

Printed in the United States of America

Contents

CHAPTER I

THE HERALDS OF PERIL

The three, the white youth, the red youth, and the white man, lay deep in the forest, watching the fire that burned on a low hill to the west, where black figures flitted now and then before the flame. They did not stir or speak for a long time, because a great horror was upon them. They had seen an army destroyed a few days before by a savage but invisible foe. They had heard continually for hours the fierce triumphant yells of the warriors and they had seen the soldiers dropping by hundreds, but the woods and thickets had hid the foe who sent forth such a rain of death.

Robert Lennox could not yet stop the quiver of his nerves when he recalled the spectacle, and Willet, the hunter, hardened though he was to war, shuddered in spite of himself at the memory of that terrible battle in the leafy wilderness. Nor was Tayoga, the young Onondaga, free from emotion when he thought of Braddock's defeat, and the blazing triumph it meant for the western tribes, the enemies of his people.

They had turned back, availing themselves of their roving commission, when they saw that the victors were not pursuing the remains of the beaten army, and now they were watching the French and Indians. Fort Duquesne was not many miles away, but the fire on the hill had been built by a party of Indians led by a Frenchman, his uniform showing when he passed between eye and flame, the warriors being naked save for the breech cloth.

"I hope it's not St. Luc," said Robert.

"Why?" asked Willet. "He was in the battle. We saw him leading on the Indian hosts."

"I know. That was fair combat, I suppose, and the French used the tools they had. The Chevalier could scarcely have been a loyal son of France if he had not fought us then, but I don't like to think of him over there by the fire, leading a band of Indians who will kill and scalp women and children as well as men along the border."

"Nor I, either, though I'm not worried about it. I can't tell who the man is, but I know it's not St. Luc. Now I see him black against the blaze, and it's not the Chevalier's figure."

Robert suddenly drew a long breath, as if he had made a surprising recognition.

"I'm not sure," he said, "but I notice a trick of movement now and then reminding me of someone. I'm thinking it's the same Auguste de Courcelles, Colonel of France, whom we met first in the northern woods and again in Quebec. There was one memorable night, as you know, Dave, when we had occasion to mark him well."

"I think you're right, Robert," said the hunter. "It looks like De Courcelles."

"I know he is right," said Tayoga, speaking for the first time. "I have been watching him whenever he passed before the fire, and I cannot mistake him."

"I wonder what he's doing here," said Robert. "He may have been in the battle, or he may have come to Duquesne a day or two later."

"I think," said Willet, "that he's getting ready to lead a band against the border, now almost defenseless."

"He is a bad man," said Tayoga. "His soul is full of wickedness and cruelty, and it should be sent to the dwelling place of the evil minded. If Great Bear and Dagaeoga say the word I will creep through the thickets and kill him."

Robert glanced at him. The Onondaga had spoken in the gentle tones of one who felt grief rather than anger. Robert knew that his heart was soft, that in ordinary life none was kinder than Tayoga. And yet he was and always would be an Indian. De Courcelles had a bad mind, and he was also a danger that should be removed. Then why not remove him?

"No, Tayoga," said Willet. "We can't let you risk yourself that way. But we might go a little closer without any great danger. Ah, do you see that new figure passing before the blaze?"

"Tandakora!" exclaimed the white youth and the red youth together.

"Nobody who knows him could mistake him, even at this distance. I think he must be the biggest Indian in all the world."

"But a bullet would bring him crashing to earth as quickly as any other," said the Onondaga.

"Aye, so it would, Tayoga, but his time hasn't come yet, though it will come, and may we be present when your Manitou deals with him as he deserves. Suppose we curve to the right through these thick bushes, and from the slope there I think we can get a much better view of the band."

They advanced softly upon rising ground, and being able to approach two or three hundred yards, saw quite clearly all those around the fire. The white man was in truth De Courcelles, and the gigantic Indian, although there could have been no mistake about him, was Tandakora, the Ojibway. The warriors, about thirty in number, were, Willet thought, a mingling of Ojibways, Pottawattomies and Ottawas. All were in war paint and

4

were heavily armed, many of them carrying big muskets with bayonets on the end, taken from Braddock's fallen soldiers. Three had small swords belted to their naked waists, not as weapons, but rather as the visible emblems of triumph.

As he looked, Robert's head grew hot with the blood pumped up from his angry heart. It seemed to him that they swaggered and boasted, although they were but true to savage nature.

"Easy, lad," said Willet, putting a restraining hand upon his shoulder. "It's their hour. You can't deny that, and we'll have to bide a while."

"But will our hour ever come, Dave? Our army has been beaten, destroyed. The colonies and mother country alike are sluggish, and now have no plans, the whole border lies at the mercy of the tomahawk and the French power in Canada not only grows all the time, but is directed by able and daring men."

"Patience, lad, patience! Our strength is greater than that of the foe, although we may be slower in using it. But I tell you we'll see our day of triumph yet."

"They are getting ready to move," whispered the Onondaga. "The Frenchman and the band will march northward."

"And not back to Duquesne?" said Willet. "What makes you think so, Tayoga?"

"What is left for them to do at Duquesne? It will be many a day before the English and Americans come against it again."

"That, alas, is true, Tayoga. They're not needed longer here, nor are we. They've put out their fire, and now they're off toward the north, just as you said they would be. Tandakora and De Courcelles lead, marching side by side. A pretty pair, well met here in the forest. Now, I wish I knew where they were going!"

"Can't the Great Bear guess?" said the Onondaga.

"No, Tayoga. How should I?"

"Doesn't Great Bear remember the fort in the forest, the one called Refuge?"

"Of course I do, Tayoga! And the brave lads, Colden and Wilton and Carson and their comrades who defended it so long and so well. That's the most likely point of attack, and now, since Braddock's army is destroyed it's too far in the wilderness, too exposed, and should be abandoned. Suppose we carry a warning!"

Robert's eyes glistened. The idea made a strong appeal to him. He had mellow memories of those Philadelphia lads, and it would be pleasant to see them again. The three, in bearing the alarm, might achieve, too, a task that would lighten, in a measure, the terror along the border. It would be a relief at least to do something while the government disagreed and delayed.

"Let's start at once for Fort Refuge," he said, "and help them to get away before the storm breaks. What do you say, Tayoga?"

"It is what we ought to do," replied the Onondaga, in his precise English of the schools.

"Come," said Willet, leading the way, and the three, leaving the fire behind them, marched rapidly into the north and east. Two miles gone, and they stopped to study the sun, by which they meant to take their reckoning.

"The fort lies there," said Willet, pointing a long finger, "and by my calculations it will take us about five days and nights to reach it, that is, if nothing gets in our way."

"You think, then," asked Robert, "that the French and Indians are already spreading a net?"

5

"The Indians might stop, Robert, my lad, to exult over their victory and to celebrate it with songs and dances, but the French leaders, whose influence with them is now overwhelming, will push them on. They will want to reap all the fruits of their great triumph by the river. I've often told you about the quality of the French and you've seen for yourself. Ligneris, Contrecoeur, De Courcelles, St. Luc and the others will flame like torches along the border."

"And St. Luc will be the most daring, skillful and energetic of them all."

"It's a fact that all three of us know, Robert, and now, having fixed our course, we must push ahead with all speed. De Courcelles, Tandakora and the warriors are on the march, too, and we may see them again before we see Fort Refuge."

"The forest will be full of warriors," said Tayoga, speaking with great gravity. "The fort will be the first thought of the western barbarians, and of the tribes from Canada, and they will wish to avenge the defeat they suffered before it."

It was not long until they had ample proof that the Onondaga's words were true. They saw three trails in the course of the day, and all of them led toward the fort. Willet and Tayoga, with their wonderful knowledge of the forest, estimated that about thirty warriors made one trail, about twenty another, and fifteen the smallest.

"They're going fast, too," said the hunter, "but we must go faster."

"They will see our traces," said Tayoga, "and by signaling to one another they will tell all that we are in the woods. Then they will set a force to destroy us, while the greater bands go on to take the fort."

"But we'll pass 'em," said Robert confidently. "They can't stop us!"

Tayoga and the hunter glanced at him. Then they looked at each other and smiled. They knew Robert thoroughly, they understood his vivid and enthusiastic nature which, looking forward with so much confidence to success, was apt to consider it already won, a fact that perhaps contributed in no small measure to the triumph wished so ardently. At last, the horror of the great defeat in the forest and the slaughter of an army was passing. It was Robert's hopeful temperament and brilliant mind that gave him such a great charm for all who met him, a charm to which even the fifty wise old sachems in the vale of Onondaga had not been insensible.

"No, Robert," said the Great Bear gravely, "I don't think anything can stop us. I've a prevision that De Courcelles and Tandakora will stand in our way, but we'll just brush 'em out of it."

They had not ceased to march at speed, while they talked, and now Tayoga announced the presence of a river, an obstacle that might prove formidable to foresters less expert than they. It was lined on both sides with dense forest, and they walked along its bank about a mile until they came to a comparatively shallow place where they forded it in water above their knees. However, their leggings and moccasins dried fast in the midsummer sun, and, experiencing no discomfort, they pressed forward with unabated speed.

All the afternoon they continued their great journey to save those at the fort, fording another river and a half dozen creeks and leaping across many brooks. Twice they crossed trails leading to the east and twice other trails leading to the west, but they felt that all of them would presently turn and join in the general march converging upon Fort Refuge. They were sure, too, that De Courcelles, Tandakora and their band were marching on a line almost parallel with them, and that they would offer the greatest danger.

Night came, a beautiful, bright summer night with a silky blue sky in which multitudes of silver stars danced, and they sought a covert in a dense thicket where they lay on their blankets, ate venison, and talked a little before they slept.

Robert's brilliant and enthusiastic mood lasted. He could see nothing but success. With the fading of the great slaughter by the river came other pictures, deep of hue, intense and charged with pleasant memories. Life recently had been a great panorama to him, bright and full of changes. He could not keep from contrasting his present position, hid in a thicket to save himself from cruel savages, with those vivid days at Quebec, his gorgeous period in New York, and the gay time with sporting youth in the cozy little capital of Williamsburg.

But the contrast, so far from making him unhappy, merely expanded his spirit. He rejoiced in the pleasures that he had known and adapted himself to present conditions. Always influenced greatly by what lay just around him, he considered their thicket the best thicket in which he had ever been hidden. The leaves of last year, drifted into little heaps on which they lay, were uncommonly large and soft. The light breeze rustling the boughs over his head whispered only of peace and ease, and the two comrades, who lay on either side of him, were the finest comrades any lad ever had.

"Tayoga," he asked, and his voice was sincerely earnest, "can you see on his star Tododaho, the founder and protector of the great league of the Hodenosaunee?"

The young Onondaga, his face mystic and reverential, gazed toward the west where a star of great size and beauty quivered and blazed.

"I behold him," he replied. "His face is turned toward us, and the wise serpents lie, coil on coil, in his hair. There are wreaths of vapor about his eyes, but I can see them shining through, shining with kindness, as the mighty chief, who went away four hundred years ago, watches over us. His eyes say that so long as our deeds are just, so long as we walk in the path that Manitou wishes, we shall be victorious. Now a cloud passes before the star, and I cannot see the face of Tododaho, but he has spoken, and it will be well for us to remember his words."

He sank back on his blanket and closed his eyes as if he, too, in thought, had shot through space to some great star. Robert and Willet were silent, sharing perhaps in his emotion. The religion and beliefs of the Indian were real and vital to them, and if Tododaho promised success to Tayoga then the promise would be fulfilled.

"I think, Robert," said Willet, "that you'd better keep the first watch. Wake me a little while before midnight, and I'll take the second."

"Good enough," said Robert. "I think I can hear any footfall Tandakora may make, if he approaches."

"It is not enough to hear the footfall of the Ojibway," said Tayoga, opening his eyes and sitting up. "To be a great sentinel and forester worthy to be compared with the greatest, Dagaeoga must hear the whisper of the grass as it bends under the lightest wind, he must hear the sound made by the little leaf as it falls, he must hear the ripple in the brook that is flowing a hundred yards from us, and he must hear the wild flowers talking together in the night. Only then can Dagaeoga call himself a sentinel fit to watch over two such sleeping foresters as the Great Bear and myself."

"Close your eyes and go to sleep without fear," said Robert in the same vein. "I shall hear Tandakora breathing if he comes within a mile of us, at the same distance I shall hear the moccasin of De Courcelles, when it brushes against last year's fallen leaf, and at half a mile I shall see the look of revenge and cruelty upon the face of the Ojibway seeking for us."

Willet laughed softly, but with evident satisfaction.

7

"You two boys are surely the greatest talkers I've heard for a long time," he said. "You have happy thoughts and you put 'em into words. If I didn't know that you had a lot of deeds, too, to your credit, I'd call you boasters, but knowing it, I don't. Go ahead and spout language, because you're only lads and I can see that you enjoy it."

"I'm going to sleep now," said Tayoga, "but Dagaeoga can keep on talking and be happy, because he will talk to himself long after we have gone to the land of dreams."

"If I do talk to myself," said Robert, "it's because I like to talk to a bright fellow, and I like to have a bright fellow talk to me. Sleep as soundly as you please, you two, because while you're sleeping I can carry on an intellectual conversation."

The hunter laughed again.

"It's no use, Tayoga," he said. "You can't put him down. The fifty wise old sachems in the vale of Onondaga proclaimed him a great orator, and great orators must always have their way."

"It is so," said the Onondaga. "The voice of Dagaeoga is like a river. It flows on forever, and like the murmur of the stream it will soothe me to deeper slumbers. Now I sleep."

"And so do I," said the hunter.

It seemed marvelous that such formal announcements should be followed by fact, but within three minutes both went to that pleasant land of dreams of which they had been talking so lightly. Their breathing was long and regular and, beyond a doubt, they had put absolute faith in their sentinel. Robert's mind, so quick to respond to obvious confidence, glowed with resolve. There was no danger now that he would relax the needed vigilance a particle, and, rifle in the hollow of his arm, he began softly to patrol the bushes.

He was convinced that De Courcelles and Tandakora were not many miles away—they might even be within a mile—and memory of a former occasion, somewhat similar, when Tayoga had detected the presence of the Ojibway, roused his emulation. He was determined that, while he was on watch, no creeping savage should come near enough to strike.

Hand on the hammer and trigger of his rifle he walked in an ever widening circle about his sleeping comrades, searching the thickets with eyes, good naturally and trained highly, and stopping now and then to listen. Two or three times he put his ear to the earth that he might hear, as Tayoga had bade him, the rustle of leaves a mile away.

His eager spirit, always impatient for action, found relief in the continuous walking, and the steady enlargement of the circle in which he traveled, acquiring soon a radius of several hundred yards. On the western perimeter he was beyond the deep thicket, and within a magnificent wood, unchoked by undergrowth. Here the trees stood up in great, regular rows, ordered by nature, and the brilliant moonlight clothed every one of them in a veil of silver. On such a bright night in summer the wilderness always had for him an elusive though powerful beauty, but he felt its danger. Among the mighty trunks, with no concealing thickets, he could be seen easily, if prowling savages were near, and, as he made his circles, he always hastened through what he called to himself his park, until he came to the bushes, in the density of which he was well hidden from any eye fifty feet away.

It was an hour until midnight, and the radius of his circle had increased another fifty yards, when he came again to the great spaces among the oaks and beeches. Halfway through and he sank softly down behind the trunk of a huge oak. Either in fact or in a sort of mental illusion, he had heard a moccasin brush a dry leaf far away. The command of Tayoga, though spoken in jest, had been so impressive that his ear was obeying it. Firm in the belief that his own dark shadow blurred with the dark trunk, and that he was safe from the sight of a questing eye, he lay there a long time, listening.

8

In time, the sound, translated from fancy into fact, came again, and now he knew that it was near, perhaps not more than a hundred yards away, the rustling of a real moccasin against a real dry leaf. Twice and thrice his ear signaled to his brain. It could not be fancy. It was instead an alarming fact.

He was about to creep from the tree, and return to his comrades with word that the enemy was near, but he restrained his impulse, merely crouching a little lower that his dark shadow might blend with the dark earth as well as the dark trunk. Then he heard several rustlings and the very low murmur of voices.

Gradually the voices which had been blended together, detached themselves and Robert recognized those of Tandakora and De Courcelles. Presently they came into the moonlight, followed by the savage band, and they passed within fifty yards of the youth who lay in the shelter of the trunk, pressing himself into the earth.

The Frenchman and the Ojibway were talking with great earnestness and Robert's imagination, plumbing the distance, told him the words they said. Tandakora was stating with great emphasis that the three whose trail they had found had gone on very fast, obviously with the intention of warning the garrison at the fort, and if they were to be cut off the band must hasten, too. De Courcelles was replying that in his opinion Tandakora was right, but it would not be well to get too far ahead. They must throw out flankers as they marched, but there was no immediate need of them. If the band spread out before dawn it would be sufficient.

Robert's fancy was so intense and creative that, beginning by imagining these things so, he made them so. The band therefore was sure to go on without searching the thickets on either right or left at present, and all immediate apprehension disappeared from his mind. Tandakora and De Courcelles were in the center of the moonlight, and although knowing them evil, he was surprised to see how very evil their faces looked, each in its own red or white way. He could remember nothing at that moment but their wickedness, and their treacherous attacks upon his life and those of his friends, and the memory clothed them about with a hideous veil through which only their cruel souls shone. It was characteristic of him that he should always see everything in extreme colors, and in his mind the good were always very good and the bad were very bad.

Hence it was to him an actual physical as well as mental relief, when the Frenchman, the Ojibway and their band, passing on, were blotted from his eyes by the forest. Then he turned back to the thicket in which his comrades lay, and bent over them for the purpose of awakening them. But before he could speak or lay a hand upon either, Tayoga sat up, his eyes wide open.

"You come with news that the enemy has been at hand!"

"Yes, but how did you know it?"

"I see it in your look, and, also when I slept, the Keeper of Dreams whispered it in my ear. An evil wind, too, blew upon my face and I knew it was the breath of De Courcelles and Tandakora. They have been near."

"They and their entire band passed not more than four hundred yards to the eastward of us. I lay in the bush and saw them distinctly. They're trying to beat us to Fort Refuge."

"But they won't do it, because we won't let 'em," said Willet, who had awakened at the talking. "We'll make a curve and get ahead of 'em again. You watched well, Robert."

"I obeyed the strict injunctions of Tayoga," said young Lennox, smiling faintly. "He bade me listen so intently that I should hear the rustle of a dry leaf when a moccasin touched it a mile away in the forest. Well, I heard it, and going whence the sound came I saw De Courcelles, Tandakora and their warriors pass by."

"You love to paint pictures with words, Robert. I see that well, but 'tis not likely that you exaggerate so much, after all. I'm sorry you won't get your share of sleep, but we must be up and away."

"I'll claim a double portion of it later on, Dave, but I agree with you that what we need most just now is silence and speed, and speed and silence."

The three, making a curve toward the east, traveled at high speed through the rest of the night, Tayoga now leading and showing all his inimitable skill as a forest trailer. In truth, the Onondaga was in his element. His spirits, like Robert's, rose as dangers grew thicker around them, and he had been affected less than either of his comrades by the terrible slaughter of Braddock's men. Mentally at least, he was more of a stoic, and woe to the vanquished was a part of the lore of all the Indian tribes. The French and their allies had struck a heavy blow and there was nothing left for the English and Americans to do but to strike back. It was all very simple.

Day came, and at the suggestion of Willet they rested again in the thickets. Robert was not really weary, at least the spirit uplifted him, though he knew that he must not overtask the body. His enthusiasm, based upon such a sanguine temperament, continued to rise. Again he foresaw glittering success. They would shake off all their foes, reach the fort in time, and lead the garrison and the people who had found refuge there safely out of the wilderness.

Where they lay the bushes were very dense. Before hiding there they had drunk abundantly at a little brook thirty or forty feet away, and now they ate with content the venison that formed their breakfast. Over the vast forest a brilliant sun was rising and here the leaves and grass were not burned much by summer heat. It looked fresh and green, and the wind sang pleasantly through its cool shadows. It appealed to Robert. With his plastic nature he was all for the town when he was in town, and now in the forest he was all for the forest.

"I can understand why you love it so well," he said to Tayoga, waving his hand at the verdant world that curved about them.

"My people and their ancestors have lived in it for more generations than anyone knows," said the Onondaga, his eyes glistening. "I have been in the white man's schools, and the white man's towns, and I have seen the good in them, but this is my real home. This is what I love best. My heart beats strongest for the forest."

"My own heart does a lot of beating for the woods," said Willet, thoughtfully, "and it ought to do so, I've spent so many years of my life in them—happy years, too. They say that no matter how great an evil may be some good will come out of it, and this war will achieve one good end."

"What is that, Great Bear?"

"It will delay the work of the ax. Men will be so busy with the rifle that they will have mighty little time for the ax. The trees will stop falling for a while, and the forest will cover again the places where it has been cleared away. Why, the game itself will increase!"

"How long do you think we'd better stay here?" asked Robert, his eager soul anxious to be on again.

"Patience! patience, my lad," replied Willet. "It's one thing that you'll have to practice. We don't want to run squarely into De Courcelles, Tandakora and their band, and meanwhile we're very comfortable here, gathering strength. Look at Tayoga there and learn from him. If need be he could lie in the same place a week and be happy."

"I hope the need will not come," laughed the Onondaga.

10

Robert felt the truth of Willet's words, and he put restraint upon himself, resolved that he would not be the first to propose the new start. He had finished breakfast and he lay on his elbow gazing up through the green tracery of the bushes at the sky. It was a wonderful sky, a deep, soft, velvet blue, and it tinted the woods with glorious and kindly hues. It seemed strange to Robert, at the moment, that a forest so beautiful should bristle with danger, but he knew it too well to allow its softness and air of innocence to deceive him.

It was almost the middle of the morning when Willet gave the word to renew the march, and they soon saw they had extreme need of caution. Evidence that warriors had passed was all about them. Now and then they saw the faint imprint of a moccasin. Twice they found little painted feathers that had fallen from a headdress or a scalplock, and once Tayoga saw a red bead lying in the grass where it had dropped, perhaps, from a legging.

"We shall have to pass by Tandakora's band and perhaps other bands in the night," said Tayoga.

"It's possible, too," said Willet, "that they know we're on our way to the fort, and may try to stop us. Our critical time will soon be at hand."

They listened throughout the afternoon for the signals that bands might make to one another, but heard nothing. Willet, in truth, was not surprised.

"Silence will serve them best," he said, "and they'll send runners from band to band. Still, if they do give signals we want to know it."

"There is a river, narrow but deep, about five miles ahead," said Tayoga, "and we'll have to cross it on our way to the fort. I think it is there that Tandakora will await us."

"It's pretty sure to be the place," said Willet. "Do you know where there's a ford, Tayoga?"

"There is none."

"Then we'll have to swim for it. That's bad. But you say it's a narrow stream?"

"Yes, Great Bear. Two minutes would carry us across it."

"Then we must find some place for the fording where the trees lean over from either side and the shadow is deep."

Tayoga nodded, and, after that, they advanced in silence, redoubling their caution as they drew near to the river. The night was not so bright as the one that had just gone before, but it furnished sufficient light for wary and watching warriors to see their figures at a considerable distance, and, now and then, they stopped to search the thickets with their own eyes. No wind blew, their footsteps made no sound and the intense stillness of the forest wove itself into the texture of Robert's mind. His extraordinary fancy peopled it with phantoms. There was a warrior in every bush, but, secure in the comradeship of his two great friends, he went on without fear.

"There is no signal," whispered Tayoga at last. "They do not even imitate the cry of bird or beast, and it proves one thing, Great Bear."

"So it does, Tayoga."

"You know as well as I do, Great Bear, that they make no sound because they have set the trap, and they do not wish to alarm the game which they expect to walk into it."

"Even so, Tayoga. Our minds travel in the same channel."

"But the game is suspicious, nevertheless," continued Tayoga in his precise school English, "and the trap will not fall."

"No, Tayoga, it won't fall, because the game won't walk into it."

"Tandakora will suffer great disappointment. He is a mighty hunter and he has hunted mighty game, but the game that he hunts now is more wary than the stag or the bear, and has greater power to strike back than either."

11

"Well spoken, Tayoga."

The hunter and the Onondaga looked at each other in the dark and laughed. Their spirits were as wild as the wilderness, and they were enjoying the prospect of the Ojibway's empty trap. Robert laughed with them. Already in his eager mind success was achieved and the crossing was made. After a while he saw dim silver through the trees, and he knew they had come to the river. Then the three sank down and approached inch by inch, sure that De Courcelles, Tandakora and their forces would be watching on the other side.

CHAPTER II

THE KINDLY BRIDGE

The thicket in which the three lay was of low but dense bushes, with high grass growing wherever the sun could reach it. In the grass tiny wild flowers, purple, blue and white were in bloom, and Robert inhaled their faint odor as he crouched, watching for the enemy who sought his life. It was a forest scene, the beauty of which would have pleased him at any other time, nor was he wholly unconscious of it now. The river itself, as Tayoga had stated, was narrow. At some points it did not seem to be more than ten or fifteen yards across, but it flowed in a slow, heavy current, showing depths below. Nor could he see, looking up and down the stream, any prospect of a ford.

Robert's gaze moved in an eager quest along the far shore, but he detected no sign of Tandakora, the Frenchman or their men. Yet he felt that Tayoga and Willet were right and that foes were on watch there. It was inevitable, because it was just the place where they could wait best for the three. Nevertheless he asked, though it was merely to confirm his own belief.

"Do you think they're in the brush, Dave?"

"Not a doubt of it, Robert," the hunter whispered back. "They haven't seen us yet, but they hope to do so soon."

"And we also, who haven't seen them yet, hope to do so soon."

"Aye, Robert, that's the fact. Ah, I think I catch a glimpse of them now. Tayoga, wouldn't you say that the reflection in the big green bush across the river is caused by a moonbeam falling on a burnished rifle barrel?"

"Not a doubt of it, Great Bear. Now, I see the rifle itself! And now I see the hands that hold it. The hands belong to a live warrior, an Ojibway, or a Pottowattomie. He is kneeling, waiting for a shot, if he should find anything to shoot at."

"I see him, too, Tayoga, and there are three more warriors just beyond him. It's certainly the band of Tandakora and De Courcelles, and they've set a beautiful trap for three who will not come into it."

"It is so, Great Bear. One may build a splendid bear trap but of what use is it if the bear stays away?"

"But what are we to do?" asked Robert. "We can't cross in the face of such a force."

"We'll go down the stream," replied Willet, "keeping hidden, of course, in the thickets, and look for a chance to pass. Of course, they've sent men in both directions along the bank, but we may go farther than any of them."

He led the way, and they went cautiously through the thickets two or three miles, all the time intently watching the other shore. Twice they saw Indian sentinels on watch, and knew that they could not risk the passage. Finally they stopped and waited a full two hours in the thickets, the contest becoming one of patience.

Meanwhile the night was absolutely silent. The wind was dead, and the leaves hung straight down. The deep, slow current of the river, although flowing between narrow banks, made no noise, and Robert's mind, colored by the conditions of the moment, began to believe that the enemy had gone away. It was impossible for them to wait so long for foresters whom they did not see and who might never come. Then he dismissed imagination and impression, and turned with a wrench to his judgment. He knew enough of the warriors of the wilderness to know that nobody could wait longer than they. Patience was one of the chief commodities of savage life, because their habits were not complex, and all the time in the world was theirs.

He took lessons, too, from Tayoga and Willet. The Onondaga, an Indian himself, had an illimitable patience, and Willet, from long practice, had acquired the ability to remain motionless for hours at a time. He looked at them as they crouched beside him, still and silent figures in the dusk, apparently growing from the earth like the bushes about them, and fixed as they were. The suggestion to go on that had risen to his lips never passed them and he settled into the same immobility.

Another hour, that was three to Robert, dragged by, and Tayoga led the way again down the stream, Robert and the hunter following without a word. They went a long distance and then the Onondaga uttered a whisper of surprise and satisfaction.

"A bridge!" he said.

"Where? I don't see it," said Robert.

"Look farther where the stream narrows. Behold the great tree that has been blown down and that has fallen from bank to bank?"

"I see it now, Tayoga. It hasn't been down long, because the leaves upon it are yet green."

"And they will hide us as we cross. Tododaho on his star has been watching over us, and has put the bridge here for our use in this crisis."

Tayoga's words were instinct with faith. He never doubted that the great Onondaga who had gone away four hundred years ago was serving them now in this, their utmost, need. Robert and Willet glanced at each other. They, too, believed. An electric current had passed from Tayoga to them, and, for the moment, their trust in Tododaho was almost as great as his. At the same time, a partial darkening of the night occurred, clouds floating up from the south and west, and dimming the moon and stars.

"How far would you say it is from one shore to the other?" asked Robert of Willet.

"About sixty feet," replied the hunter, "but it's a long tree, and it will easily bear the weight of the three of us all the way. We may be attacked while we're upon it, but if so we have our rifles."

"It is the one chance that Tododaho has offered to us, and we must take it," said Tayoga, as he led the way upon the natural bridge. Robert followed promptly and Willet brought up the rear.

The banks were high at that point, and the river flowed rather more swiftly than usual. Robert, ten feet beyond the southern shore, looked down at a dark and sullen current, seeming in the dim moonlight to have interminable depths. It was only about fifteen feet below him, but his imagination, heightened by time and place, made the distance three or fourfold greater.

He felt a momentary fear lest he slip and fall into the dark stream, and he clung tightly to an upthrust bough.

The fallen tree swayed a little with the weight of the three, but Robert knew that it was safe. It was not the bridge that they had to fear, but what awaited them on the farther shore. Tayoga stopped, and the tense manner in which he crouched among the boughs and leaves showed that he was listening with all his ears.

"Do you hear them?" Robert whispered.

"Not their footsteps," Tayoga whispered back, "but there was a soft call in the woods, the low cry of a night bird, and then the low cry of another night bird replying. It was the warriors signaling to one another, the first signal they have given."

"I heard the cries, too," said Willet, behind Robert, "and no doubt Tandakora and De Courcelles feel they are closing in on us. It's a good thing this tree was blown down but lately, and the leaves and boughs are so thick on it."

"It was so provided by Tododaho in our great need," said Tayoga.

"Do you mean that we're likely to be besieged while we're still on our bridge?" asked Robert, and despite himself he could not repress a shiver.

"Not a siege exactly," replied Willet, "but the warriors may pass on the farther shore, while we're still in the tree. That's the reason why I spoke so gratefully of the thick leaves still clinging to it."

"They come even now," said Tayoga, in the lowest of whispers, and the three, stopping, flattened themselves like climbing animals against the trunk of the tree, until the dark shadow of their bodies blurred against the dusk of its bark. They were about halfway across and the distance of the stream beneath them seemed to Robert to have increased. He saw it flowing black and swift, and, for a moment, he had a horrible fear lest he should fall, but he tightened his grasp on a bough and turning his eyes away from the water looked toward the woods.

"The warriors come," whispered Tayoga, and Robert, seeing, also flattened himself yet farther against the tree, until he seemed fairly to sink into the bark. Their likeness to climbing animals increased, and it would have required keen eyes to have seen the three as they lay along the trunk, deep among the leaves and boughs thirty feet from either shore.

Tandakora, De Courcelles and about twenty warriors appeared in the forest, walking a little distance back from the stream, where they could see on the farther bank, and yet not be seen from it. The moon was still obscured, but a portion of its light fell directly upon Tandakora, and Robert had never beheld a more sinister figure. The rays, feeble, were yet strong enough to show his gigantic figure, naked save for the breech cloth, and painted horribly. His eyes, moreover, were lighted up either in fact or in Robert's fancy with a most wicked gleam, as if he were already clutching the scalps of the three whom he was hunting so savagely.

"Now," whispered Tayoga, "Tododaho alone can save us. He holds our fate in the hollow of his hand, but he is merciful as well as just."

Robert knew their danger was of the uttermost, but often, in the extreme crises of life and death, one may not feel until afterward that fate has turned on a hair.

De Courcelles was just behind Tandakora, but the light did not fall so clearly upon him. The savage had a hideous fascination for Robert, and the moon's rays seemed to follow him. Every device and symbol painted upon the huge chest stood out like carving, and all the features of the heavy, cruel face were disclosed as if by day. But Robert noticed with extraordinary relief that the eyes so full of menace were seeking the three among the woods on the farther shore, and were paying little attention to the tree. It was likely that neither Tandakora nor De Courcelles would dream that they were upon it, but it was

14

wholly possible that the entire band should seek to cross that way, and reach the southern shore in the quest of their prey.

The three in the depths of the boughs and leaves did not stir. The rising wind caused the foliage to rustle about them again. It made the tree sway a little, too, and as Robert could not resist the temptation to look downward once, the black surface of the river seemed to be dancing back and forth beneath him. But, save the single glance, his eyes all the while were for the Ojibway and the Frenchman.

Tandakora and De Courcelles came a little closer to the bank. Apparently they were satisfied that no one was on the farther shore, and that they were in no danger of a bullet, as presently they emerged fully into the open, and stood there, their eyes questing. Then they looked at the bridge, and, for a few instants, Robert was sure they would attempt the crossing upon it. But in a minute or so they walked beyond it, and then he concluded that the crisis had passed. After all, it would be their plan to hold their own shore, and prevent the passage of the three.

Yet Tandakora and De Courcelles were cruelly deliberate and slow. They walked not more than fifteen feet beyond the end of the tree, and then stood a while talking. Half of the warriors remained near them, standing stolidly in the background, and the others went on, searching among the woods and thickets. The two glanced at the tree as they talked. Was it possible that they would yet come back and attempt the crossing? Again Robert quivered when he realized that in truth the crisis had not passed, and that Tandakora and De Courcelles might reconsider. Once more, he pressed his body hard against the tree, and held tightly to a small bough which arched an abundant covering of leaves over his head. The wind rustled among those leaves, and sang almost in words, but whether they told him that Tandakora and De Courcelles would go on or come upon the bridge he did not know.

Five minutes of such intense waiting that seemed nearer to an hour, and the leaders, with the band, passed on, disappearing in the undergrowth that lined the stream. But for another five minutes the three among the boughs did not stir. Then Tayoga whispered over his shoulder:

"Great is the justice of Tododaho and also great is his mercy. I did not doubt that he would save us. I felt within me all the time that he would cause Tandakora and De Courcelles to leave the bridge and seek us elsewhere."

Robert was not one to question the belief of Tayoga, his sagacious friend. If it was not Tododaho who had sent their enemies away then it was some other spirit, known by another name, but in essence the same. His whole being was permeated by a sort of shining gratitude.

"At times," he said, "it seems that we are favored by our God, who is your Manitou."

"Now is the time for us to finish the crossing," said Willet, alive to the needs of the moment. "Lead, Tayoga, and be sure, Robert, not to give any bough a shake that might catch the eye of a lurking savage in the forest."

The Onondaga resumed the slow advance, so guiding his movements that he might neither make the tree quiver nor bring his body from beneath the covering of leaves. Robert and the hunter followed him in close imitation. Thus they gained the bank, and the three drew long breaths of deep and intense relief, as they stepped upon firm ground. But they could not afford to linger. Tayoga still in front, they plunged into the depths of the forest, and advanced at speed a half hour, when they heard a single faint cry behind them.

"They've found our trail at the end of the natural bridge," said Willet.

"It is so," said Tayoga, in his precise school English.

15

"And they're mad, mad clean through," said the hunter. "That single cry shows it. If they hadn't been so mad they'd have followed our trail without a sound. I wish I could have seen the faces of the Ojibway and the Frenchman when they came back and noticed our trace at the end of the tree. They're mad in every nerve and fiber, because they did not conclude to go upon it. It was only one chance in a thousand that we'd be there, they let that one chance in a thousand go, and lost."

The great frame of the hunter shook with silent laughter. But Robert, in very truth, saw the chagrin upon the faces of Tandakora and De Courcelles. His extraordinary imagination was again up and leaping and the picture it created for him was as glowing and vivid as fact. They had gone some distance, and then they had come back, continually searching the thickets of the opposite shore with their powerful and trained eyesight. They had felt disappointed because they had seen no trace of the hunted, who had surely come by this time against the barrier of the river. Frenchman and Ojibway were in a state of angry wonder at the disappearance of the three who had vanished as if on wings in the air, leaving no trail. Then Tandakora had chanced to look down. His eye in the dusky moonlight had caught the faint imprint of a foot on the grass, perhaps Robert's own, and the sudden shout had been wrenched from him by his anger and mortification. Now Robert, too, was convulsed by internal laughter.

"It was our great luck that they did not find us on the tree," he said.

"No, it was not luck," said Tayoga.

"How so?"

"They did not come upon the tree because Tododaho would not let them."

"I forgot. You're right, Tayoga," said Robert sincerely.

"We'll take fresh breath here for five minutes or so," said the hunter, "and then we'll push on at speed, because we have not only the band of Tandakora and De Courcelles to fear. There are others in the forest converging on Fort Refuge."

"Great Bear is right. He is nearly always right," said Tayoga. "We have passed one barrier, but we will meet many more. There is also danger behind us. Even now the band is coming fast."

They did not move until the allotted time had passed. Again Robert's mind painted a picture in glowing colors of the savage warriors, led by Tandakora and De Courcelles, coming at utmost speed upon their trail, and his muscles quivered, yet he made no outward sign. To the eye he was as calm as Tayoga or Willet.

An hour after the resumption of their flight they came to a shallow creek with a gravelly bed, a creek that obviously emptied into the river they had crossed, and they resorted to the commonest and most effective of all devices used by fugitives in the North American wilderness who wished to hide their trail. They waded in the stream, and, as it led in the general direction in which they wished to go, they did not leave the water until they had covered a distance of several miles. Then they emerged upon the bank and rested a long time.

"When Tandakora and De Courcelles see our traces disappear in the creek and fail to reappear on the other side," said Willet, "they'll divide their band and send half of it upstream, and half downstream, looking everywhere for our place of entry upon dry land, but it'll take 'em a long time to find it. Robert, you and Tayoga might spread your blankets, and if you're calm enough, take a nap. At any rate, it won't hurt you to stretch yourselves and rest. I can warn you in time, when an enemy comes."

The Onondaga obeyed without a word, and soon slept as if his will had merely to give an order to his five senses to seek oblivion. Robert did not think he could find slumber, but closing his eyes in order to rest better, he drifted easily into unconsciousness.

Meanwhile Willet watched, and there was no better sentinel in all the northern wilderness. The wind was still blowing lightly, and the rustling of the leaves never ceased, but he would have detected instantly any strange note, jarring upon that musical sound.

The hunter looked upon the sleeping lads, the white and the red. Both had a powerful hold upon his affection. He felt that he stood to them almost in the relationship of a father, and he was proud, too, of their strength and skill, their courage and intelligence. Eager as he was to reach Fort Refuge and save the garrison and people there, he was even more eager to save the two youths from harm.

He let them sleep until the gold of the morning sun was gilding the eastern forest, when the three drew further upon their supplies of bread and venison and once more resumed the journey through the pathless woods towards their destination. There was no interruption that day, and they felt so much emboldened that near sundown Tayoga took his bow and arrows, which he carried as well as his rifle, and stalked and shot a deer, the forest being full of game. Then they lighted a fire and cooked delicate portions of the spoil in a sheltered hollow. But they did not eat supper there. Instead, they took portions of the cooked food and as much as they could conveniently carry of the uncooked, and, wading along the bed of a brook, did not stop until they were three or four miles from the place in which they had built the fire. Then they sat down and ate in great content.

"We will fare well enough," said Willet, "if it doesn't rain. 'Tis lucky for us that it's the time of year when but little rain falls."

"But rain would be as hard upon those who are hunting us as upon us," said Robert.

"'Tis true, lad, and I'm glad to see you always making the best of everything. It's a spirit that wins."

"And now, Great Bear," said Tayoga, his eyes twinkling, "you have talked enough. It is only Dagaeoga who can talk on forever."

"That's so about Robert, but what do you mean by saying I've talked enough?"

"It is time for you to sleep. You watched last night while we slept, and now your hour has come. While you slumber Dagaeoga and I will be sentinels who will see and hear everything."

"Why the two of you?"

"Because it takes both of us to be the equal of the Great Bear."

"Come, now, Tayoga, that's either flattery or irony, but whatever it is I'll let it pass. I'll own that I'm sleepy enough and you two can arrange the rest between you."

He was asleep very soon, his great figure lying motionless on his blanket, and the two wary lads watched, although they sat together, and, at times, talked. Both knew there was full need for vigilance. They had triumphed for the moment over Tandakora and De Courcelles, but they expected many other lions in the path that led to Fort Refuge. It was important also, not only that they should arrive there, but that they should arrive in time. It was true, too, that they considered the danger greater by night than by day. In the day it was much easier to see the approach of an enemy, but by night one must be very vigilant indeed to detect the approach of a foe so silent as the Indian.

The two did not yet mention a division of the watch. Neither was sleepy and they were content to remain awake much longer. Moreover, they had many things of interest to talk about and also they indulged in speculation.

"Do you think it possible, Tayoga," asked Robert, "that the garrison, hearing of the great cloud now overhanging the border, may have abandoned the fort and gone east with the refugees?"

"No, Dagaeoga, it is not likely. It is almost certain that the young men from Philadelphia have not heard of General Braddock's great defeat. French and savage runners could have reached them with the news, could have taunted them from the forest, but they would not wish to do so; they seek instead to gather their forces first, to have all the effect of surprise, to take the fort, its garrison and the people as one takes a ripe apple from a tree, just when it is ready to fall."

"That rout back there by Duquesne was a terrible affair for us, Tayoga, not alone because it uncovers the border, but because it heartens all our enemies. What joy the news must have caused in Quebec, and what joy it will cause in Paris, too, when it reaches the great French capital! The French will think themselves invincible and so will their red allies."

"They would be invincible, Dagaeoga, if they could take with them the Hodenosaunee."

"And may not this victory of the French and their tribes at Duquesne shake the faith of the Hodenosaunee?"

"No, Dagaeoga. The fifty sachems will never let the great League join Onontio. Champlain and Frontenac have been gone long, but their shadows still stand between the French and the Hodenosaunee, and there is Quebec, the lost Stadacona of the Ganegaono, whom you call the Mohawks. As long as the sun and stars stand in the heavens the Keepers of the Eastern Gate are the enemies of the French. Even now, as you know, they fight by the side of the Americans and the English."

"It is true. I was wrong to question the faith of the great nations of the Hodenosaunee. If none save the Mohawks fight for us it is at least certain that they will not fight against us, and even undecided, while we're at present suffering from disaster, they'll form a neutral barrier, in part, between the French and us. Ah, that defeat by Duquesne! I scarcely see yet how it happened!"

"A general who made war in a country that he did not know, with an enemy that he did not understand."

"Well, we'll learn from it. We were too sure. Pride, they say, goes before a fall, but they ought to add that those who fall can rise again. Perhaps our generals will be more cautious next time, and won't walk into any more traps. But I foresee now a long, a very long war. Nearly all of Europe, if what comes across the Atlantic be true, will be involved in it, and we Americans will be thrown mostly upon our own resources. Perhaps it will weld our colonies together and make of them a great nation, a nation great like the Hodenosaunee."

"I think it will come to pass, Dagaeoga. The mighty League was formed by hardship and self-denial. A people who have had to fight long and tenaciously for themselves grows strong. So it has been said often by the fifty sachems who are old and very wise, and who know all that it is given to men to know. Did you hear anything stirring in the thicket, Dagaeoga?"

"I did, Tayoga. I heard a rustling, the sound of very light footfalls, and I see the cause."

"A black bear, is it not, seeing what strangers have invaded the bush! Now, he steals away, knowing that we are the enemies most to be dreaded by him. Doubtless there are other animals among the bushes, watching us, but we neither see nor hear them. It is time to divide the watch, for we must save our strength, and it is not well for both to remain awake far into the night."

It was arranged that Robert should sleep first and the Onondaga gave his faithful promise to awaken him in four hours. The two lads meant to take the burden of the watch upon themselves, and, unless Willet awoke, of his own accord, he was to lie there until day.

18

Robert lay down upon his blanket, went to sleep in an instant, and the next instant Tayoga awakened him. At least it seemed but an instant, although the entire four hours had passed. Tayoga laughed at the dubious look on his face.

"The time is up. It really is," he said. "You made me give my faithful promise. Look at the moon, and it will tell you I am no teller of a falsehood."

"I never knew four hours to pass so quickly before. Has anything happened while I slept?"

"Much, Dagaeoga. Many things, things of vast importance."

"What, Tayoga! You astonish me. The forest seems quiet."

"And so it is. But the revolving earth has turned one-sixth of its way upon itself. It has also traveled thousands and thousands of miles in that vast circle through the pathless void that it makes about the sun. I did not know that such things happened until I went to the white man's school at Albany, but I know them now, and are they not important, hugely important?"

"They're among the main facts of the universe, but they happen every night."

"Then it would be more important if they did not happen?"

"There'd be a big smash of some kind, but as I don't know what the kind would be I'm not going to talk about it. Besides, I can see that you're making game of me, Tayoga. I've lived long enough with Indians to know that they love their joke."

"We are much like other people. I think perhaps that in all this great world, on all the continents and islands, people, whether white or red, brown or black, are the same."

"Not a doubt of it. Now, stop your philosophizing and go to sleep."

"I will obey you, Dagaeoga," said Tayoga, and in a minute he was fast asleep.

Robert watched his four hours through and then awakened the Onondaga, who was sentinel until day. When they talked they spoke only in whispers lest they wake Willet, whose slumbers were so deep that he never stirred. At daybreak Tayoga roused Robert, but the hunter still slept, his gigantic bulk disposed at ease upon his blanket. Then the two lads seized him by either shoulder and shook him violently.

"Awake! Awake, Great Bear!" Tayoga chanted in his ear. "Do you think you have gone into a cave for winter quarters? Lo, you have slept now, like the animal for which you take your name! We knew you were exhausted, and that your eyes ached for darkness and oblivion, but we did not know it would take two nights and a day to bring back your wakefulness. Dagaeoga and I were your true friends. We watched over you while you slept out your mighty sleep and kept away from you the bears and panthers that would have devoured you when you knew it not. They came more than once to look at you, and truly the Great Bear is so large that he would have made breakfast, dinner and supper for the hungriest bear or panther that ever roamed the woods."

Willet sat up, sleep still heavy on his eyelids, and, for a moment or two, looked dazed.

"What do you mean, you young rascals?" he asked. "You don't say that I've been sleeping here two nights and a day?"

"Of course you have," replied Robert, "and I've never seen anybody sleep so hard, either. Look under your blanket and see how your body has actually bored a hole into the ground."

Then Willet began to laugh.

"I see, it's a joke," he said, "though I don't mind. You're good lads, but it was your duty to have awakened me in the night and let me take my part in the watch."

"You were very tired," said Robert, "and we took pity on you. Moreover, the enemy is all about us, and we knew that the watch must be of the best. Tayoga felt that at such a time he could trust me alone, and I felt with equal force that I could trust him alone. We could not put our lives in the hands of a mere beginner."

Willet laughed again, and in the utmost good humor.

"As I repeat, you're sprightly lads," he said, "and I don't mind a jest that all three of us can enjoy. Now, for breakfast, and, truth to say, we must take it cold. It will not do to light another fire."

They ate deer meat, drank water from a brook, and then, refreshed greatly by their long rest, started at utmost speed for Fort Refuge, keeping in the deepest shadows of the wilderness, eager to carry the alarm to the garrison, and anxious to avoid any intervening foe. The day was fortunate, no enemy appearing in their path, and they traveled many miles, hope continually rising that they would reach the fort before a cloud of besiegers could arrive.

Thus they continued their journey night and day, seeing many signs of the foe, but not the foe himself, and the hope grew almost into conviction that they would pass all the Indian bands and gain the fort first.

CHAPTER III

THE FLIGHT

They were within twenty-four hours of the fort, when they struck a new trail, one of the many they had seen in the forest, but Tayoga observed it with unusual attention.

"Why does it interest you so much?" asked Robert. "We've seen others like it and you didn't examine them so long."

"This is different, Dagaeoga. Wait a minute or two more that I may observe it more closely."

Young Lennox and Willet stood to one side, and the Onondaga, kneeling down in the grass, studied the imprints. It was late in the afternoon, and the light of the red sun fell upon his powerful body, and long, refined, aristocratic face. That it was refined and aristocratic Robert often felt, refined and aristocratic in the highest Indian way. In him flowed the blood of unnumbered chiefs, and, above all, he was in himself the very essence and spirit of a gentleman, one of the finest gentlemen either Robert or Willet had ever known. Tayoga, too, had matured greatly in the last year under the stern press of circumstance. Though but a youth in years he was now, in reality, a great Onondaga warrior, surpassed in skill, endurance and courage by none. Young Lennox and the hunter waited in supreme confidence that he would read the trail and read it right.

Still on his knees, he looked up, and Robert saw the light of discovery in the dusky eyes.

"What do you read there, Tayoga?" he asked.

"Six men have passed here."

"Of what tribe were they?"

"That I do not know, save as it concerns one."

"I don't understand you."

"Five were of the Indian race, but of what tribe I cannot say, but the sixth was a white man."

"A Frenchman. It certainly can't be De Courcelles, because we've left him far behind, and I hope it's not St. Luc. Maybe it's Jumonville, De Courcelles' former comrade. Still, it doesn't seem likely that any of the Frenchmen would be with so small a band."

"It is not one of the Frenchmen, and the white man was not with the band."

"Now you're growing too complex for my simple mind, Tayoga. I don't understand you."

"It is one trail, but the Indians and the white man did not pass over it at the same time. The Indian imprints were made seven or eight hours ago, those of the white man but an hour or so since. Stoop down, Great Bear, and you will see that it is true."

"You're right, Tayoga," said Willet, after examining minutely.

"It follows, then," said the young Onondaga, in his precise tones, "that the white man was following the red men."

"It bears that look."

"And you will notice, Great Bear, and you, too, Dagaeoga, that the white man's moccasin has made a very large imprint. The owner of the foot is big. I know of none other in the forest so big except the Great Bear himself."

"Black Rifle!" exclaimed Robert, with a flash of insight.

"It can be none other."

"And he's following on the trail of these Indians, intending to ambush them when they camp tonight. He hunts them as we would hunt wolves."

Robert shuddered a little. It was a time when human life was held cheap in the wilderness, but he could not bring himself to slay except in self-defense.

"We need Black Rifle," said Willet, "and they'll need him more at the fort. We've an hour of fair sunlight left, and we must follow this trail as fast as we can and call him back. Lead the way, Tayoga."

The young Onondaga, without a word, set out at a running walk, and the others followed close behind. It was a plain trail. Evidently the warriors had no idea that they were followed, and the same was true of Black Rifle. Tayoga soon announced that both pursuers and pursued were going slowly, and, when the last sunlight was fading, they stopped at the crest of a hill and called, imitating first the cry of a wolf, and then the cry of an owl.

"He can't be more than three or four hundred yards away," said Willet, "and he may not understand either cry, but he's bound to know that they mean something."

"Suppose we stand out here where he can see us," said Robert. "He must be lurking in the thickets just ahead."

"The simplest way and so the right way," said Willet. "Come forth, you lads, where the eyes of Black Rifle may look upon you."

The three advanced from the shelter of the woods, and stood clearly outlined in an open space. A whistle came from a thicket scarce a hundred yards before them, and then they saw the striking figure of the great, swarthy man emerging. He came straight toward them, and, although he would not show it in his manner, Robert saw a gleam of gladness in the black eyes.

"What are you doing here, you three?" he asked.

"Following you," replied Robert in his usual role of spokesman.

"Why?"

"Tayoga saw the trail of the Indians overlaid by yours. We knew you were pursuing them, and we've come to stop you."

"By what right?"

"Because you're needed somewhere else. You're to go with us to Fort Refuge."

"What has happened?"

"Braddock's army was destroyed near Fort Duquesne. The general and many of his officers were killed. The rest are retreating far into the east. We're on our way to Fort Refuge to save the garrison and people if we can, and you're to go with us."

Black Rifle was silent a moment or two. Then he said:

"I feared Braddock would walk into an ambush, but I hardly believed his army would be annihilated. I don't hold it against him, because he turned my men and me away. How could I when he died with his soldiers?"

"He was a brave man," said Robert.

"I'm glad you found me. I'll leave the five Indians, though I could have ambushed 'em within the hour. The whole border must be ablaze, and they'll need us bad at Fort Refuge."

The three, now four, slept but little that night and they pressed forward all the next day, their anxiety to reach the fort before an attack could be made, increasing. It did not matter now if they arrived exhausted. The burden of their task was to deliver the word, to carry the warning. At dusk, they were within a few miles of the fort. An hour later they noticed a thread of blue smoke across the clear sky.

"It comes from the fort," said Tayoga.

"It's not on fire?" said Robert, aghast.

"No, Dagaeoga, the fort is not burning. We have come in time. The smoke rises from the chimneys."

"I say so, too," said Willet. "Unless there's a siege on now, we're ahead of the savages."

"There is no siege," said Tayoga calmly. "Tododaho has held the warriors back. Having willed for us to arrive first, nothing could prevent it."

"Again, I think you're right, Tayoga," said Robert, "and now for the fort. Let our feet devour the space that lies between."

He was in a mood of high exaltation, and the others shared his enthusiasm. They went faster than ever, and soon they saw rising in the moonlight the strong palisade and the stout log houses within it. Smoke ascended from several chimneys, and, uniting, made the line across the sky that they had beheld from afar. From their distant point of view they could not yet see the sentinels, and it was hard to imagine a more peaceful forest spectacle.

"At any rate, we can save 'em," said Robert.

"Perhaps," said Willet gravely, "but we come as heralds of disaster occurred, and of hardships to come. It will be a task to persuade them to leave this comfortable place and plunge into the wilderness."

"It's fortunate," said Robert, "that we know Colden and Wilton and Carson and all of them. We warned 'em once when they were coming to the place where the fort now is, and they didn't believe us, but they soon learned better. This time they'll know that we're making no mistake."

As they drew near they saw the heads of four sentinels projecting above the walls, one on each side of the square. The forest within rifle shot had also been cleared away, and Black Rifle spoke words of approval.

"They've learned," he said. "The city lads with the white hands have become men."

"A fine crowd of boys," said Willet, with hearty emphasis. "You'll see 'em acting with promptness and courage. Now, we want to tell 'em we're here without getting a bullet for our pains."

"Suppose you let me hail 'em," said Robert. "I'll stand on the little hill there—a bullet from the palisades can't reach me—and sing 'em a song or two."

"Go ahead," said the hunter.

Standing at his full height, young Lennox began to shout:

"Awake! Awake! Up! Up! We're friends! We're friends!"

His musical voice had wonderful carrying power, and the forest, and the open space in which the fort stood, rang with the sound. Robert became so much intoxicated with his own chanting that he did not notice its effect, until Willet called upon him to stop.

"They've heard you!" exclaimed the hunter. "Many of them have heard you! All of them must have heard you! Look at the heads appearing above the palisade!"

The side of the palisade fronting them was lined with faces, some the faces of soldiers and others the faces of civilians. Robert uttered a joyful exclamation.

"There's Colden!" he exclaimed. "The moonlight fell on him just then, and I can't be mistaken."

"And if my eyes tell me true, that's young Wilton beside him," said the hunter. "But come, lads, hold up your hands to show that we're friends, and we'll go into the fort."

They advanced, their hands, though they grasped rifles, held on high, but Robert, exalted and irrepressible, began to sing out anew:

"Hey, you, Colden! And you, too, Wilton and Carson! It's fine to see you again, alive and well."

There was silence on the wall, and then a great shout of welcome.

"It's Lennox, Robert Lennox himself!" cried someone.

"And Willet, the big hunter!"

"And there's Black Rifle, too!"

"And Tayoga, the Onondaga!"

"Open the gate for 'em! Let 'em come in, in honor."

The great gate was thrown wide, and the four entered quickly, to be surrounded at once by a multitude, eager for news of the outside world, from which they had been shut off so long. Torches, held aloft, cast a flickering light over young soldiers in faded uniforms, men in deerskin, and women in home-made linsey. Colden, and his two lieutenants, Wilton and Carson, stood together. They were thin, and their faces brown, but they looked wiry and rugged. Colden shook Robert's hand with great energy.

"I'm tremendously glad to see you," he exclaimed, "and I'm equally glad to see Mr. Willet, the great Onondaga, and Black Rifle. You're the first messengers from the outside world in more than a month. What news of victory do you bring? We heard that a great army of ours was marching against Duquesne."

Robert did not answer. He could not, because the words choked in his throat, and a silence fell over the crowd gathered in the court, over soldiers and men and women and children alike. A sudden apprehension seized the young commander and his lips trembled.

"What is it, Lennox, man?" he exclaimed. "Why don't you speak? What is it that your eyes are telling me?"

"They don't tell of any victory," replied Robert slowly.

"Then what do they tell?"

"I'm sorry, Colden, that I have to be the bearer of such news. I would have told it to you privately, but all will have to know it anyhow, and know it soon. There has been a great battle, but we did not win it."

"You mean we had to fall back, or that we failed to advance? But our army will fight again soon, and then it will crush the French and Indian bands!"

"General Braddock's army exists no longer."

"What? It's some evil jest. Say it's not true, Lennox!"

"It's an evil jest, but it's not mine, Colden. It's the jest of fate. General Braddock walked into a trap—it's twice I've told the terrible tale, once to Black Rifle and now to you—and he and his army were destroyed, all but a fragment of it that is now fleeing from the woods."

The full horror of that dreadful scene in the forest returned to him for a moment, and, despite himself, he made tone and manner dramatic. A long, deep gasp, like a groan, came from the crowd, and then Robert heard the sound of a woman on the outskirts weeping.

"Our army destroyed!" repeated Colden mechanically.

"And the whole border is laid bare to the French and Indian hosts," said Robert. "Many bands are converging now upon Fort Refuge, and the place cannot be held against so many."

"You mean abandon Fort Refuge?"

"Aye, Colden, it's what wiser men than I say, Dave here, and Tayoga, and Black Rifle."

"The lad is speaking you true, Captain Colden," said Willet. "Not only must you and your garrison and people leave Fort Refuge, but you must leave it tomorrow, and you must burn it, too."

Again Robert heard the sound of a woman weeping in the outskirts of the crowd.

"We held it once against the enemy," protested Colden.

"I know," said Willet, "but you couldn't do it now. A thousand warriors, yes, more, would gather here for the siege, and the French themselves would come with cannon. The big guns would blow your palisades to splinters. Your only safety is in flight. I know it's a hard thing to destroy the fort that your own men built, but the responsibility of all these women and children is upon you, and it must be done."

"So it is, Mr. Willet. I'm not one to gainsay you. I think we can be ready by daylight. Meanwhile you four rest, and I'll have food served to you. You've warned us and we can count upon you now to help us, can't we?"

"To the very last," said Willet.

After the first grief among the refugees was over the work of preparation was carried on with rapidity and skill, and mostly in silence. There were enough men or well grown boys among the settlers to bring the fighting force up to a hundred. Colden and his assistants knew much of the forest now, and they were willing and anxious, too, to take the advice of older and far more experienced men like Black Rifle and Willet.

"The fighting spirit bottled up so long in our line has surely ample opportunity to break out in me," said Wilton to Robert toward morning. "As I've told you before, Lennox, if I have any soldierly quality it's no credit of mine. It's a valor suppressed in my Quaker ancestors, but not eradicated."

"That is, if you fight you fight with the sword of your fathers and not your own."

"You put it well, Lennox, better than I could have stated it myself.
What has become of that wonderful red friend of yours?"

"Tayoga? He has gone into the forest to see how soon we can expect Tandakora, De Courcelles and the Indian host."

24

The Onondaga returned at dawn, saying that no attack need be feared before noon, as the Indian bands were gathering at an appointed place, and would then advance in great force.

"They'll find us gone by a good six hours," said Willet, "and we must make every minute of those six hours worth an ordinary day, because the warriors, wild at their disappointment, will follow, and at least we'll have to beat off their vanguard. It's lucky all these people are used to the forest."

Just as the first rim of the sun appeared they were ready. There were six wagons, drawn by stout horses, in which they put the spare ammunition and their most valuable possessions. Everybody but the drivers walked, the women and children in the center of the column, the best of the scouts and skirmishers in the woods on the flanks. Then at the command of Colden the whole column moved into the forest, but Tayoga, Willet and a half dozen others ran about from house to house, setting them on fire with great torches, making fifty blazes which grew rapidly, because the timbers were now dry, uniting soon into one vast conflagration.

Robert and Colden, from the edge of the forest, watched the destruction of Fort Refuge. They saw the solid log structures fall in, sending up great masses of sparks as the burning timbers crashed together. They saw the strong blockhouse go, and then they saw the palisade itself flaming. Colden turned away with a sigh.

"It's almost like burning your own manor house which you built yourself, and in which you expected to spend the remainder of your life," he said. "It hurts all the more, too, because it's a sign that we've lost the border."

"But we'll come back," said Robert, who had the will to be cheerful.

"Aye, so we will," said Colden, brightening. "We'll sweep back these French and Indians, and we'll come here and rebuild Fort Refuge on this very spot. I'll see to it, myself. This *is* a splendid place for a fort, isn't it, Lennox?"

"So it is," replied Robert, smiling, "and I've no doubt, Colden, that you'll supervise the rebuilding of Fort Refuge."

And in time, though the interval was great, it did come to pass.

Colden was not one to be gloomy long, and there was too much work ahead for one to be morbid. Willet had spoken of the precious six hours and they were, in, truth, more precious than diamonds. The flight was pushed to the utmost, the old people or the little children who grew weary were put in the wagons, and the speed they made was amazing for the wilderness. Robert remained well in the rear with Tayoga, Willet and Black Rifle, and they continually watched the forest for the first appearance of the Indian pursuit. That, in time, it would appear they never doubted, and it was their plan to give the vanguard of the warriors such a hot reception that they would hesitate. Besides the hundred fighting men, including the soldiers and boys large enough to handle arms, there were about a hundred women and children. Colden marched with the main column, and Wilton and Carson were at the rear. Black Rifle presently went ahead to watch lest they walk into an ambush, while Tayoga, Robert and Willet remained behind, the point from which the greatest danger was apprehended.

"Isn't it likely," asked Robert, "that the Indians will see the light of the burning fort, and that it will cause them to hasten?"

"More probably it will set them to wondering," replied the hunter, "and they may hesitate. They may think a strong force has come to rescue the garrison and people."

"But whatever Tandakora and the officer of Onontio may surmise," said Tayoga, "our own course is plain, and that is to march as fast as we can."

"And hope that a body of Colonial troops and perhaps the Mohawks will come to help us," said Willet. "Colonel William Johnson, as we all know, is alert and vigorous, and it would be like him to push westward for the protection of settlers and refugees. 'Twould be great luck, Tayoga, if that bold young friend of yours, Daganoweda, the Mohawk chief, should be in this region."

"It is not probable," said the Onondaga. "The Keepers of the Eastern Gate are likely to remain in their own territory. They would not, without a strong motive, cross the lands of the other nations of the Hodenosaunee, but it is not impossible. They may have such a motive."

"Then let us hope that it exists!" exclaimed Robert fervently. "The sight of Daganoweda and a hundred of his brave Mohawks would lift a mighty load from my mind."

Tayoga smiled. A compliment to the Mohawks was a compliment to the entire Hodenosaunee, and therefore to the Onondagas as well. Moreover the fame and good name of the Mohawks meant almost as much to him as the fame and good name of the Onondagas.

"The coming of Daganoweda would be like the coming of light itself," he said.

They were joined by Wilton, who, as Robert saw, had become a fine forest soldier, alert, understanding and not conceited because of his knowledge. Robert noted the keen, wary look of this young man of Quaker blood, and he felt sure that in the event of an attack he would be among the very best of the defenders.

"The spirit of battle, bursting at last in you, Will, from its long confinement, is likely to have full chance for gratification," he said.

"So it will, Lennox, and I tremble to think of what that released spirit may do. If I achieve any deed of daring and valor bear in mind that it's not me, but the escaped spirit of previous ages taking violent and reckless charge of my weak and unwilling flesh."

"Suppose we form a curtain behind our retreating caravan," said Robert. "A small but picked force could keep back the warriors a long time, and permit our main column to continue its flight unhampered."

"A good idea! an idea most excellent!" exclaimed Willet.

As a matter of form, the three being entirely independent in their movements, the suggestion was made to Colden, and he agreed at once and with thorough approval. Thirty men, including Willet, Robert, Tayoga and Wilton, were chosen as a fighting rear guard, and the hunter himself took command of it. Spreading out in a rather long line to prevent being flanked, they dropped back and let the train pass out of sight on its eastern flight.

They were now about ten miles from the burned fort, and, evidences of pursuit not yet being visible, Robert became hopeful that the caution of Tandakora and De Courcelles would hold them back a long time. He and Tayoga kept together, but the thirty were stretched over a distance of several hundred yards, and now they retreated very slowly, watching continually for the appearance of hostile warriors.

"They have, of course, a plain trail to follow," Robert said. "One could not have a better trace than that made by wagon wheels. It's just a matter of choice with them whether they come fast or not."

"I think we are not likely to see them before the night," said Tayoga. "Knowing that the column has much strength, they will prefer the darkness and ambush."

"But they're not likely to suspect the screen that we have thrown out to cover the retreat."

"No, that is the surprise we have prepared for them. But even so, we, the screen, may not come into contact with them before the dark."

Tayoga's calculation was correct. The entire day passed while the rear guard retreated slowly, and all the aspects of the forest were peaceful. They saw no pursuing brown figures and they heard no war cry, nor the call of one band to another. Yet Robert felt that the night would bring a hostile appearance of some kind or other. Tandakora and De Courcelles when they came upon the site of the burned fort would not linger long there, but would soon pass on in eager pursuit, hoping to strike a fleeing multitude, disorganized by panic. But he smiled to himself at the thought that they would strike first against the curtain of fire and steel, that is, the thirty to whom he belonged.

When night came he and Tayoga were still together and Willet was a short distance away. He watched the last light of the sun die and then the dusk deepen, and he felt sure that the approach of the pursuing host could not be long delayed. His eyes continually searched the thickets and forest in front of them for a sight of the savage vanguard.

"Can you see Tododaho upon his star?" he asked Tayoga in all earnestness.

"The star is yet faint in the heavens," replied the Onondaga, "and I can only trace across its face the mists and vapors which are the snakes in the hair of the great chieftain, but Tododaho will not desert us. We, his children, the Onondagas, have done no harm, and I, Tayoga, am one of them. I feel that all the omens and presages are favorable."

The reply of the Onondaga gave Robert new strength. He had the deepest respect for the religion of the Hodenosaunee, which he felt was so closely akin to his own, and Tododaho was scarcely less real to him than to Tayoga. His veins thrilled with confidence that they would drive back, or at least hold Tandakora and De Courcelles, if they came.

The last and least doubt that they would come was dispelled within an hour when Tayoga suddenly put a hand upon his arm, and, in a whisper, told him to watch a bush not more than a hundred yards away.

"A warrior is in the thicket," he said. "I would not have seen him as he crept forward had not a darker shadow appeared upon the shadow of the night. But he is there, awaiting a chance to steal upon us and fire."

"And others are near, seeking the same opportunity."

"It is so, Dagaeoga. The attack will soon begin."

"Shall we warn Willet?"

"The Great Bear has seen already. His eyes pierce the dark and they have noted the warrior, and the other warriors. Lie down, Dagaeoga, the first warrior is going to fire."

Robert sank almost flat. There was a report in the bush, a flash of fire, and a bullet whistled high over their heads. From a point on their right came an answering report and flash, and the warrior in the bush uttered his death cry. Robert, who was watching him, saw him throw up his hands and fall.

"It was the bullet of the Great Bear that replied," said Tayoga. "It was rash to fire when such a marksman lay near. Now the battle begins."

The forest gave forth a great shout, penetrating and full of menace, coming in full volume, and indicating to the shrewd ears of Tayoga the presence of two or three hundred warriors. Robert knew, too, that a large force was now before them. How long could the thirty hold back the Indian hosts? Yet he had the word of Tayoga that Tododaho looked down upon them with benignity and that all the omens and presages were favorable. There was a flash at his elbow and a rifle sang its deadly song in his ear. Then Tayoga uttered a sigh of satisfaction.

"My bullet was not wasted," he said.

27

Robert waited his opportunity, and fired at a dusky figure which he saw fall. He was heart and soul averse to bloodshed, but in the heat of action, and in self-defense, he forgot his repugnance. He was as eager now for a shot as Tayoga, Willet, or any other of the thirty. Tayoga, who had reloaded, pulled trigger again and then a burst of firing came from the savage host. But the thirty, inured to the forest and forest warfare, were sheltered well, and they took no hurt. The Indians who were usually poor marksmen, fired many bullets after their fashion and wasted much lead.

"They make a great noise, inflict no wounds, and do not advance," whispered Tayoga to Robert.

"Doubtless they are surprised much at meeting our line in the forest, and think us many times more numerous than we are."

"And we may fill their minds with illusions," said Robert hopefully. "They may infer from our strong resistance that reënforcements have come, that the Mohawks are here, or that Colonel Johnson himself has arrived with Colonial troops."

"It may be that Waraiyageh will come in time," said Tayoga. "Ah, they are trying to pass around our right flank."

His comment was drawn by distant shots on their right. The reports, however, did not advance, and the two, reassured, settled back into their places. Three or four of the best scouts and skirmishers were at the threatened point, and they created the effect of at least a dozen. Robert knew that the illusion of a great force confronting them was growing in the Indian mind, and his heart glowed with satisfaction. While they held the savage host the fugitive train was putting fresh miles between them and pursuit. Suddenly he raised his own rifle and fired. Then he uttered a low cry of disappointment.

"It was Tandakora himself," he said. "I couldn't mistake his size, but it was only a glimpse, and I missed."

"The time of the Ojibway has not come," said Tayoga with conviction, "but it will come before this war is over."

"The sooner the better for our people and yours, Tayoga."

"That is so, Dagaeoga."

They did not talk much more for a long time because the combat in the forest and the dark deepened, and the thirty were so active that there was little time for question or answer. They crept back and forth from bush to bush and from log to log, firing whenever they saw a flitting form, and reloading with quick fingers. Now and then Willet, or some other, would reply with a defiant shout to the yells of the warriors, and thus, while the combat of the sharpshooters surged to and fro in the dim light, many hours passed.

But the thirty held the line. Robert knew that the illusion of at least a hundred, doubtless more, was created in the minds of the warriors, and, fighting with their proverbial caution, they would attempt no rush. He had a sanguine belief now that they could hold the entire host until day, and then the fleeing train would be at least twenty miles farther on. A few of the thirty had been wounded, though not badly enough to put them out of the combat, but Robert himself had not been touched. As usual with him in moments of success or triumph his spirits flamed high, and his occasional shout of defiance rose above the others.

"In another hour," said Tayoga, "we must retreat."

"Why?" asked Robert. "When we're holding 'em so well?"

"By day they will be able to discover how few we are, and then, although they may not be able to force our front, they will surely spread out and pass around our flanks. I do not see the Great Bear now, but I know he thinks so, too, and it will not be long before we hear from him."

Within five minutes Willet, who was about a hundred yards away, uttered a low whistle, which drew to him Robert, Tayoga and others, and then he passed the word by them to the whole line to withdraw swiftly, but in absolute silence, knowing that the longer Tandakora and De Courcelles thought the defenders were in their immediate front the better it was for their purpose. Seven of the thirty were wounded, but not one of them was put out of the combat. Their hurts merely stung them to renewed energy, and lighted higher in them the fire of battle.

Under the firm leadership of Willet they retreated as a group, wholly without noise, vanishing in the thickets, and following fast on the tracks left by the wagons. When the sun rose they stopped and Tayoga went back to see if the Indian host was yet coming. He returned in an hour saying there was no indication of pursuit, and Robert exulted.

"We've come away, and yet we are still there!" he exclaimed.

"What do you mean?" asked Willet.

"We abandoned our position, but we left the great illusion there for the warriors. They think we're still before 'em and so long as that illusion lasts it will hold 'em. So you see, Dave, an illusion is often fully as good as reality."

"It may be for a little while, but it doesn't last as long. Within another hour Tandakora and De Courcelles will surely find out that we've gone, and then, raging mad, they'll come on our trail."

"And we'll meet 'em with a second stand, I suppose?"

"If we can find a good place for defense."

One of the men, Oldham, who had been sent ahead, soon returned with news that the train had crossed a deep creek with rather high banks.

"It was a hard ford," he said, "but I followed the trail some distance on the other side, and they seem to have made the passage without any bad accident."

"Was the far bank of the creek thick with forest?" asked Willet.

"Trees and undergrowth are mighty dense there," replied Oldham.

"Then that's the place for our second stand. If we can hold the creek against 'em for three or four hours more it will be another tremendous advantage gained. With high banks and the woods and thickets on 'em so dense, we ought to create what Robert would call a second illusion."

"We will!" exclaimed Robert. "We can do it!"

"At least, we'll try," said Willet, and he led the little force at speed toward the creek.

CHAPTER IV

A FOREST CONCERT

The deep creek with its high banks and interwoven forest and thickets on the other side formed an excellent second line of defense, and Willet, with the instinct of a true commander, made the most of it, again posting his men at wide intervals until they covered a distance of several hundred yards, at the same time instructing them to conceal themselves carefully, and let the enemy make the first move. He allowed Robert and Tayoga to remain together, knowing they were at their best when partners.

The two lay behind the huge trunk of a tree torn down by some old hurricane and now almost hidden by vegetation and trailing vines. They were very comfortable there, and, uplifted by their success of the night they were sanguine of an equal success by day.

29

To the right Robert caught occasional glimpses of Willet, moving about in the bushes, but save for these stray glances he watched the other side of the stream. Luckily it was rather open there, and no savage, however cunning, could come within fifty yards of it without being seen by the wary eyes in the thickets.

"How long do you think it will be before they come?" Robert asked of Tayoga, for whose forest lore he had an immense respect.

"Three hours, maybe four," replied the Onondaga. "Tandakora and De Courcelles may or may not know of this creek, but when they see it they are sure to advance with caution, fearing a trap."

"What a pity our own people don't show the same wisdom!"

"You are thinking of the great slaughter at Duquesne. Every people has its own ways, and the soldiers have not yet learned those of the forest, but they *will* learn."

"At a huge cost!"

"Perhaps there is no other way? You will notice the birds on the bushes on the far side of the stream, Dagaeoga?"

"Aye, I see 'em. They're in uncommon numbers. What a fine lot of fellows with glossy plumage! And some of 'em are singing away as if they lived for nothing else!"

"I see that Dagaeoga looks when he is told to look and sees when he is told to see. The birds are at peace and are enjoying themselves."

"That is, they're having a sunlight concert, purely for their own pleasure."

"It is so. They feel joy and know that danger is not present. They are protected by the instinct that Manitou, watching over the least of his creatures, has given to them."

"Why this dissertation on birds at such a time, Tayoga?"

"Dissertation is a very long word, but I am talking for Dagaeoga's own good. He has learned much of the forest, but he can learn more, and I am here to teach him."

"Wondrous good of you, Tayoga, and, in truth, your modesty also appeals to me. Proceed with your lesson in woodcraft, although it seems to me that you have chosen a critical time for it."

"The occasion is most fitting, because it comes out of our present danger. We wish to see the approach of our enemies who will lie down among the grass and bushes, and creep forward very silently. We will not see them, perhaps, but others will give warning."

"Oh, you mean that the birds, alarmed by the warriors, will fly away?"

"Nothing else, Dagaeoga."

"Then why so much circumlocution?"

"Circumlocution is another very long word, Dagaeoga. It is the first time that I have heard it used since we left the care of our teacher in Albany. But I came to the solution by a circular road, because I wished you to see it before I told it to you. You did see it, and so I feel encouraged over the progress of my pupil."

"Thanks, Tayoga, I appreciate the compliment, and, as I said before, your modesty also appeals to me."

"You waste words, Dagaeoga, but you have always been a great talker. Now, watch the birds."

Tayoga laughed softly. The Indian now and then, in his highest estate, used stately forms of rhetoric, and it pleased the young Onondaga, who had been so long in the white man's school, to employ sometimes the most orotund English. It enabled him to develop his vein of irony, with which he did not spare Robert, just as Robert did not spare him.

"I will watch the birds," said young Lennox. "They're intelligent, reasoning beings, and I'll lay a wager that while they're singing away there they're not singing any songs that make fun of their friends."

"Of that I'm not sure, Dagaeoga. Look at the bird with the red crest, perched on the topmost tip of the tall, green bush directly in front of us. I can distinguish his song from those of the others, and it seems that the note contains something saucy and ironic."

"I see him, Tayoga. He is an impudent little rascal, but I should call him a most sprightly and attractive bird, nevertheless. Observe how his head is turned on one side. If we were only near enough to see his eyes I'd lay another wager that he is winking."

"But his head is not on one side any longer, Dagaeoga. He has straightened up. If you watch one object a long time you will see it much more clearly, and so I am able to observe his actions even at this distance. He has ceased to sing. His position is that of a soldier at attention. He is suspicious and watchful."

"You're right, Tayoga. I can see, too, that the bird's senses are on the alert against something foreign in the forest. All the other birds, imitating the one who seems to be their leader, have ceased singing also."

"And the leader is unfolding his wings."

"So I see. He is about to fly away. There he goes like a flash of red flame!"

"And there go all the rest, too. It is enough. Tandakora, De Courcelles and the savages have come."

Robert and Tayoga crouched a little lower and stared over the fallen log. Presently the Onondaga touched the white youth on the arm. Robert, following his gaze, made out the figure of a warrior creeping slowly through a dense thicket toward the creek.

"It is likely that Great Bear sees him, too," said Tayoga, "but we will not fire. He will not come nearer than fifty yards, because good cover is lacking."

"I understand that the contest is to be one of patience. So they can loose their bullets first. I see the bushes moving in several places now, Tayoga."

"It is probable that their entire force has come up. They may wait at least an hour before they will try a ford."

"Like as not. Suppose we eat a little venison, Tayoga, and strengthen ourselves for the ordeal."

"You have spoken well, Dagaeoga."

They ate strips of venison contentedly, but did not neglect to keep a wary watch upon the creeping foe. Robert knew that Tandakora and De Courcelles were trying to discover whether or not the line of the creek was defended, and if Willet and his men remained well hidden it would take a long time for them to ascertain the fact. He enjoyed their perplexity, finding in the situation a certain sardonic humor.

"The Ojibway and the Frenchman would give a good deal to know just what is in the thickets here," he whispered to Tayoga. "But the longer they must take in finding out the better I like it."

"They will delay far into the afternoon," said Tayoga. "The warriors and the Frenchmen have great patience. It would be better for the Americans and the English if they, too, like the French, learned the patience of the Indians."

"The birds gave us a warning that they had come. You don't think it possible, Tayoga, that they will also give the savages warning that we are here?"

"No, Dagaeoga, we have been lying in the thickets so long now, and have been so quiet that the birds have grown used to us. They feel sure we are not going to do them any harm, and while they may have flown away when we first came they are back now, as you can see with your own eyes, and can hear with your own ears."

Almost over Robert's head a small brown bird on a small green bough was singing, pouring out a small sweet song that was nevertheless clear and penetrating. Within the radius of his sight a half dozen more were trilling and quavering, and he knew that others were pouring out their souls farther on, as the low hum of their many voices came to his ears. Now and then he saw a flash of blue or brown or gray, as some restless feathered being shot from one bough to another. The birds, unusual in number and sure that there was no hostile presence, were having a grand concert in honor of a most noble day.

Robert listened and the appeal to his imagination and higher side was strong. Overhead the chorus of small sweet voices went on, as if there were no such things as battle or danger. Tayoga also was moved by it.

"By the snakes in the hair of the wise Tododaho," he said, "it is pleasant to hear! May the wilderness endure always that the birds can sing in it, far from men, and in peace!"

"May it not be, Tayoga, that the warriors watching the thickets here will see the birds so thick, and will conclude from it that no defenders are lying in wait?"

"De Courcelles might, but Tandakora, who has lived his whole life in the forest, will conclude that the birds are here, unafraid, because we have been so long in the bushes."

Time went on very slowly and the forest on either side of the creek was silent, save for the singing of the birds among the bushes in which the defenders lay hidden. Robert, from whom the feeling of danger departed for the moment, was almost tempted into? a doze by the warmth of the thicket and the long peace. His impressions, the pictures that passed before his mental and physical eye, were confused but agreeable. He was lying on a soft bank of turf that sloped up to a huge fallen trunk, and warm, soothing winds stole about among the boughs, rustling the leaves musically. The birds were singing in increased volume, and, though his eyes were half veiled by drooping lids, he saw them on many boughs.

"'Tis not their daily concert," he said to Tayoga "In very truth it must be their grand, annual affair I believe that a great group on our right is singing against another equally great group on our left. I can't recall having heard ever before such a volume of song in the woods. It's in my mind that a contest is going on, for a prize, perhaps. Doubtless juicy worms are awaiting the winners."

Tayoga laughed.

"You are improving, Dagaeoga," he said in precise tones. "You do not merely fight and eat and sleep like the white man. You are developing a soul. You are beginning to understand the birds and animals that live in the woods. Almost I think you worthy to be an Onondaga."

"I know you can pay me what is to you no higher compliment, but I have a notion the end of the concert is not far away. It seems to me the volume of song from the group on the left is diminishing."

"And you notice no decrease on our right?"

"No, Tayoga. The grand chorus there is as strong as ever, and unless my ears go wrong, I detect in it a triumphant note."

"Then the test of song which you have created is finished, and the prize has been won by the group on the right. It is a fine conceit that you have about the birds, Dagaeoga. I like it, and we will see it to the end."

The song on their left died, the one on their right swelled anew, and then died in its turn. Soon the birds began to drift slowly away. Robert watched some of them as they disappeared among the green boughs farther on.

"I also am learning to read the signs, Tayoga," he said, "and, having observed 'em, I conclude that our foes are about to make an advance, or at least, have crept forward a little more. The birds, used to our presence, know we are neither dangerous nor hostile, but they do not know as much about those on the other side of the creek. While the advance of the warriors is not yet sufficient to threaten 'em, it's enough to make 'em suspicious, and so they are flying away slowly, ready to return if it be a false alarm."

"Good! Very good, Dagaeoga! I can believe that your conclusions are true, and I can say to you once more that almost you are worthy to be an Onondaga. If you will look now toward the spot where the banks shelve down, and the grass grows high you will see four warriors on their hands and knees approaching the creek. If they reach the water without being fired upon they will assume that we are not here. Then the entire force will rush across the stream and take up the trail."

"But the creeping four will be fired upon."

"I think so, too, Dagaeoga, because there is no longer any reason for us to delay, and the rifle of the Great Bear will speak the first word."

There was a report near them, and one of the warriors, sinking flat in the grass, lay quite still. Robert, through the bushes, saw Willet, smoking rifle in hand. The three savages who lived began a swift retreat, and the others behind them uttered a great cry of grief and rage. They fired a dozen shots or so, but the bullets merely clipped leaves and twigs in the thickets. Nobody among the defenders save Willet pulled trigger, but his single shot was a sufficient warning to Tandakora and De Courcelles. They knew that the creek was held strongly.

Now ensued another long combat in which the skill, courage and ingenuity of warriors and hunters were put to the supreme test. Many shots were fired, but faces and bodies were shown only for an instant. Nevertheless a bullet now and then went home. One of Willet's men was killed and three more sustained slight wounds. Several of the warriors were slain, and others were wounded, but Robert had no means of telling the exact number of their casualties, as it was an almost invisible combat, which Willet and Tayoga, as the leaders, used all their skill to prolong to the utmost with the smallest loss possible. What they wanted was time, time for the fugitive train, now far away among the hills.

So deftly did they manage the defense of the creek that the entire afternoon passed and Tandakora and De Courcelles were still held in front of it, not daring to make a rush, and Willet, Robert and Tayoga glowed with the triumph they were achieving at a cost relatively so small. Night arrived, fortunately for them thick and black, and Willet gathered up his little force. They would have taken away with them the body of the slain man, but that was impossible, and, covering it up with brush and stones, they left it. Then still uplifted and exulting, they slipped away on the trail of the wagons, knowing that the Indian horde might watch for hours at the creek before they discovered the departure of the defenders.

"You see, Dagaeoga," said Tayoga to Robert, "that there is more in war than fighting. Craft and cunning, wile and stratagem are often as profitable as the shock of conflict."

"So I know, Tayoga. I learned it well in the battle by Duquesne. What right had a force of French and Indians which must have been relatively small to destroy a fine army like ours!"

"No right at all," said Willet, "but it happened, nevertheless. We'll learn from it, though it's a tremendous price to pay for a lesson."

"Do we make a third stand somewhere, Dave?" asked Robert, "and delay them yet another time?"

33

"I scarcely see a chance for it," replied the hunter. "We must have favorable ground or they'd outflank us. How old does the trail of the wagons look, Tayoga?"

"They are many, many hours ahead," replied the Onondaga. "They have made good use of the time we have secured for them."

"Another day and night and they should be safe," said Willet. "Tandakora and De Courcelles will scarcely dare follow deep into the fringe of settlements. What is it, Tayoga?"

The Onondaga had stopped and, kneeling down, he was examining the trail as minutely as he could in the dusk.

"Others have come," he replied tersely.

"What do you mean by 'others'?" asked Willet.

"Those who belong neither to pursued nor pursuers, a new force, white men, fifteen, perhaps. They came down from the north, struck this trail, for which they were not looking, and have turned aside from whatever task they were undertaking to see what it means."

"And so they're following the fugitive train. Possibly it's a band of French."

"I do not think so, Great Bear. The French do not roam the forest alone. The warriors are always with them, and this party is composed wholly of white men."

"Then they must be ours, perhaps a body of hunters or scouts, and we need 'em. How long would you say it has been since they passed?"

"Not more than two hours."

"Then we must overtake 'em. Do you lead at speed, Tayoga, but on the bare possibility that they're French, look out for an ambush."

"The new people, whoever they are," said Robert, "are trailing the train, we're trailing them, and the French and Indians are trailing us. It's like a chain drawing its links through the forest."

"But the links are of different metals, Robert," said Willet.

They talked but little more, because they needed all their breath now for the pursuit, as Tayoga was leading at great speed, the broad trail in the moonlight being almost as plain as day. It was a pleasure to Robert to watch the Onondaga following like a hound on the scent. His head was bent forward a little, and now and then when the brightest rays fell across them, Robert could see that his eyes glittered. He was wholly the Indian, his white culture gone for the moment, following the wilderness trail as his ancestors had done for centuries before him.

"Do the traces of the new group grow warmer?" asked Robert.

"They do," replied Tayoga. "We are advancing just twice as fast as they. We will overtake them before midnight."

"White men, and only by the barest possibility French," said Robert. "So the chances are nine out of ten that they're our own people. Now, I wonder what they are and what they're doing here."

"Patience, Dagaeoga," said the young Onondaga. "We will learn by midnight. How often have I told you that you must cultivate patience before you are worthy to be an Onondaga?"

"I'll bear it in mind, O worthy teacher. Your great age and vast learning compel me to respect your commands."

The new trail, which was like a narrow current in the broad stream of that left by the flying train, was now rapidly growing warmer. The speed of the thirty was so great that it became evident to Tayoga that they would overtake the strange band long before midnight.

"They stopped here and talked together a little while," he said, when they had been following the trail about two hours. "They stood by the side of the path. Their footprints are gathered in a group. They knew by the wagon tracks that white settlers, fleeing, were ahead of them, and they may have thought of turning back to see who followed. That is why they drew up in a group, and talked. At last they concluded to keep on following the train, and they cannot be more than a half hour ahead now."

Willet knelt down for the first time, and examined the traces with the greatest care and attention.

"The leader stood here by this fallen log," he said, "He had big feet, as anybody can see, and I believe I can make a good guess at his identity. I hope to Heaven I'm right!"

"Whom do you mean?" exclaimed Robert eagerly.

"I won't say just yet, because if I'm wrong you won't know the mistake I've made. But come on, lads. 'Twill not take long to decide the question that interests us so much."

He led the way with confidence, and when they had gone about a mile he sank down in a thicket beside the trail, the others imitating him. Then the hunter emitted a sharp whistle.

"I think I'll soon get an answer to that," he said, "and it'll not come from French or Indian."

They waited a minute or two and then the whistling note, clear and distinct, rose from a point ahead of them. Willet whistled a second time, and the second reply soon came in similar fashion.

"Now, lads," he said, rising from the bush, "we'll up and join 'em. It's the one I expected, and right glad I am, too."

He led the way boldly, making no further effort at concealment. Robert saw outlined in the moonlight on a low hill in front of them a group of fifteen or sixteen white men, all in hunter's garb, all strong, resolute figures, armed heavily. One, a little in advance of the others, and whom the lad took at once to be the leader, was rather tall, with a very powerful figure and a bold, roving eye. He was looking keenly at the approaching group and as they drew near his eyes lighted up with recognition and pleasure.

"By all that's glorious, it's Dave Willet, the Great Bear himself, the greatest hunter and marksman in all the northern province! Of a certainty it's none other!"

"Yes, Rogers, it's Willet," said the hunter, extending his hand, "though you complimented me too prettily. But glad am I, too, to see you here. You're no beauty, but your face is a most welcome sight."

Then Robert understood. It was Robert Rogers from the New Hampshire grants, already known well, and destined to become famous as one of the great partisan leaders of the war, a wild and adventurous spirit who was fully a match for Dumas and Ligneris or St. Luc himself, a man whose battles and hairbreadth escapes surpassed fiction. Around him gathered spirits dauntless and kindred, and here already was the nucleus of the larger force that he was destined to lead in so many a daring deed. Now his fierce face showed pleasure, as he shook the hunter's powerful hand with his own hand almost as powerful.

"It's a joy to meet you in these woods, Dave," he said. "But who are the two likely lads with you? Lads, I call 'em because their faces are those of lads, though their figures have the stature and size of men."

"Rogers, this is Tayoga, of the clan of the Bear, of the nation Onondaga, of the great League of the Hodenosaunee, a friend of ours, and

35

no braver or more valiant youth ever trod moccasin. Tayoga, this is Robert Rogers of the New Hampshire grants."

The sunburnt face of Rogers shone with pleasure.

"I've heard of the lad," he said, "and I know he's all that you claim for him, Dave."

"And the other youth," continued Willet, "is Robert Lennox, in a way a ward of mine, in truth almost a son to me. What Tayoga is among the Onondagas, he is among the white people of New York. I can say no more."

"That's surely enough," said Rogers, "and glad am I to meet you, Lennox. I've come from the north and the east, from Champlain and George, with my brave fellows, hearing of Braddock's defeat and thinking we might be needed, and by chance we struck this broad trail. It's plain enough that it's made by settlers withdrawing from the border, but whether 'tis a precaution or they're pursued closely we don't know. We thought once of turning back to see. But you know, Dave."

Willet explained rapidly and again the fierce face of Rogers shone with pleasure.

"'Twas in truth a fortunate chance that guided us down here," he said.

"It was Tododaho himself," said Tayoga with reverence.

Then Willet also called rapidly the names of his hunters and scouts, who had remained in a little group in the rear, while the leaders talked.

"Dave," said Rogers, "you and I will be joint leaders, if you say so. We've now nearly two score stout fellows ready for any fray, and since you've twice held back Tandakora, De Courcelles and their scalp hunters, our united bands should be able to do it a third time. I agree with you that the best way to save the train is to fight rear guard actions, and never let the train itself be attacked."

"If we had about twenty more good men," said Willet, "we might not only defend a line but push back the horde itself. What say you to sending Tayoga, our swiftest runner, to the wagons for a third force?"

"A good plan, a most excellent plan, Dave! And while he's about it, tell him to make it thirty instead of twenty. Then we'll burn the faces of these Indian warriors. Aye, Dave, we'll scorch 'em so well that they'll be glad to turn back!"

It was arranged in a minute or two and Tayoga disappeared like one of his own arrows in the forest and the darkness, while the others followed, but much more slowly. It would not escape the sharp eyes of the warriors that a reënforcement had come, but, confident in their numbers, they would continue the pursuit with unabated zeal.

The united bands of hunters and scouts fell back slowly, and for a long time. Robert looked with interest at Rogers' men. They were the picked survivors of the wilderness, the forest champions, young mostly, lean, tough of muscle, darkened by wind and weather, ready to follow wherever their leader led, ready to risk their lives in any enterprise, no matter how reckless. They affiliated readily with Willet's own band, and were not at all averse to being overtaken by the Indian horde.

After dawn they met Tayoga returning with thirty-five men, rather more than they had expected, and also with the news that the train was making great speed in its flight. Willet and Rogers looked over the seventy or more brave fellows, with glistening eyes, and Robert saw very well that, uplifted by their numbers, they were more than anxious for a third combat. In an hour or so they found a place suitable for an ambush, a long ravine, lined and filled with thickets which the wagons evidently had crossed with difficulty, and here they took their stand, all of the force hidden among the bushes and weeds. Robert, at the advice of Willet, lay down in a secure place and went to sleep.

"You're young, lad," he said, "and not as much seasoned in the bark as the rest of us who are older. I'll be sure to wake you when the battle begins, and then you'll be so much the better for a nap that you'll be a very Hercules in the combat."

Robert, trained in wilderness ways, knew that it was best, and he closed his eyes without further ado. When he opened them again it was because the hunter was shaking his shoulder, and he knew by the position of the sun that several hours had passed.

"Have they come?" he asked calmly.

"We've seen their skirmishers in the woods about two hundred yards away," replied the hunter. "I believe they suspect danger here merely because this is a place where danger is likely to be, but 'twill not keep them from attacking. You can hold your rifle ready, lad, but you'll have no use for it for a good quarter of an hour. They'll do a lot of scouting before they try to pass the ravine, but our fellows are happy in the knowledge that they'll try to pass it."

Robert suppressed as much as he could the excitement one was bound to feel at such a time, and ate a little venison to stay him for the combat, imitating the coolness and providence of Tayoga, who was also strengthening his body for the ordeal.

"About noon, isn't it?" he asked of the Onondaga.

"A little after it," Tayoga replied.

"When did they come up?"

"Just now. I too have slept, although my sleep was shorter than yours."

"Have you seen Tandakora or De Courcelles?"

"I caught one glimpse of Tandakora. My bullet will carry far, but alas! it will not carry far enough to reach the Ojibway. It is not the will of Tododaho that he should perish now. As I have said, his day will come, though it is yet far away."

"What will happen here, Tayoga?"

"The forces of Tandakora and De Courcelles will be burned worse than before. The man Rogers, whom some of the Mohawks call the Mountain Wolf, is like a Mohawk warrior himself, always eager to fight. He will want to push the battle and Great Bear, having so many men now, will be willing."

The words of Tayoga came to pass. After a long delay, accompanied by much scouting and attempts to feel out the defense, Tandakora and De Courcelles finally charged the ravine in force and suffered a bitter repulse. Seventy or eighty rifles, aimed by cool and experienced sharpshooters, poured in a fire which they could not withstand, and so many warriors were lost that the Ojibway and the Frenchman retreated. The Great Bear and the Mountain Wolf would not allow their eager men to follow, lest in their turn they fall into an ambush.

Later in the day the Indian horde returned a second time to the attack, with the same result, and when night came Tayoga and several others who went forward to scout reported that they had withdrawn several miles. The white leaders then decided in conference that they had done enough for their purpose, and, after a long rest on their arms, withdrew slowly in the path of the retreating train, ready for another combat, if pursued too closely, but feeling sure that Tandakora and De Courcelles would not risk a battle once more.

They overtook the train late that evening and their welcome was enough to warm their hearts and to repay them for all the hardships and dangers endured. Colden was the first to give them thanks, and his fine young face showed his emotion.

"I'm sorry I couldn't have been back there with you," he said, when he heard the report Robert made; "you had action, and you faced the enemy, while we have merely been running over the hills."

"In truth you've made a good run of it," said Robert, "and as I see it, it was just as necessary for you to run as it was for us to fight. We had great luck, too, in the coming of Rogers and his men."

That night the train, for the first time since it began its flight, made a real camp. Willet, Rogers and all the great foresters thought it safe, as they were coming now so near to the settled regions, and the faces of the pursuers had been scorched so thoroughly. Scouts and skirmishers were thrown out on all sides, and then fires were built of the fallen brushwood that lay everywhere in the forest. The ample supplies in the wagons were drawn upon freely, and the returning victors feasted at their leisure.

It was a happy time for Robert. His imaginative mind responded as usual to time and place. They had won one victory. It was no small triumph to protect the fugitive train, and so they would win many more. He already saw them through the flame of his sanguine temperament, and the glow of the leaping fires helped in the happy effect. All around him were cheerful faces and he heard the chatter of happy voices, their owners happy because they believed themselves released from a great and imminent danger.

"Has anything been heard of Black Rifle?" Robert asked of Tayoga.

"He has not come back," replied the Onondaga, "but they think he will be here in the morning."

The dawn brought instead fifty dusky figures bare to the waist and painted in all the terrible imagery of Indians who go to war. Some of the women cried out in fright, but Tayoga said:

"Have no fear. These be friends. The warriors of our great brother nation, the Ganeagaono, known to you as the Mohawks, have come to aid us."

The leader of the Mohawks was none other than the daring young chief, Daganoweda himself, flushed with pride that he had come to the help of his white brethren, and eager as always for war. He gravely saluted Robert, Willet and Tayoga.

"Dagaeoga is a storm bird," he said. "Wherever he goes battle follows."

"Either that," laughed Robert, "or because I follow battle. How could I keep from following it, when I have Willet on one side of me and Tayoga on the other, always dragging me to the point where the combat rages fiercest?"

"Did you meet Black Rifle?" asked Willet.

"It was he who told us of your great need," replied Daganoweda. "Then while we came on at the speed of runners to help you, he continued north and east in the hope that he would meet Waraiyageh and white troops."

"Do you know if Colonel William Johnson is in this region or near it?"

"He lay to the north with a considerable force, watching for the French and Indians who have been pouring down from Canada since their great taking of scalps by Duquesne. Black Rifle will find him and he will come, because Waraiyageh never deserts his people, but just when he will arrive I cannot say."

Ample food was given to the Mohawks and then, burning for battle, Daganoweda at their head, they went on the back trail in search of Tandakora, De Courcelles and their savage army.

"We could not have a better curtain between us and the enemy," said Willet. "War is their trade and those fifty Mohawks will sting and sting like so many hornets."

The train resumed its flight an hour after sunrise, although more slowly now and with less apprehension, and about the middle of the afternoon the uniforms of Colonial militia appeared in the forest ahead. All set up a great shout, because they believed them to be the vanguard of Johnson. They were not mistaken, as a force of a hundred men, better equipped and drilled than usual, met them, at their head Colonel William Johnson himself, with the fierce young Mohawk eagle, Joseph Brant, otherwise Thayendanegea, at his side. The somber figure of Black Rifle, who had brought him, stood not far away.

Colonel Johnson was in great good humor, thoroughly delighted to find the train safe and to meet such warm friends of his again. He was first presented duly to Captain Colden and his young officers, paid them some compliments on their fine work, talked with them a while and then conversed more intimately with Tayoga, Robert and Willet.

"The train is now entirely safe," he said. "Even if Tandakora and De Courcelles could brush away the screen of the Mohawks, they dare not risk an encounter with such a force as we have here. They will turn aside for easier game."

"And there will be no battle!" exclaimed young Brant, in deep disappointment. "Ah! why did I not have the chance to go forward with my cousin, Daganoweda?"

Colonel Johnson laughed, half in pride and half in amusement, and patted his warlike young Mohawk brother-in-law on the shoulder.

"All in good time, Joseph, my lad," he said. "Remember that you are scarce twelve and you may have fifty years of fighting before you. No one knows how long this conflagration in America may last. As for you, Tayoga and Lennox, and you, Willet, your labors with the train are over. But there is a fierce fire burning in the north, and it is for us to put it out. You have lost one commander, Braddock, but you may find another. I can release you from your obligations to Governor Dinwiddie of Virginia. Will you go with me?"

The three assented gladly, and they saw that their service of danger was but taking a new form.

CHAPTER V

GATHERING FORCES

The eyes of all the warlike young men now turned northward. The people whom they had rescued scattered among their relatives and friends, awaiting the time when they could return to the wilderness, and rebuild their homes there, but Colden, Wilton, Carson and their troop were eager for service with Colonel William Johnson. In time orders arrived from the Governor of Pennsylvania, directing them to join the force that was being raised in the province of New York to meet the onrush of the savages and the French, and they rejoiced. Meanwhile Robert, Tayoga and Willet made a short stay at Mount Johnson, and in the company of its hospitable owner and his wife refreshed themselves after their great hardships and dangers.

Colonel Johnson's activities as a host did not make him neglect his duties as a commander. Without military experience, save that recently acquired in border war, he nevertheless showed indomitable energy as a leader, and his bluff, hearty manner endeared him to Colonials and Mohawks alike. A great camp had been formed on the low grounds by Albany, and Robert and his comrades in time proceeded there, where a numerous force of men from New York and New England and many Mohawks were gathered. It was their plan to march against the great French fortress of Crown Point on Lake Champlain, which Robert heard would be defended by a formidable French and Indian army under Baron Dieskau, an elderly Saxon in the French service.

Robert also heard that St. Luc was with Dieskau, and that he was leading daring raids against little bands of militia on their way from New England to the camp near Albany. Two were practically destroyed, half of their numbers being killed, while the rest were sent as prisoners into Canada. Two more succeeded in beating off the Frenchman, though with large loss, but he was recognized by everybody as a great danger, and Daganoweda and the best of the Mohawks went forth to meet him.

Rogers with his partisan band and Black Rifle also disappeared in the wilderness, and Robert looked longingly after them, but he and his friends were still held at the Albany camp, as the march of the army was delayed, owing to the fact that five provincial governors, practically independent of one another, had a hand in its management, and they could not agree upon a plan. Braddock's great defeat had a potent influence in the north, and now they were all for caution.

While they delayed Robert went into Albany one bright morning to see Mynheer Jacobus Huysman, who showed much anxiety about him these days. The little Dutch city looked its best, a comfortable place on its hills, inhabited by comfortable people, but swarming now with soldiers and even with Mohawks, all of whom brought much business to the thrifty burghers. Albany had its profit out of everything, the river commerce, the fur trade, and war itself.

Robert, as he walked along, watched with interest the crowd which was, in truth, cosmopolitan, despite the smallness of the place. Some of the Colonials had uniforms of blue faced with red, of which they were very proud, but most of them were in the homespun attire of every day. They were armed with their own rifles. Only the English had bayonets so far. The Americans instead carried hatchets or tomahawks at their belts, and the hatchet had many uses. Every man also carried a big jack or clasp knife which, too, had its many uses.

The New Englanders, who were most numerous in the camp, were of pure British blood, a race that had become in the American climate tall, thin and very muscular, enduring of body and tenacious of spirit, religious, ambitious, thinking much of both worldly gain and the world hereafter. Among them moved the people of Dutch blood from the province of New York, generally short and fat like their ancestors, devoted to good living, cheerful in manner, but hard and unscrupulous in their dealing with the Indians, and hence a menace to the important alliance with the Hodenosaunee.

There were the Germans, also, most of them descendants of the fugitives from the Palatinate, after it had been ravaged by the generals of Louis XIV, a quiet, humble people, industrious, honest, sincerely religious, low at present in the social scale, and patronized by the older families of English or Dutch blood, perhaps not dreaming that their race would become some day the military terror of the world.

The Mohawks, who passed freely through the throng, were its most picturesque feature. The world bred no more haughty savages than they. Tall men, with high cheek bones, and fierce eyes, they wore little clothing in the summer weather, save now and then a blanket of brilliant color for the sake of adornment. There were also some Onondagas, as proud as the Mohawks, but not so fierce.

A few Virginians and Marylanders, come to cooperate with the northern forces, were present, and they, like the New Englanders, were of pure British blood. Now and then a Swede, broad of face, from the Jersey settlements could be seen, and there was scarcely a nation in western Europe that did not have at least one representative in the streets of Albany.

It pleased Robert to see the great variety of the throng. It made a deep impression upon his imaginative mind. Already he foresaw the greatness of America, when these races were blended in a land of infinite resources. But such thoughts were driven from his mind by a big figure that loomed before him and a hearty voice that saluted him.

"Day dreaming, Master Lennox?" said the voice. "One does not have much time for dreams now, when the world is so full of action."

It was none other than Master Benjamin Hardy, portly, rubicund, richly but quietly dressed in dark broadcloth, dark silk stockings and shoes of Spanish leather with large silver buckles. Robert was unaffectedly glad to see him, and they shook hands with warmth.

"I did not know that you were in Albany," said young Lennox.

"But I knew that you were here," said Master Hardy.

"I haven't your great resources for collecting knowledge."

"A story reached me in New York concerning the gallant conduct of one Robert Lennox on the retreat from Fort Refuge, and I wished to come here myself and see if it be true."

"I did no better than a hundred others. How is the wise Master Jonathan Pillsbury?"

"As wise as ever. He earnestly urged me, when I departed for this town, not to be deceived by the glamour of the military. 'Bear in mind, Master Benjamin,' he said, 'that you and I have been associates many years, and your true path is that of commerce and gain. The march and the battlefield are not for you any more than they are for me.' Wise words and true, and it was not for me to gainsay them. So I gave him my promise that I would not march with this brave expedition to the lakes."

The merchant's words were whimsical, but Robert felt that he was examining him with critical looks, and he felt, too, that a protecting influence was once more about him. He could not doubt that Master Hardy was his sincere friend, deeply interested in him. He had given too many proofs of it, and a sudden curiosity about his birth, forgotten amid the excitement of continued action, rose anew. He was about to ask questions, but he remembered that they would not be answered, and so he held his peace, while the merchant walked on with him toward the house of Mynheer Jacobus Huysman.

"You are bent upon going with the army?" said Mr. Hardy. "Haven't you had enough of battle? There was a time, after the news of Braddock's defeat came, when I feared that you had fallen, but a message sent by the young Englishman, Grosvenor, told me you were safe, and I was very thankful. It is natural for the young to seek what they call adventure, and to serve their country, but you have done much already, Robert. You might go with me now to New York, and still feel that you are no shirker."

"You are most kind, Mr. Hardy. I believe that next to Willet and Tayoga you are the greatest and best of my friends. Why, I know not, nor do I ask now, but the fact is patent, and I thank you many times over, although I can't accept your offer. I'm committed to this expedition and there my heart lies, too. Willet and Tayoga go with it. So do Black Rifle and Rogers, I think, and Colonel Johnson, who is also my good friend, is to lead it. I couldn't stay behind and consider myself a true man."

Master Benjamin Hardy sighed.

"Doubtless you are right, Robert," he said, "and perhaps at your age I should have taken the same view, despite Jonathan's assertion that my true ways are the ways of commerce and gain. Nevertheless, my interest in this struggle is great. It is bound to be since it means vast changes in the colonies, whatever its result."

"What changes do you have in mind, Mr. Hardy?"

"Mental changes more than any other, Robert. The war in its sweep bids fair to take in almost all the civilized world we know. We are the outpost of Britain, Canada is the outpost of France, and in a long and desperate strife such as this promises to be we are sure to achieve greater mental stature, and to arrive at a more acute consciousness of our own strength and resources. Beyond that I don't care to predict. But come, lad, we'll not talk further of such grave matters, you and I. Instead we'll have a pleasant hour with Mynheer Jacobus Huysman, a man of no mean quality, as you know."

Mynheer Jacobus was at home, and he gave them a great welcome, glancing at one and at the other, and then back again, apparently rejoiced to see them together.

Then he ordered a huge repast, of which they ate bountifully, and upon which he made heavy inroads himself. When the demands of hospitality were somewhat satisfied, he put aside knife and fork, and said to Mr. Hardy:

"And now, old friend, it iss no impertinence on my part to ask what hass brought you to Albany."

Master Benjamin, who was gravely filling a pipe, lighted it, took one puff, and replied:

"No, Jacobus, it is no impertinence. No question that you might ask me could be an impertinence. You and I are old friends, and I think we understand each other. I have to say in reply that I have come here on a matter of army contracts, to get a clearer and better view of the war which is going to mean so much to all of us, and to attend to one or two matters personal to myself."

Robert, excusing himself, had risen and was looking out of a window at a passing company of soldiers. Mynheer Jacobus glanced at him and then glanced back at the merchant.

"It iss a good lad," he said, "und you watch over him as well as you can."

"Aye, I do my best," replied Hardy in the same subdued tones, "but he is bold of spirit, full of imagination and adventurous, and, though I would fain keep him out of the war, I cannot. Yet if I were his age I would go into it myself."

"It iss the way of youth. He lives in times troubled und full of danger, yet he hass in the hunter, Willet, and the Onondaga, Tayoga, friends who are a flaming sword on each side of him. Willet hass a great mind. He iss as brave as a lion und full of resource."

"Right well do I know it, Jacobus."

"And the young Onondaga, Tayoga, is of the antique mold. Do I not know it, I who haf taught him so long? Often I could think he was a young Greek or Roman of the best type, reincarnated und sent to the forest. He does haf the lofty nature, the noble character und simplicity of a young Roman of the republic, before it was corrupted by conquest. I tell you, Benjamin Hardy, that we do not value the red men at their true worth, especially those of the Hodenosaunee!"

"Right well do I know that, too, Jacobus. I had a fair reading in the classics, when I was a schoolboy, and I should call the lad, Tayoga, more Greek in spirit than Roman. I have found in him the spiritual quality, the love of beauty and the kindliness of soul which the books say the Greeks had and which the Romans lacked."

"It iss fairly put, Benjamin, und I bethink me you are right. But there iss one thing which you do not know, but which you ought to know, because it iss of much importance."

"What is it?" asked Hardy, impressed by the manner of Jacobus.

"It iss the fact that Adrian Van Zoon arrived in Albany this morning."

The merchant started slightly in surprise, and then his face became a mask.

"Adrian Van Zoon is a merchant like myself," he said. "He has a right to come to Albany. Perhaps he feels the necessity, too, as no doubt he is interested in large contracts for the army."

"It iss true, Benjamin, but you und I would rather he had not come. He arrived but this morning on his own sloop, the *Dirkhoeven*, und I feel that wherever Adrian Van Zoon iss the air becomes noxious, full of poisonous vapors und dangerous to those about him."

"You're right, Jacobus. I see that your faculties are as keen as ever. You can see through a mill stone, and you can put together much larger figures than two and two."

Mynheer Jacobus smiled complacently.

"I haf not yet reached my zenith," he said, "und I am very glad I am not yet an old man, because I am so full of curiosity."

"I don't take your meaning, Jacobus."

"I would not like to die before this great und long war iss ended because I wish to see how it does end. Und I want to see the nature of the mighty changes which I feel are coming in the world."

"What changes, for instance, Jacobus?"

"The action of the New World upon the Old, und the action of the old monarchies upon one another. All things change, Benjamin. You und I know that. The veil of majesty that wraps around kings und thrones iss not visible to us here in der American forest, und maybe for dot reason we see the changes coming in Europe better than those who are closer by. France is the oldest of all the old und great monarchies und for dot reason the French monarchy iss most overripe. Steeped in luxury und corruption, the day of its decay hass set in."

"But the French people are valiant and great, Jacobus. Think not that we have in them a weak antagonist."

"I said nothing of the French nation, Benjamin, mein friend. I spoke of the French throne. The French leaders in Canada are brave und enterprising. They will inflict on us many defeats, but the French throne will not give to them the support to which they as Frenchmen are entitled."

"You probably see the truth, Jacobus, and it's to our advantage. Perhaps 'tis better that the French throne should decay. But we'll return to affairs closer by. You've had Van Zoon watched?"

"My stable boy, Peter, hass not let him out of sight, since he landed from the *Dirkhoeven*. Peter is not a lad of brilliant appearance, which iss perhaps all the better for our purpose, but he will keep Van Zoon in sight, if it iss humanly possible, without being himself suspected."

"Well done, Jacobus, but I might have known that you would take all needful precautions."

Robert came back from the window, and they promptly changed the current of the talk, speaking now of the army, its equipment, and the probable time of its march to meet Dieskau. Presently they left Mynheer Huysman's house, and Robert and the merchant went toward the camp on the flats. Here they beheld a scene of great activity and of enormous interest to Robert.

Few stranger armies have ever been gathered than that which Colonel William Johnson was preparing to lead against Crown Point. The New Englanders brought with them all their characteristics, their independence, their love of individualism and their piety. Despite this piety it was an army that swore hugely, and, despite its huge swearing, it was an honest army. It survives in written testimony that the greatest swearers were from the provinces of New York and Rhode Island, and Colonel Ephraim Williams, an officer among them writing at the time, said that the language they most used was "the language of Hell." And, on the other hand, a New York officer testified that not a housewife in Albany or its suburbs could mourn the loss of a single chicken. Private property everywhere was absolutely safe, and, despite the oaths and rough appearance of the men, no woman was insulted.

"They're having prayer meeting now," said Mr. Hardy, as they came upon the flats. "I've learned they have sermons twice a week—their ministers came along with them— prayers every day, and the singing of songs many times. They often alternate the psalm singing with the military drill, but I'm not one to decry their observances. Religious fervor is a great thing in battle. It made the Ironsides of Cromwell invincible."

Five hundred voices, nearly all untrained, were chanting a hymn. They were the voices of farmers and frontiersmen, but the great chorus had volume and majesty, and Robert was not one to depreciate them. Instead he was impressed. He understood the character of both New Englanders and New Yorkers. Keen for their own, impatient of control, they were nevertheless capable of powerful collective effort. A group of Mohawks standing by were also watching with grave and serious attention. When they raised a chant to Manitou they demanded the utmost respect, and they gave it also, without the asking, to the white man when he sang in his own way to his own God.

It was when they turned back to the town that they were hailed in a joyous voice, and Robert beheld the young English officer, Grosvenor, whom he had known in New York, Grosvenor, a little thinner than of old, but more tanned and with an air of experience. His pleasure at meeting Robert again was great and unaffected. He shook hands with him warmly and exclaimed:

"When I last saw you, Lennox, it was at the terrible forest fight, where we learned our bitter lesson. I saw that you escaped, but I did not know what became of you afterward."

"I've had adventures, and I'll tell you of 'em later," said Robert.
"Glad I am to see you, although I had not heard of your coming to
Albany."

"I arrived but this morning. No British troops are here. I understand this army is to be composed wholly of Colonials—pardon the word, I use it for lack of a better—and of Mohawks. But I was able to secure in New York a detail on the staff of Colonel Johnson. My position perhaps will be rather that of an observer and representative of the regular troops, but I hope, nevertheless, to be of some service. I suppose I won't see as much of you as I would like, as you're likely to be off in the forest in front of the army with those scouting friends of yours."

"It's what we can do best," said Robert, "but if there's a victory ahead I hope we'll all be present when it's gained."

Jacobus Huysman insisted that all his old friends be quartered with him, while they were in Albany, and as there was little at present for Grosvenor to do, he was added by arrangement with Colonel Johnson to the group. They sat that evening on the portico in the summer dusk, and Master Alexander McLean, the schoolmaster, joined them, still regarding Robert and Tayoga as lads under his care, and soon including Grosvenor also. But the talk was pleasant, and they were deep in it when a man passed in the street and a shadow fell upon them all.

It was Adrian Van Zoon, heavy, dressed richly as usual, and carrying a large cane, with a gold head. To the casual eye he was a man of importance, aware of his dignity, and resolute in the maintenance of it. He bowed with formal politeness to the group upon the portico, and walked majestically on. Mynheer Jacobus watched him until he was out of sight, going presumably to his inn, and then his eyes began to search for another figure. Presently it appeared, lank, long and tow-headed, the boy, Peter, of whom he had spoken. Mynheer Huysman introduced him briefly to the others, and he responded, in every case, with a pull at a long lock on his forehead. His superficial appearance was that of a simpleton, but Robert noticed sharp, observant eyes under the thick eyebrows. Mynheer Jacobus, Willet and Master Hardy, excusing themselves for a few minutes, went into an inner room.

"What has Mynheer Van Zoon been doing, Peter?" asked Jacobus.

"He has talked with three contractors for the army," replied the lad. "He also had a short conversation with Colonel Ephraim Williams of the Massachusetts militia."

"Williams is a thoroughly honest man," said Mr. Hardy. "His talk with Van Zoon could only have been on legitimate business. We'll dismiss him. What more have you seen, Peter?"

"Late in the afternoon he went to his schooner, the *Dirkhoeven*, which is anchored in the river. I could not follow him there, but I saw him speaking on the deck to a man who did not look like a sailor. They were there only a minute, then they went into the cabin, and when Mynheer Van Zoon came ashore he came alone."

"And the man who did not look like a sailor was left on the ship. It may mean nothing, or it may mean anything, but my mind tells me it hath an unpleasant significance. Now, I wish I knew this man who is lying hid in the *Dirkhoeven*. Perhaps it would be better, Jacobus, to instruct Peter to follow the lad, Lennox, and give the alarm if any threat or menace appears."

"I think it is the wiser course, Benjamin, and I will even instruct Peter in such manner."

He spoke a few sentences to Peter, who listened with eagerness, apparently delighted with the task set for him. When Mynheer Huysman had finished the lad slipped out at a back door, and was gone like a shadow.

"An admirable youth for our purpose," said Mynheer Jacobus Huysman. "He likes not work, but if he is to watch or follow anyone he hangs on like a hound. In Albany he will become the second self of young Lennox, whose first self will not know that he has a second self."

They returned to the portico. Robert glanced curiously at them, but not one of the three offered any explanation. He knew, however, that their guarded talk with Peter had to do with himself, and he felt a great emotion of gratitude. If he was surrounded by dangers he was also surrounded by powerful friends. If chance had put him on the outskirts of the world it had also given him comrades who were an armor of steel about him.

Tayoga and he occupied their old bedroom at Mynheer Jacobus Huysman's that night, and once when Robert glanced out of the window he caught a glimpse of a dark figure lurking in the shrubbery. It was a man who did not look like a sailor, but as he did not know of the conversation in the inner room the shadow attracted little attention from him. It disappeared in an instant, and he thought no more about it.

Robert and his comrades were back in the camp next day, and now they saw Colonel Johnson at his best, a man of wonderful understanding and tact. He was soon able to break through the reserve of the New England citizen officers who were not wont to give their confidence in a hurry, and around great bowls of lemon punch they talked of the campaign. The Mohawks, as of old, told him all their grievances, which he remedied when just, and persuaded them into forgetting when unjust.

Robert, Tayoga and Willet, in their capacity of scouts and skirmishers, could go about practically as they pleased. Colonel Johnson trusted them absolutely and they talked of striking out into the wilderness on a new expedition to see what lay ahead of the army. Adrian Van Zoon, they learned definitely, had started for New York on the *Dirkhoeven*, and Robert felt relief. Yet the lank lad, Peter, still followed him, and, as had been predicted truly, was his second self, although his first self did not know it.

He had been at Albany several days when he returned alone from the flats to the town late one evening. At a dark turn in the road he heard a report, and a bullet whistled very near him. It was followed quickly by a second report, but not by the whistling of any bullet. He had a pair of pistols in his belt, and, taking out one and cocking it, he searched the woods, though he found nothing. He concluded then that it was a random bullet fired by some returning hunter, and that the second shot was doubtless of the same character. But the first hunter had been uncommonly careless and he hastened his steps from a locality which had been so dangerous, even accidentally.

Inured, however, as he was to risks, the incident soon passed entirely out of his mind. Yet an hour or two later the lad, Peter, sat in a back room with Mynheer Jacobus Huysman, and told him with relish of the occurrence at the dark turn of the road.

"I was fifty or sixty yards behind in the shadow of the trees," he said. "I could see Master Lennox very well, though he could not see me. The figure of a man appeared in the woods near me and aimed a pistol at Master Lennox. I could not see his face well, but I knew it was the man on the boat who was talking to Mynheer Van Zoon. I uttered a cry which did not reach Master Lennox, but which did reach the man with the pistol. It disturbed his aim, and his bullet flew wide. Then I fired at him, but if I touched him at all it was but lightly. He made off through the woods and I followed, but his speed was so great I could not overtake him."

"You haf done well, Peter. Doubtless you haf saved the life of young Master Lennox, which was the task set for you to do. But it iss not enough. You may haf to save it a second und yet a third time."

The pale blue eyes of Peter glistened. Obviously he liked his present task much better than the doing of chores.

"You can trust me, Mynheer Huysman," he said importantly. "I will guard him, and I will do more. Is there anybody you want killed?"

"No, no, you young savage! You are to shoot only in self-defense, or in defense of young Lennox whom you are to protect. Bear that in mind."

"Very well, Mynheer. Your orders are law to me."

Peter went out of the room and slid away in the darkness. Mynheer Jacobus Huysman watched his departure and sighed. He was a good man, averse to violence and bloodshed, and he murmured:

"The world iss in a fever. The nations fight among themselves und even the lads talk lightly of taking life."

Peter reported to him again the next night, when Robert was safely in bed.

"I followed Master Lennox to the parade ground again," he said. "The Onondaga, Tayoga, the hunter, Willet, and the Englishman, Grosvenor, were with him. They watched the drill for a while, and spoke with Colonel Johnson. Then Master Lennox wandered away alone to the north edge of the drill ground, where there are some woods. Since I have received your instructions, Mynheer, I always examine the woods, and I found in them a man who might have been in hiding, or who might have been lying there for the sake of the shade, only I am quite sure it was not the latter. Just when Master Lennox came into his view I spoke to him, and he seemed quite angry. He asked me impatiently to go away, but I stood by and talked to him until Master Lennox was far out of sight."

"You saw the man well, then, Peter?"

"I did, Mynheer Huysman, and I cannot be mistaken. It was the same that talked with Mynheer Van Zoon on the deck of the *Dirkkoeven*."

"I thought so. And what kind of a looking man was he, Peter?"

"About thirty, I should say, Mynheer, well built and strong, and foreign."

"Foreign! What mean you, Peter?"

46

"French."

"What? French of France or French of Canada?"

"That I cannot say with certainty, Mynheer, but French he was I do believe and maintain."

"Then he must be a spy as well as a threat to young Lennox. This goes deeper than I had thought, but you haf done your work well, Peter. Continue it."

He held out a gold coin, which Peter pocketed with thanks, and went forth the next morning to resume with a proud heart the task that he liked.

Robert, all unconscious that a faithful guardian was always at his heels, was passing days full of color, variety and pleasure. Admission into the society of Albany was easy to one of his manner and appearance, who had also such powerful friends, and there were pleasant evenings in the solid Dutch houses. But he knew they could not last long. Daganoweda and a chosen group of his Mohawks came back, reporting the French and Indian force to be far larger than the one that had defeated Braddock by Duquesne, and that Baron Dieskau who led it was considered a fine general. Unless Waraiyageh made up his mind to strike quickly Dieskau would strike first.

The new French and Indian army, Daganoweda said, numbered eight thousand men, a great force for the time, and for the New World, and it would be both preceded and followed by clouds of skirmishers, savages from the regions of the Great Lakes and even from beyond. They were flushed with victory, with the mighty taking of scalps, at Braddock's defeat, and they expected here in the north a victory yet greater. They were already assuming control of Champlain and George, the two lakes which from time immemorial, long before the coming of the white man, had formed the line of march between what had become the French colonies and the British colonies. It was equally vital now to possess this passage. Whoever became the rulers of the lakes might determine in their favor the issue of the war in America, and the youths in Johnson's army were eager to go forward at once and fight for the coveted positions.

But further delay was necessary. The commander still had the difficult task of harmonizing the provincial governors and legislatures, and he also made many presents to the Indians to bind them to the cause. Five of the Six Nations, alarmed by the French successes and the slowness of the Americans and English, still held neutral, but the Mohawks were full of zeal, and the best of their young chiefs and warriors stood by Johnson, ready to march when he marched, and to cover his van with their skirmishers and patrols.

Meanwhile the army drilled incessantly. The little troop of Philadelphians under Colden, Wilton and Carson were an example. They had seen much hard service already, although they spoke modestly of the dangers over which they had triumphed in the forest. It was their pride, too, to keep their uniforms neat, and to be as soldierly in manner as possible. They had the look of regulars, and Grosvenor, the young Englishman who had been taken on Colonel Johnson's staff, spoke of them as such.

New York and the four New England Colonies, whatever their lack of cooperation, showed energy. The governors issued proclamations, and if not enough men came, more were drafted from the regiments of militia. Bounties of six dollars for every soldier were offered by Massachusetts, and that valiant colony, as usual, led the way in energy.

They were full days for Robert. He listened almost incessantly to the sound of drum and fife, the drill master's word of command, or to voices raised in prayer, preaching or the singing of psalms. Recruits were continually coming in, awkward plowboys, but brave and enduring, waiting only to be taught. Master Benjamin Hardy was compelled to return to New York, departing with reluctance and holding an earnest conference with Mynheer Jacobus Huysman before he went.

"The man, who is most certainly a French spy, is somewhere about," said Mynheer Jacobus. "Peter haf seen him twice more, but he haf caught only glimpses. But you can trust Peter even as I do. His whole heart iss in the task I have set him. He wass born Dutch but hiss soul iss Iroquois! He iss by nature a taker of scalps."

Master Benjamin laughed.

"Just at present," he said, "'tis the nature that suits us best. Most urgent business calls me back to New York, and, after all, I can't do more here than you are doing, old friend."

When they had bidden each other good-by in the undemonstrative manner of elderly men who have long been friends, Master Jacobus strolled down the main street of Albany and took a long look at a substantial house standing in fine grounds. Then he shook his head several times, and, walking on, met its owner, whom he greeted with marked coolness, although the manner of the other toward him had been somewhat effusive.

"I gif you good day, Hendrik Martinus," he said, "und I hear that you are prospering. I am not one to notice fashions myself, but others haf spoken to me of the beautiful new shawls your daughters are wearing und of the brooches und necklaces they haf."

The face of Martinus, a man of about fifty, turned a deep red, but the excessive color passed in a few moments, and he spoke carelessly. In truth, his whole manner was lighter and more agile than that of the average man of Dutch blood.

"I am not so sure, Mynheer Jacobus, that you did not take notice yourself," he said. "Mynheer Jacobus is grave and dignified, but many a grave and dignified man has a wary eye for the ladies."

Mynheer Jacobus Huysman frowned.

"And as for shawls and brooches and necklaces," continued Martinus, "it is well known that war brings legitimate profits to many men. It makes trade in certain commodities brisk. Now I'd willingly wager that your friend, Master Benjamin Hardy, whom you have just seen on his way to New York, will be much the richer by this war."

"Master Hardy has ships upon the seas, and important contracts for the troops."

"I have no ships upon the seas, but I may have contracts, too."

"It may well be so, Hendrik," said Mynheer Jacobus, and without another word he passed on. When he had gone a hundred yards he shook himself violently, and when he had gone another hundred yards he gave himself a second shake of equal vigor. An hour later he was in the back room talking with the lad, Peter.

"Peter," he said, "you haf learned to take naps in the day und to keep awake all through the night?"

"Yes, Mynheer," replied Peter, proudly.

"Then, Peter, you vass an owl, a watcher in the dark."

"Yes, Mynheer."

"Und I gif you praise for watching well, Peter, und also gold, which iss much more solid than praise. Now I gif you by und by more praise und more gold which iss still more solid than praise. The lad, Robert Lennox, will be here early tonight to take supper with me, und I will see that he does not go out again before the morrow. Now, do you, Peter, watch the house of Hendrik Martinus all night und tell me if anyone comes out or goes in, und who und what he may be, as nearly as you can."

"Yes, Mynheer," said Peter, and a sudden light flickered in the pale blue eyes.

No further instructions were needed. He left the house in silence, and Mynheer Jacobus Huysman trusted him absolutely.

CHAPTER VI

THE DARK STRANGER

Robert arrived at the house of Jacobus Huysman about dark and Tayoga came with him. Willet was detained at the camp on the flats, where he had business with Colonel Johnson, who consulted him often. The two lads were in high good spirits, and Mynheer Jacobus, whatever he may have been under the surface, appeared to be so, too. Robert believed that the army would march very soon now. The New York and New England men alike were full of fire, eager to avenge Braddock's defeat and equally eager to drive back and punish the terrible clouds of savages which, under the leadership of the French, were ravaging the border, spreading devastation and terror on all sides.

"There has been trouble, Mynheer Huysman," said Robert, "between Governor Shirley of Massachusetts, who has been in camp several days, and Colonel Johnson. I saw Governor Shirley when he was in the council at Alexandria, in Virginia, and I know, from what I've heard, that he's the most active and energetic of all the governors, but they say he's very vain and pompous."

"Vanity and pomp comport ill with a wilderness campaign," said Mynheer Jacobus, soberly. "Of all the qualities needed to deal with the French und Indians I should say that they are needed least. It iss a shame that a man should demand obeisance from others when they are all in a great crisis."

"The Governor is eager to push the war," said Robert, "yet he demands more worship of the manner from Colonel Johnson than the colonel has time to give him. 'Tis said, too, that the delays he makes cause dissatisfaction among the Mohawks, who are eager to be on the great war trail. Daganoweda, I know, fairly burns with impatience."

Mynheer Jacobus sighed.

"We will not haf the advantage of surprise," he said. "Of that I am certain. I do believe that the French und Indians know of all our movements und of all we do."

"Spies?" said Robert.

"It may be," replied Mynheer Jacobus.

Robert was silent. His first thought was of St. Luc, who, he knew, would dare anything, and it was just the sort of adventure that would appeal to his bold and romantic spirit. But his thought passed on. He had no real feeling that St. Luc was in the camp. Mynheer Jacobus must be thinking of another or others. But Huysman volunteered no explanation. Presently he rose from his chair, went to a window and looked out. Tayoga observed him keenly.

The Onondaga, trained from his childhood to observe all kinds of manifestations, was a marvelous reader of the minds of men, and, merely because Mynheer Jacobus Huysman interrupted a conversation to look out into the dark, he knew that he expected something. And whatever it was it was important, as the momentary quiver of the big man's lip indicated.

The Indian, although he may hide it, has his full share of curiosity, and Tayoga wondered why Mynheer Jacobus watched. But he asked no question.

The Dutchman came back from the window, and asked the lads in to supper with him. His slight air of expectancy had disappeared wholly, but Tayoga was not deceived. "He has merely been convinced that he was gazing out too soon," he said to himself. "As surely as Tododaho on his star watches over the Onondagas, he will come back here after supper and look from this window, expecting to see something or somebody."

The supper of Mynheer Jacobus was, in reality, a large dinner, and, as it was probably the last the two lads would take with him before they went north, he had given to it a splendor and abundance even greater than usual. Tayoga and Robert, as became two such stout youths, ate bountifully, and Mynheer Jacobus Huysman, whatever his secret troubles may have been, wielded knife and fork with them, knife for knife and fork for fork.

But Tayoga was sure that Mynheer Jacobus was yet expectant, and still, without making it manifest, he watched him keenly. He noted that the big man hurried the latter part of the supper, something which the Onondaga had never known him to do before, and which, to the observant mind of the red youth, indicated an expectancy far greater than he had supposed at first.

Clearly Mynheer Jacobus was hastening, clearly he wished to be out of the room, and it was equally clear to Tayoga that he wanted to go back to his window, the one from which he could see over the grounds, and into the street beyond.

"Will you take a little wine?" he said to Robert, as he held up a bottle, through which the rich dark red color shone.

"Thank you, sir, no," replied Robert.

"Und you, Tayoga?"

"I never touch the firewater of the white man, call they it wine or call they it whiskey."

"Good. Good for you both. I merely asked you for the sake of politeness, und I wass glad to hear you decline. But as for me, I am old enough to be your father, und I will take a little."

He poured a small glass, drank it, and rose.

"Your old room iss ready," he said, "und now, if you two lads will go to it, you can get a good und long night's sleep."

Robert was somewhat surprised. He felt that they were being dismissed, which was almost like the return of the old days when they were schoolboys, but Tayoga touched him on the elbow, and his declaration that he was not sleepy died on his lips. Instead, he said a polite good-night and he and Tayoga went away as they were bid.

"Now, what did he mean? Why was he so anxious to get rid of us?" asked Robert, when they were again in their room.

"Mynheer Jacobus expects something," replied the Onondaga, gravely. "He expects it to come out of the night, and appear at a window of the room in which we first sat, the window that looks over the garden, and to the street behind us."

"How do you know that?" asked Robert, astonished.

Tayoga explained what he had seen.

"I do not doubt you. It's convincing," said Robert, "but I'd not have noticed it."

"We of the red nations have had to notice everything in order that we might live. As surely as we sit here, Dagaeoga, Mynheer Jacobus is at the window, watching. When I lie down on the bed I shall keep my clothes on, and I shall not sleep. We may be called."

"I shall do the same, Tayoga."

Nevertheless, as time passed, young Lennox fell asleep, but the Onondaga did not close his eyes. What was time to him? The red race always had time to spare, and nature and training had produced in him illimitable patience. He had waited by a pool a whole day and night for a deer to come down to drink. He heard the tall clock standing on the floor in the corner strike ten, eleven, and then twelve, and a half hour later, when he was as wide awake as ever, there was a knock at the door. But he had first heard the approaching footsteps of the one who came and knocked, and he was already touching the shoulder of Robert, who sat up at once, sleep wholly gone from him.

"It is Mynheer Jacobus," said Tayoga, "and he wants us."

Then he opened the door and the large red face of Mynheer Huysman looked into the room, which was illuminated by the moonlight.

"Come, you lads," he said, in sharp, eager tones, "und bring your pistols with you."

Robert and Tayoga snatched up their weapons, and followed him into the sitting-room, where the tall lank youth, Peter, stood.

"You know Peter," he said, "und Peter knows you. Now, listen to what he hass to tell, but first pledge me that you will say nothing of it until I give you leave. Do you?"

"We do," they replied together.

"Then, Peter, tell them what you haf seen, but be brief, because it may be that we must act quickly."

"Obeying the instructions of Mynheer Jacobus Huysman, whom I serve," said Peter, smoothly, evidently enjoying his importance of the moment, "I watched tonight the house of Mynheer Hendrik Martinus, who is not trusted by my master. The building is large, and it stands on ground with much shrubbery that is now heavy with leaf. So it was difficult to watch all the approaches to it, but I went about it continuously, hour after hour. A half hour ago, I caught a glimpse of a man, strong, and, as well as I could tell in the night, of a dark complexion. He was on the lawn, among the shrubbery, hiding a little while and then going on again. He came to a side door of the house, but he did not knock, because there was no need. The door opened of itself, and he went in. Then the door closed of itself, and he did not come out again. I waited ten minutes and then hurried to the one whom I serve with the news."

Mynheer Jacobus turned to Tayoga and Robert.

"I haf long suspected," he said, "that Hendrik Martinus iss a spy in the service of France, a traitor for his own profit, because he loves nothing but himself und his. He has had remarkable prosperity of late, a prosperity for which no one can account, because he has had no increase of business. Believing that a Frenchman wass here, a spy who wished to communicate with him, I set Peter to watch his house, und the result you know."

"Then it is for us to go there and seize this spy," said Robert.

"It iss what I wish," said Mynheer Huysman, "und we may trap a traitor und a spy at the same time. It is well to haf money if you haf it honestly, but Hendrik Martinus loves money too well."

He took from a drawer a great double-barreled horse pistol, put it under his coat, and the four, quietly leaving the house, went toward that of Hendrik Martinus. There was no light except that of the moon and, in the distance, they saw a watchman carrying a lantern and thumping upon the stones with a stout staff.

"It iss Andrius Tefft," said Mynheer Jacobus. "He hass a strong arm und a head with but little in it. It would be best that he know nothing of this, or he would surely muddle it."

They drew back behind some shrubbery, and Andrius Tefft, night watchman, passed by without a suspicion that one of Albany's most respected citizens was hiding from him. The light of his lantern faded in the distance, and the four proceeded rapidly towards the house of Hendrik Martinus, entering its grounds without hesitation and spreading in a circle about it. Robert, who lurked behind a small clipped pine in the rear saw a door open, and a figure slip quietly out. It was that of a man of medium height, and as he could see by the moonlight, of dark complexion. He had no doubt that it was a Frenchman, the fellow whom Peter had seen enter the house.

Robert acted with great promptness, running forward and crying to the fugitive to halt. The man, quick as a flash, drew a pistol and fired directly at him. The lad felt the bullet graze his scalp, and, for a moment, he thought he had been struck mortally. He staggered, but recovered himself, and raising his own pistol, fired at the flying figure which was now well beyond him. He saw the man halt a moment, and quiver, but in an instant he ran on again faster than ever, and disappeared in an alley. A little later a swift form followed in pursuit and Robert saw that it was Tayoga.

Young Lennox knew that it was useless for him to follow, as he felt a little dizzy and he was not yet sure of himself. He put his hand to his hair, where the bullet had struck, and, taking it away, looked anxiously at it. There was no blood upon either palm or finger, and then he realized, with great thankfulness, that he was merely suffering a brief weakness from the concussion caused by a heavy bullet passing so close to his skull. He heard a hasty footstep, and Mynheer Huysman, breathing heavily and anxious, stood before him. Other and lighter footsteps indicated that Peter also was coming to his aid.

"Haf you been shot?" exclaimed Mynheer Jacobus

"No, only shot at," replied Robert, whimsically, "though I don't believe the marksman could come so close to me again without finishing me. I think it was Peter's spy because I saw him come out of the house, and cried to him to halt, but he fired first. My own bullet, I'm sure, touched him, and Tayoga is in pursuit, though the fugitive has a long lead."

"We'll leave it to Tayoga, because we haf to," said Mynheer Jacobus. "If anybody can catch him the Onondaga can, though I think he will get away. But come now, we will talk to Hendrik Martinus und Andrius Tefft who hass heard the shots und who iss coming back. You lads, let me do all of the talking. Since the spy or messenger or whatever he iss hass got away, it iss best that we do not tell all we know."

The watchman was returning at speed, his staff pounding quick and hard on the stones, his lantern swinging wildly. The houses there were detached and nobody else seemed to have heard the shots, save Hendrik Martinus and his family. Martinus, fully dressed, was coming out of his house, his manner showing great indignation, and the heads of women in nightcaps appeared at the windows.

"What is this intrusion, Mynheer Huysman? Why are you in my grounds? And who fired those two pistol shots I heard?"

"Patience, Hendrik! Patience!" replied Mynheer Jacobus, in a smooth suave manner that surprised Robert. "My young friend, Master Lennox, here, saw a man running across your grounds, after having slipped surreptitiously out of your house. Suspecting that he had taken und carried from you that which he ought not to haf, Master Lennox called to him to stop. The reply wass a pistol bullet und Master Lennox, being young und like the young prone to swift anger, fired back. But the man hass escaped with hiss spoil, whatefer it iss, und you only, Hendrik, know what it iss."

Hendrik Martinus looked at Jacobus Huysman and Jacobus Huysman looked squarely back at him. The angry fire died out of the eyes of Martinus, and instead came a swift look of comprehension which passed in an instant. When he spoke again his tone was changed remarkably:

"Doubtless it was a robber," he said, "and I thank you, Mynheer Jacobus, and Master Lennox, and your boy Peter, for your attempt to catch him. But I fear that he has escaped."

"I will pursue him und capture him," exclaimed Mynheer Andrius Tefft, who stood by, listening to their words and puffing and blowing.

"I fear it iss too late, Andrius," said Mynheer Jacobus Huysman, shaking his head. "If anyone could do it, it would be you, but doubtless Mynheer Hendrik hass not lost anything that he cannot replace, und it would be better for you, Andrius, to watch well here und guard against future attempts."

"That would be wise, no doubt," said Martinus, and Robert thought he detected an uneasy note in his voice.

"Then I will go," said Andrius Tefft, and he walked on, swinging his lantern high and wide, until its beams fell on every house and tree and shrub.

"I will return to my house," said Mynheer Martinus. "My wife and daughters were alarmed by the shots, and I will tell them what has happened."

"It iss the wise thing to do," said Mynheer Huysman, gravely, "und I would caution you, Hendrik, to be on your guard against robbers who slip so silently into your house und then slip out again in the same silence. The times are troubled und the wicked take advantage of them to their own profit."

"It is true, Mynheer Jacobus," said Martinus somewhat hastily, and he walked back to his own house without looking Huysman in the eyes again.

Mynheer Huysman, Robert and Peter returned slowly.

"I think Hendrik understands me," said Mynheer Huysman; "I am sorry that we did not catch the go-between, but Hendrik hass had a warning, und he will be afraid. Our night's work iss not all in vain. Peter, you haf done well, but I knew you would. Now, we will haf some refreshment und await the return of Tayoga."

"I believe," said Robert, "that in Albany, when one is in doubt what to do one always eats. Is it not so?"

"It iss so," replied Mynheer Jacobus, smiling, "und what better could one do? While you wait, build up the body, because when you build up the body you build up the mind, too, und at the same time it iss a pleasure."

Robert and Peter ate nothing, but Mynheer Jacobus partook amply of cold beef and game, drank a great glass of home-made beer, and then smoked a long pipe with intense satisfaction. One o'clock in the morning came, then two, then three, and Mynheer Jacobus, taking the stem of his pipe from his mouth, said:

"I think it will not be long now before Tayoga iss here. Long ago he hass either caught hiss man or hiss man hass got away, und he iss returning. I see hiss shadow now in the shrubbery. Let him in, Peter."

Tayoga entered the room, breathing a little more quickly than usual, his dark eyes showing some disappointment.

"It wass not your fault that he got away, Tayoga," said Mynheer Jacobus soothingly. "He had too long a start, und doubtless he was fleet of foot. I think he iss the very kind of man who would be fleet of foot."

"I had to pick up his trail after he went through the alley," said Tayoga, "and I lost time in doing so. When I found it he was out of the main part of the town and in the outskirts, running towards the river. Even then I might have caught him, but he sprang into the stream and swam with great skill and speed. When I came upon the bank, he was too far away for a shot from my pistol, and he escaped into the thickets on the other shore."

"I wish we could have caught him," said Mynheer Jacobus. "Then we might have uncovered much that I would like to know. What iss it, Tayoga? You haf something more to tell!"

"Before he reached the river," said the Onondaga, "he tore in pieces a letter, a letter that must have been enclosed in an envelope. I saw the little white pieces drift away before the wind. I suppose he was afraid I might catch him, and so he destroyed the letter which must have had a tale to tell. When I came back I looked for the pieces, but I found only one large enough to bear anything that had meaning." He took from his tunic a fragment of white paper and held it up. It bore upon it two words in large letters:

"ACHILLE GARAY"

"That," said Robert, "is obviously the name of a Frenchman, and it seems to me it must have been the name of this fugitive spy or messenger to whom the letter was addressed. Achille Garay is the man whom we want. Don't you think so, Mynheer Huysman?"

"It iss truly the one we would like to capture," said Mynheer Jacobus, "but I fear that all present chance to do so hass passed. Still, we will remember. The opportunity may come again. Achille Garay! Achille Garay! We will bear that name in mind! Und now, lads, all of you go to bed. You haf done well, too, Tayoga. Nobody could haf done better."

Robert, when alone the next day, met Hendrik Martinus in the street. Martinus was about to pas? without speaking, but Robert bowed politely and said:

"I'm most sorry, Mr. Martinus, that we did not succeed in capturing your burglar last night, but my Onondaga friend followed him to the river, which he swam, then escaping. 'Tis true that he escaped, but nevertheless Tayoga salvaged a piece of a letter that he destroyed as he ran, and upon the fragment was written a name which we're quite sure was that of the bold robber."

Robert paused, and he saw the face of Martinus whiten.

"You do not ask me the name, Mynheer Martinus," he said. "Do you feel no curiosity at all about it?"

"What was it?" asked Martinus, thickly.

"Achille Garay."

Martinus trembled violently, but by a supreme effort controlled himself.

"I never heard it before," he said. "It sounds like a French name."

"It is a French name. I'm quite confident of it. I merely wanted you to understand that we haven't lost all trace of your robber, that we know his name, and that we may yet take him."

"It does look as if you had a clew," said Martinus. He was as white as death, though naturally rubicund, and without another word he walked on. Robert looked after him and saw the square shoulders drooping a little. He had not the slightest doubt of the man's guilt, and he was filled with indignant wonder that anyone's love of money should be strong enough to create in him the willingness to sell his country. He was sure Mynheer Jacobus was right. Martinus was sending their military secrets into Canada for French gold, and yet they had not a particle of proof. The man must be allowed to go his way until something much more conclusive offered. Both he and Tayoga talked it over with Willet, and the hunter agreed that they could do nothing for the present.

"But," he said, "the time may come when we can do much."

Then Martinus disappeared for a while from Robert's mind, because the next day he met the famous old Indian known in the colonies as King Hendrik of the Mohawks. Hendrik, an ardent and devoted friend of the Americans and English, had come to Albany to see Colonel William Johnson, and to march with him against the French and Indians. There was no hesitation, no doubt about him, and despite his age he would lead the Mohawk warriors in person into battle. Willet, who had known him long, introduced Robert, who paid him the respect and deference due to an aged and great chief.

Hendrik, who was a Mohegan by birth but by adoption a Mohawk, adoption having all the value of birth, was then a full seventy years of age. He spoke English fluently, he had received education in an American school, and a substantial house, in which he had lived for many years, stood near the Canajoharie or upper castle of the Mohawks. He had been twice to England and on each occasion had been received by the king, the head of one

54

nation offering hospitality to the allied head of another. A portrait of him in full uniform had been painted by a celebrated London painter.

He had again put on his fine uniform upon the occasion of his meeting with Colonel Johnson on the Albany flats, and when Robert saw him he was still clothed in it. His coat was of superfine green cloth, heavily ornamented with gold epaulets and gold lace. His trousers were of the same green cloth with gold braid all along the seams, and his feet were in shoes of glossy leather with gold buckles. A splendid cocked hat with a feather in it was upon his head. Beneath the shadow of the hat was a face of reddish bronze, aged but intelligent, and, above all, honest.

Hendrik in an attire so singular for a Mohawk might have looked ridiculous to many a man, but Robert, who knew so much of Indian nature, found him dignified and impressive.

"I have heard of you, my son," said Hendrik, in the precise, scholarly English which Tayoga used. "You are a friend of the brave young chief, Daganoweda, and to you, because of your gift of speech, has been given the name, Dagaeoga. The Onondaga, Tayoga, of the clan of the Bear, is your closest comrade, and you are also the one who made the great speech in the Vale of Onondaga before the fifty sachems against the missionary, Father Drouillard, and the French leader, St. Luc. They say that words flowed like honey from your lips."

"It was the occasion, not any words of mine," said Robert modestly.

"I was ill then, and could not be present," continued the old chief gravely, "and another took my place. I should have been glad could I have heard that test of words in the Vale of Onondaga, because golden speech is pleasant in my ears, but Manitou willed it otherwise, and I cannot complain, as I have had much in my long life. Now the time for words has passed. They have failed and the day of battle is at hand. I go on my last war trail."

"No! No, Hendrik!" exclaimed Willet. "You will emerge again the victor, covered with glory."

"Yes, Great Bear, it is written here," insisted the old Mohawk, tapping his forehead. "It is my last war trail, but it will be a great one. I know it. How I know it I do not know, but I know it. The voice of Manitou has spoken in my ear and I cannot doubt. I shall fall in battle by the shores of Andiatarocte (the Iroquois name of Lake George) and there is no cause to mourn. I have lived the three score years and ten which the Americans and English say is the allotted age of man, and what could be better for a Mohawk chief, when the right end for his days has come, than to fall gloriously at the head of his warriors? I have known you long, Great Bear. You have always been the friend of the Hodenosaunee. You have understood us, you have never lied to us, and tricked us, as the fat traders do. I think that when I draw my last breath you will not be far away and it will be well. I could not wish for any better friend than Great Bear to be near when I leave this earth on my journey to the star on which the mighty Hayowentha, the Mohawk chief of long ago, lives."

Willet was much affected, and he put his hand on the shoulder of his old friend.

"I hope you are wrong, Hendrik," he said, "and that many years of good life await you, but if you do fall it is fitting, as you say, to fall at the head of your warriors."

The old chief smiled. It was evident that he had made his peace with his Manitou, and that he awaited the future without anxiety.

"Remember the shores of Andiatarocte," he said. "They are bold and lofty, covered with green forest, and they enclose the most beautiful of all the lakes. It is a wonderful lake. I have known it more than sixty years. The mountains, heavy with the great forest, rise all around it. Its waters are blue or green or silver as the skies over it change. It is full of islands, each like a gem in a cluster. I have gone there often, merely to sit on a great cliff a half mile above its waters, and look down on the lake, Andiatarocte, the Andiatarocte of the Hodenosaunee that Manitou gave to us because we strive to serve him. It is a great and glorious gift to me that I should be allowed to die in battle there and take my flight from its shores to Hayowentha's star, the star on which Hayowentha sits, and from which he talks across infinite space, which is nothing to them, to the great Onondaga chieftain Tododaho, also on his star to which he went more than four centuries ago."

The face of the old chief was rapt and mystic. The black eyes in the bronzed face looked into futurity and infinity. Robert was more than impressed, he had a feeling of awe. A great Indian chief was a great Indian chief to him, as great as any man, and he did not doubt that the words of Hendrik would come true. And like Hendrik himself he did not see any cause for grief. He, too, had looked upon the beautiful shores of Andiatarocte, and it was a fitting place for a long life to end, preparatory to another and eternal life among the stars.

He gravely saluted King Hendrik with the full respect and deference due him, to which the chief replied, obviously pleased with the good manners of the youth, and then he and the hunter walked to another portion of the camp.

"A great man, a really great man!" said Willet.

"He made a great speech here in Albany more than a year ago to a congress of white men, and he has made many great speeches. He is also a great warrior, and for nearly a half century he has valiantly defended the border against the French and their Indians."

"I wonder if what he says about falling in battle on the shores of Andiatarocte will come true."

"We'll wait and see, Robert, we'll wait and see, but I've an idea that it will. Some of these Indians, especially the old, seem to have the gift of second sight, and we who live so much in the woods know that many strange things happen."

A few days of intense activity followed. The differences between Governor Shirley and the commander, Colonel William Johnson, were composed, and the motley army would soon march forward to the head of Andiatarocte to meet Dieskau and the French. It was evident that the beautiful lake which both English and French claimed, but which really belonged to the Hodenosaunee, had become one of two keys to the North American lock, the other being its larger and scarcely less beautiful sister, Champlain. They and their chains of rivers had been for centuries the great carry between what had become the French and English colonies, and whoever became the ruler of these two lakes would become the ruler of the continent.

It was granted to Robert with his extraordinary imaginative gifts to look far into the future. He had seen the magnificence of the north country, its world of forest and fertile land, its network of rivers and lakes, a region which he believed to be without an equal anywhere on earth, and he knew that an immense and vigorous population was bound to spring up there. He had his visions and dreams, and perhaps his youth made him dream all the more, and more magnificently than older men whose lives had been narrowed by the hard facts of the present. It was in these brilliant, glowing dreams of his that New York might some day be as large as London, with a commerce as large, and that Boston and Philadelphia and other places for which the sites were not yet cleared, would be a match for the great cities of the Old World.

And yet but few men in the colonies were dreaming such dreams, which became facts in a period amazingly short, as the history of the world runs. Perhaps the dream was in the wise and prophetic brain of Franklin or in the great imagination of Jefferson, but there is little to prove that more than a few were dreaming that way. To everybody, almost, the people on the east coast of North America were merely the rival outposts of France and England.

But the army that was starting for the green shores of Andiatarocte bore with it the fate of mighty nations, and its march, hidden and obscure, compared with that of many a great army in Europe, was destined to have a vast influence upon the world.

It was a strange composite force. There were the militiamen from New England, tall, thin, hardy and shrewd, accustomed to lives of absolute independence, full of confidence and eager to go against the enemy. Many of the New Yorkers were of the same type, but the troops of that province also included the Germans and the Dutch, most of the Germans still unable to speak the English language. There was the little Philadelphia troop under Colden, trained now, the wild rangers from the border, and the fierce Mohawks led by King Hendrik and Daganoweda. Colonel Johnson, an Irishman by birth, but more of an American than many of those born on the soil, was the very man to fuse and lead an army of such varying elements.

Robert now saw Waraiyageh at his best. He soothed the vanity of Governor Shirley. He endeared himself to the New England officers and their men. He talked their own languages to the men of German and Dutch blood, and he continued to wield over the Mohawks an influence that no other white man ever had. The Mohawk lad, Joseph Brant, the great Thayendanegea of the future, was nearly always with him, and Tayoga himself was not more eager for the march.

Now came significant arrivals in the camp, Robert Rogers, the ranger, at the head of his men, and with him Black Rifle, dark, saturnine and silent, although Robert noticed that now and then his black eyes flashed under the thick shade of his long lashes. They brought reports of the greatest activity among the French and Indians about the northern end of Andiatarocte, and that Dieskau was advancing in absolute confidence that he would equal the achievement of Dumas, St. Luc, Ligneris and the others against Braddock. All about him were the terrible Indian swarms. Every settler not slain had fled with his people for their lives. Only the most daring and skillful of the American forest runners could live in the woods, and the price they paid was perpetual vigilance. Foremost among the Indian leaders was Tandakora, the huge Ojibway, and he spared none who fell into his hands. Torture and death were their fate.

The face of Colonel Johnson darkened when Rogers told him the news. "My poor people!" he groaned. "Why were we compelled to wait so long?" And by his "people" he meant the Mohawks no less than the whites. The valiant tribe, and none more valiant ever lived, was threatened with destruction by the victorious and exultant hordes.

Refugees poured into Albany, bringing tales of destruction and terror. Albany itself would soon be attacked by Dieskau, with his regulars, his cannon, his Canadians and his thousands of Indians, and it could not stand before them. Robert, Tayoga and Willet were with Colonel Johnson, when Rogers and Black Rifle arrived, and they saw his deep grief and anger.

"The army will march in a few more days, David, old friend," he said, "but it must move slowly. One cannot take cannon and wagons through the unbroken forest, and so I am sending forward two thousand men to cut a road. Then our main force will advance, but we should do something earlier, something that will brush back these murderous swarms. David, old friend, what are we to do?"

Willet looked around in thought, and he caught the flashing eyes of Rogers. He glanced at Black Rifle and his dark eyes, too, were sparkling under their dark lashes. He understood what was in their minds, and it appealed to him.

"Colonel Johnson," he said, "one must burn the faces of the French and Indians, and show them a victory is not theirs until they've won it. Let

57

Mr. Rogers here take the rangers he has, other picked ones from the camp, Robert, Tayoga and me, perhaps also a chosen band of Mohawks under Daganoweda, and go forward to strike a blow that will delay Dieskau."

The somber face of Waraiyageh lightened.

"David Willet," he said, "you are a man. I have always known it, but it seems to me that every time I meet you you have acquired some new virtue of the mind. 'Tis a daring task you undertake, but a noble one that I think will prove fruitful. Perhaps, though, you should leave the lads behind."

Then up spoke Robert indignantly.

"I've been through a thousand dangers with Dave, and I'll not shirk a new one. I have no commission in the army and it cannot hold me. I shall be sorry to go without your permission, Colonel Johnson, but go I surely will."

"For more centuries than man knows, my ancestors have trod the war trail," said Tayoga, "and I should not be worthy to have been born a son of the clan of the Bear, of the nation Onondaga, of the great League of the Hodenosaunee, if I did not go now upon the greatest war trail of them all, when the nations gather to fight for the lordship of half a world. When the Great Bear and the Mountain Wolf and Dagaeoga and the others leave this camp for the shores of Andiatarocte I go with them!"

He stood very erect, his head thrown back a little, his eyes flashing, his face showing unalterable resolve. Colonel Johnson laughed mellowly.

"What a pair of young eagles we have!" he exclaimed in a pleased tone. "And if that fiery child, Joseph Brant, were here he would be wild to go too! And if I let him go on such a venture Molly Brant would never forgive me. Well, it's a good spirit and I have no right to make any further objection. But do you, Dave Willet, and you, Rogers, and you, Black Rifle, see that they take no unnecessary risks."

Grosvenor also was eager to go, but they thought his experience in the woods was yet too small for him to join the rangers, and, to his great disappointment, the band was made up without him. Then they arranged for their departure.

CHAPTER VII

ON THE GREAT TRAIL

Robert appreciated fully all the dangers they were sure to encounter upon their perilous expedition to the lakes. Having the gift of imagination, he saw them in their most alarming colors, but having a brave heart also, he was more than willing, he was eager to encounter them with his chosen comrades by his side. The necessity of striking some quick and sharp blow became more apparent every hour, or the lakes, so vital in the fortunes of the war, would soon pass into the complete possession of the French and Indians.

The band was chosen and equipped with the utmost care. It included, of course, all of Rogers' rangers, Robert, Tayoga, Willet and Black Rifle, making a total of fifty white men, all of tried courage and inured to the forest. Besides there were fifty Mohawks under Daganoweda, the very pick of the tribe, stalwart warriors, as tough as hickory, experienced in every art of wilderness trail and war, and eager to be at the foe. Every white man was armed with a rifle, a pistol, a hatchet and a knife, carrying also a pouch containing many bullets, a large horn of powder, a blanket folded tightly and a knapsack full of food. The Mohawks were armed to the teeth in a somewhat similar fashion, and, it being midsummer and the weather warm, they were bare to the waist. Rogers, the ranger,

was in nominal command of the whole hundred, white and red, but Willet and
Daganoweda in reality were on an equality, and since the three knew one another well
and esteemed one another highly they were sure to act in perfect coordination. Black
Rifle, it was understood, would go and come as he pleased. He was under the orders of no
man.

"I give you no instructions," said Colonel William Johnson to the three leaders,
"because I know of none to be given under such circumstances. No man can tell what
awaits you in the forest and by the lakes. I merely ask you in God's name to be careful!
Do not walk into any trap! And yet 'tis foolish of me to warn Robert Rogers, David
Willet, Black Rifle and Daganoweda, four foresters who probably haven't their equal in
all North America. But we can ill afford to lose you. If you do not see your way to strike
a good blow perhaps it would be better to come back and march with the army."

"You don't mean that, William, old friend," said Willet, smiling and addressing him
familiarly by his first name. "In your heart you would be ashamed of us if we returned
without achieving at least one good deed for our people. And turning from William, my
old friend, to Colonel William Johnson, our commander, I think I can promise that a high
deed will be achieved. Where could you find a hundred finer men than these, fifty white
and fifty red?"

Daganoweda, who understood him perfectly, smiled proudly and glanced at the ranks
of Mohawks who stood impassive, save for their eager, burning eyes.

"But be sure to bring back the good lads, Robert and Tayoga," said
Mynheer Jacobus Huysman, who stood with Colonel William Johnson. "I
would keep them from going, if I could, but I know I cannot and perhaps
I am proud of them, because I know they will not listen to me."

King Hendrik of the Mohawks, in his gorgeous colored clothes, was also present, his
bronzed and aged face lighted up with the warlike gleam from his eyes. Evidently his
mind was running back over the countless forays and expeditions he had led in the course
of fifty years. He longed once more for the forests, the beautiful lakes and the great war
trail. His seventy years had not quenched his fiery spirit, but they had taken much of his
strength, and so he would abide with the army, going with it on its slow march.

"My son," he said, with the gravity and dignity of an old Indian sachem, to
Daganoweda, "upon this perilous chance you carry the honor and fortune of the
Ganeagaono, the great warlike nation of the Hodenosaunee. It is not necessary for me to
bid you do your duty and show to the Great Bear, the Mountain Wolf, Black Rifle and the
other white men that a young Mohawk chief will go where any other will go, and if need
be will die with all his men before yielding a foot of ground. I do not bid you do these
things because I know that you will do them without any words from me, else you would
not be a Mohawk chief, else you would not be Daganoweda, son of fire and battle."

Daganoweda smiled proudly. The wise old sachem had struck upon the most
responsive chords in his nature.

"I will try to bear myself as a Mohawk should," he said simply.

Colden and Grosvenor were also there.

"I'm sorry our troop can't go with you," said the young Philadelphian, "but I'm not one
to question the wisdom and decision of our commander-in-chief. Doubtless we'd be a
drag upon such a band as yours, but I wish we could have gone. At least, we'll be with the
army which is going to march soon, and perhaps we'll overtake you at Lake George
before many days."

"And I," said Grosvenor to Robert and Tayoga, "am serving on the staff of the
commander. I'm perhaps the only Englishman here and I'm an observer more than
anything else. So I could be spared most readily, but the colonel will not let me go. He

says there is no reason why we should offer a scalp without price to Tandakora, the Ojibway."

"And I abide by what I said," laughed Colonel Johnson, who heard. "You're in conditions new to you, Grosvenor, though you've had one tragic and dreadful proof of what the Indians can do, but there's great stuff in you and I'm not willing to see it thrown away before it's developed. Don't be afraid the French and Indians won't give you all the fighting you want, though I haven't the slightest doubt you'll stand up to it like a man."

"Thank you, sir," said Grosvenor, modestly.

The lad, Peter, was also eager to go, and he was soothed only by the promise of Mynheer Jacobus Huysman that he might join the army on the march to Lake George.

Then the leaders gave the word and the hundred foresters, fifty white and fifty red, plunged into the great northern wilderness which stretched through New York into Canada, one of the most beautiful regions on earth, and at that particular time the most dangerous, swarming with ruthless Indians and daring French partisans.

It was remarkable how soon they reached the wilds after leaving Albany. The Dutch had been along the Hudson for more than a century, and the English had come too, but all of them had clung mostly to the river. Powerful and warlike tribes roamed the great northern forests, and the French colonies in the north and the English colonies in the south had a healthy respect for the fighting powers of one another. The doubtful ground between was wide and difficult, and anyone who ventured into it now had peril always beside him.

The forest received the hundred, the white and the red, and hid them at once in its depths. It was mid-summer, but there was yet no brown on the leaves. A vast green canopy overhung the whole earth, and in every valley flowed brooks and rivers of clean water coming down from the firm hills. The few traces made by the white man had disappeared since the war. The ax was gone, and the scalp-hunters had taken its place.

Robert, vivid of mind, quickly responsive to the externals of nature, felt all the charm and majesty that the wilderness in its mightiest manifestations had for him. He did not think of danger yet, because he was surrounded by men of so much bravery and skill. He did not believe that in all the world there was such another hundred, and he was full of pride to be the comrade of such champions.

Daganoweda and the Mohawks reverted at once to the primitive, from which they had never departed much. The young Mohawk chieftain was in advance with Willet. He had a blanket but it was folded and carried in a small pack on his back. He was bare to the waist and his mighty chest was painted in warlike fashion. All his warriors were in similar attire or lack of it.

Daganoweda was happy. Robert saw his black eyes sparkling, and he continually raised his nose to scent the wind like some hunting animal. Robert knew that in his fierce heart he was eager for the sight of a hostile band. The enemy could not come too soon for Daganoweda and the Mohawks. Tayoga's face showed the same stern resolve, but the Onondaga, more spiritual than the Mohawk, lacked the fierceness of Daganoweda.

When they were well into the wilderness they stopped and held a consultation, in which Rogers, Willet, Black Rifle, Daganoweda, Robert and Tayoga shared. They were to decide a question of vital importance—their line of march. They believed that Dieskau and the main French army had not yet reached Crown Point, the great French fortress on Lake Champlain, but there was terrible evidence that the swarms of his savage allies were not only along Champlain but all around Lake George, and even farther south. Unquestionably the French partisan leaders were with them, and where and when would it be best for the American-Iroquois force to strike?

"I think," said Willet, "that St. Luc himself will be here. The Marquis de Vaudreuil, the new Governor General of Canada, knows his merit and will be sure to send him ahead of Dieskau."

Robert felt the thrill that always stirred him at the mention of St. Luc's name. Would they meet once more in the forest? He knew that if the Chevalier came all their own skill and courage would be needed to meet him on equal terms. However kindly St. Luc might feel toward him he would be none the less resolute and far-seeing in battle against the English and Americans.

"I think we should push for the western shore of Andiatarocte," said Willet. "What is your opinion, Daganoweda?"

"The Great Bear is right. He is nearly always right," replied the Mohawk. "If we go along the eastern shore and bear in toward Champlain we might be trapped by the French and their warriors. West of Andiatarocte the danger to us would not be so great, while we would have an equal chance to strike."

"Well spoken, Daganoweda," said Rogers. "I agree with you that for the present it would be wise for us to keep away from Oneadatote (the Indian name for Lake Champlain) and keep to Andiatarocte. The Indians are armed at Crown Point on Oneadatote, which was once our own Fort Saint Frederick, founded by us, but plenty of them spread to the westward and we'll be sure to have an encounter."

The others were of a like opinion, and the line of march was quickly arranged. Then they settled themselves for the night, knowing there was no haste, as the French and Indians would come to meet them, but knowing also there was always great need of caution, since if their foes were sure to come it was well to know just when they would come. The Mohawks asked for the watch, meaning to keep it with three relays of a dozen warriors each, a request that Rogers and Willet granted readily, and all the white forest runners prepared for sleep, save the strange and terrible man whom they commonly called Black Rifle.

Black Rifle, whose story was known in some form along the whole border, was a figure with a sort of ominous fascination for Robert, who could not keep from watching him whenever he was within eye-shot. He had noticed that the man was restless and troubled at Albany. The presence of so many people and the absence of the wilderness appeared to vex him. But since they had returned to the forest his annoyance and uneasiness were gone. He was confident and assured, he seemed to have grown greatly in size, and he was a formidable and menacing figure.

Black Rifle did not watch with the Mohawk sentinels, but he was continually making little trips into the forest, absences of ten or fifteen minutes, and whenever he returned his face bore a slight look of disappointment. Robert knew it was because he had found no Indian sign, but to the lad himself the proof that the enemy was not yet near gave peace. He was eager to go on the great war trail, but he was not fond of bloodshed, though to him more perhaps than to any other was given the vision of a vast war, and of mighty changes with results yet more mighty flowing from those changes. His heart leaped at the belief that he should have a part in them, no matter how small the part.

He lay on the grass with his blanket beneath him, his head on a pillow of dead leaves. Not far away was Tayoga, already asleep. They had built no fires, and as the night was dark the bronze figures of the Indian sentinels soon grew dim. Rogers and Willet also slept, but Robert still lay there awake, seeing many pictures through his wide-open eyes, Quebec, the lost Stadacona of the Mohawks, the St. Lawrence, Tandakora, the huge Ojibway who had hunted him so fiercely, St. Luc, De Courcelles, and all the others who had passed out of his life for a while, though he felt now, with the prescience of old King Hendrik, that they were coming back again. His path would lie for a long time away from cities and the gay and varied life that appealed to him so much, and would lead once more through the wilderness, which also appealed to him, but in another way. Hence when he slept his wonderfully vivid imagination did not permit him to sleep as soundly as the others.

He awoke about midnight and sat up on his blanket, looking around at the sleeping forms, dim in the darkness. He distinguished Tayoga near him, just beyond him the mighty figure of Willet, then that of Rogers, scarcely less robust, and farther on some of the white men. He did not see Black Rifle, but he felt sure that he was in the forest, looking for the signs of Indians and hoping to find them. Daganoweda also was invisible and it was likely that the fiery young Mohawk chief was outside the camp on an errand similar to that of Black Rifle. He was able to trace on the outskirts the figures of the sentinels, shadowy and almost unreal in the darkness, but he knew that the warriors of the Ganeagaono watched with eyes that saw everything even in the dusk, and listened with ears that heard everything, whether night or day.

He fell again into a doze or a sort of half sleep in which Tarenyawagon, the sender of dreams, made him see more pictures and see them much faster than he ever saw them awake. The time of dreams did not last more than half an hour, but in that period he lived again many years of his life. He passed once more through many scenes of his early boyhood when Willet was teaching him the ways of the forest. He met Tayoga anew for the first time, together they went to the house of Mynheer Jacobus Huysman in Albany, and together they went to the school of Alexander McLean; then he jumped over a long period and with Willet and Tayoga had his first meeting with St. Luc and Tandakora. He was talking to the Frenchman when he came out of that period of years which was yet less than an hour, and sat up.

All the others save the sentinels were asleep, but his delicate senses warned him that something was moving in the forest. It was at first an instinct rather than anything seen or heard, but soon he traced against the misty background of the dusk the shadowy figures of moving Mohawks. He saw the tall form of Daganoweda, who had come back from the forest, and who must have come because he had something to tell. Then he made out behind the Mohawk chief, Black Rifle, and, although he could not see his features, the white man nevertheless looked swart and menacing, an effect of the day carried over into the night.

It was Robert's first impulse to lie down again and pretend not to know, but he remembered that he was in the full confidence of them all, a trusted lieutenant, welcomed at any time, anywhere, and so remembering, he arose and walked on light foot to the place where Daganoweda stood talking with the others. The Mohawk chief gave him one favoring glance, telling him he was glad that he had come. Then he returned his attention to a young Indian warrior who stood alert, eager and listening.

"Haace (Panther), where did you find the sign that someone had passed?" he asked.

"Two miles to the north *Gao* (the wind) brought me a sound," replied Haace. "It was light. It might have been made by the boughs of *Oondote* (a tree) rubbing together, but the ears of Haace told him it was not so. I crept through *Gabada* (the forest) to the place, whence the sound had come, and lo! it and whatever had made it were gone, but I found among the bushes traces to show that moccasins had passed."

Fire leaped up in the black eyes of Daganoweda.

"Did you follow?" he asked.

"For a mile, and I found other traces of moccasins passing. The traces met and fused into one trail. All the owners of the moccasins knelt and drank at a *Dushote* (a spring), and as they were very thirsty they must have come far."

"How do you know, Haace?"

"Because the imprints of their knees were sunk deep in the earth, showing that they drank long and with eagerness. *Oneganosa* (the water) was sweet to their lips, and they would not have drunk so long had they not been walking many miles. I would have followed further, but I felt that I should come back and tell to my chief, Daganoweda, what I had seen."

"You have done well, Haace. Some day the Panther will turn into a chief."

The black eyes of the young warrior flashed with pleasure, but he said nothing, silence becoming him when he was receiving precious words of praise from his leader.

"I saw sign of the savages too," said Black Rifle. "I came upon the coals of a dead fire about two days' old. By the side of it I found these two red beads that had dropped from the leggings or moccasins of some warrior. I've seen beads of this kind before, and they all come from the French in Canada."

"Then," said Robert, speaking for the first time, "you've no doubt the enemy is near?"

"None in the world," replied Black Rifle, "but I think they're going west, away from us. It's not likely they know yet we're here, but so large a band as ours can't escape their notice long."

"If they did not find that we are here," said Daganoweda proudly, "we would soon tell it to them ourselves, and in such manner that they would remember it."

"That we would," said Black Rifle, with equal emphasis. "Now, what do you think, Daganoweda? Should we wake the Great Bear and the Mountain Wolf?"

"No, Black Rifle. Let them sleep on. They will need tomorrow the sleep they get tonight. Man lives by day in the sleep that he has at night, and we wish the eyes of them all to be clear and the arms of them all to be strong, when the hour of battle, which is not far away, comes to us."

"You're right, Daganoweda, right in both things you say, right that they need all their strength, and right that we'll soon meet St. Luc, at the head of the French and Indians, because I'm as sure as I know that I'm standing here that he's now leading 'em. Shall we finish out the night here, and then follow on their trail until we can bring 'em to battle on terms that suit us?"

"Yes, Black Rifle. That is what the Great Bear and the Mountain Wolf would say too, and so I shall not awake them. Instead, I too will go to sleep."

Daganoweda, as much a Viking as any that ever lived in Scandinavia, lay down among his men and went quickly to the home over which Tarenyawagon presided. Haace, filled with exultation that he had received the high approval of his chief, slid away among the trees on another scout, and, in like manner, the forest swallowed up Black Rifle. Once more the camp was absolutely silent, only the thin and shadowy figures of the bronze sentinels showing through the misty gloom. Robert lay down again and Tarenyawagon, the sender of dreams, held him in his spell. His excited brain, even in sleep, was a great sensitive plate, upon which pictures, vivid and highly colored, were passing in a gorgeous procession.

Now, Tarenyawagon carried him forward and not back. They met St. Luc in battle, and it was dark and bloody. How it ended he did not know, because a veil was dropped over it suddenly, and then he was in the forest with Tayoga, fleeing for his life once more from Tandakora, De Courcelles and their savage band. Nor was it given to him to know how the pursuit ended, because the veil fell again suddenly, and when it was lifted he was in a confused and terrible battle not far from a lake, where French soldiers, American soldiers and English soldiers were mingled in horrible conflict. For some strange reason, one that he wondered at then, he stood among the French, but while he wondered, and while the combat increased in ferocity the veil slipped down and it was all gone like a mist. Then came other pictures, vivid in color, but vague in detail, that might or might not be scenes in his future life, and he awoke at last to find the dawn had come.

Tayoga was already awake and handed him a piece of venison.

"Eat, Dagaeoga," he said, "and drink at the little spring in the wood on our right. I have learned what Haace and Black Rifle saw in the night, and we march in half an hour."

Robert did more than drink at the spring; he also bathed his face, neck and hands at the little brook that ran away from it, and although Tarenyawagon had been busy shifting his kaleidoscope before him while he slept, he was as much refreshed as if he had slumbered without dreams. The dawn, clear but hot in the great forest, brought with it zeal and confidence. They would follow on the trail of the French and Indian leaders, and he believed, as surely as a battle came, that Willet, Rogers, Daganoweda and their men would be the victors.

As soon as the brief and cold breakfast was finished the hundred departed silently. The white rangers wore forest dress dyed green that blended with the foliage, and the Mohawks still wore scarcely anything at all. It was marvelous the way in which they traveled, and it would not have been possible to say that white man or red man was the better. Robert heard now and then only the light brush of a moccasin. A hundred men flitted through the greenwood and they passed like phantoms.

In a brief hour they struck the trail that Haace had found, and followed it swiftly, but with alert eyes for ambush. Presently other little trails flowed into it, some from the east, and some from the west, and the tributaries included imprints, which obviously were those of white men. Then the whole broad trail, apparently a force of about one hundred, curved back toward the west.

"They go to Andiatarocte," said Daganoweda. "Perhaps they meet another force there."

"It's probably so," said Willet. "Knowing that our army is about to advance they wouldn't come to the southwest shore of the lake unless they were in strength. I still feel that St. Luc is leading them, but other Frenchmen are surely with him. It behooves us to use all the caution of which white men and red together are capable. In truth, there must be no ambush for us. Besides the loss which we should suffer it would be a terrible decrease of prestige for it to be known that the Mountain Wolf and Daganoweda, the most warlike of all the chiefs of the Ganeagaono, were trapped by the French and their savage allies."

Willet spoke artfully and the response was instantaneous. The great chest of Daganoweda swelled, and a spark leaped from his eyes.

"It will never be told of us," he said, "because it cannot happen. There are not enough of the French and their savage allies in the world to trap the Great Bear, the Mountain Wolf, Daganoweda, and the lads Tayoga and Dagaeoga."

Willet smiled. It was the reply that he had expected. Moreover, both his words and those of the chief were heard by many warriors, and he knew that they would respond in every fiber to the battle cry of their leader. His contemptuous allusion to the allies of the French as "savages" met a ready response in their hearts, since the nations of the Hodenosaunee considered themselves civilized and enlightened, which, in truth, they were in many respects.

Robert always remembered the place at which they held their brief council. They stood in a little grove of oaks and elms, clear of underbrush. The trees were heavy with foliage, and the leaves were yet green. The dawn had not yet fully come, and the heavens, save low down in the east, were still silver, casting a silvery veil which gave an extraordinary and delicate tint to the green of foliage. In the distance on the right was the gleam of water, silver like the skies, but it was one of the beautiful lakelets abundant in that region and not yet Andiatarocte, which was still far away. The bronze figures of the Indians, silent and impassive as they listened to their chief, fitted wonderfully into the wilderness scene, and the white men in forest green, their faces tanned and fierce, were scarcely less wild in look and figure. Robert felt once more a great thrill of pride that he had been chosen a member of such a company.

They talked less than five minutes. Then Black Rifle, alone as usual because he preferred invariably to be alone, disappeared in the woods to the right of the great trail. Three young warriors, uncommonly swift of foot, soon followed him, and three more as nimble of heel as the others, sank from sight in the forest to the left. Both right and left soon swallowed up several of the rangers also, who were not inferior as scouts and trailers to the Mohawks.

"The wings of our force are protected amply now," said Tayoga, in his precise school English. "When such eyes as those of our flankers are looking and watching, no ambush against us is possible. Now our main force will advance with certainty."

Twenty men had been sent out as scouts and the remaining eighty, eager for combat, white and red, advanced on the main trail, not fast but steadily. Now and then the cries of bird or beast, signals from the flankers, came from right or left, and the warriors with Daganoweda responded.

"They are telling us," said Tayoga to Robert, "that they have not yet found a hostile presence. The enemy has left behind him no skirmishers or rear guard. It may be that we shall not overtake them until we approach the lake or reach it."

"How do you know that we will overtake them at all, Tayoga? They may go so fast that we can't come up."

"I know it, Dagaeoga, because if they are led by St. Luc, and I think they are, they will not try to get away. If they believe we are not about to overtake them they will wait for us at some place they consider good."

"You're probably right, Tayoga, and it's likely that we'll be in battle before night. One would think there is enough country here on this continent for the whole world without having the nations making war over any part of it. As I have said before, here we are fighting to secure for an English king or a French king mountains and lakes and rivers and forests which neither of them will ever see, and of the existence of which, perhaps, they don't know."

"And as I have told you before, Dagaeoga, the mountains and lakes and rivers and forests for which the English and French kings have their people fight, belong to neither, but to the great League of the Hodenosaunee and other red nations."

"That's true, Tayoga. Sometimes I'm apt to forget it, but you know I'm a friend of the Hodenosaunee. If I had the power I'd see that never an acre of their country was filched from them by the white men."

"I know it well, Dagaeoga."

The pursuit continued all the morning, and the great trail left by the French and Indians broadened steadily. Other trails flowed into and merged with it, and it became apparent that the force pursued was larger than the force pursuing. Yet Willet, Rogers and Daganoweda did not flinch, clinging to the trail, which now led straight toward Andiatarocte.

CHAPTER VIII

ARESKOUI'S FAVOR

In the dusk of the evening the whole force came to the crest of a hill from which through a cleft they caught a glimpse of the shimmering waters of the lake, called by the Iroquois Andiatarocte, by the French, St. Sacrement, and by the English, George. It was not Robert's first view of it, but he always thrilled at the prospect.

"Both Andiatarocte and Oneadatote must be ours," he said to Tayoga. "They're too fine and beautiful to pass into possession of the French."

"What about the Hodenosaunee? Do you too forget, Dagaeoga?"

"I don't forget, Tayoga. When I said 'ours' I meant American, Hodenosaunee and English combined. You've good eyes, and so tell me if I'm not right when I say I see a moving black dot on the lake."

"You do see it, my friend, and also a second and a third. The segment of the lake that we can see from here is very narrow. At this distance it does not appear to be more than a few inches across, but I know as surely as Tododaho sits on his star watching over us, that those are canoes, or perhaps long boats, and that they belong to our enemies."

"A force on the water coöperating with that on land?"

"It seems so, Dagaeoga."

"And they mean to become the rulers of the lakes! With their army powerfully established at Crown Point, and their boats on both Andiatarocte and Oneadatote, it looks as if they were getting a great start in that direction."

"Aye, Dagaeoga. The French move faster than we. They seize what we both wish, and then it will be for us to put them out, they being in possession and intrenched. Look, Black Rifle comes out of the forest! And Haace is with him! They have something to tell!"

It was the honor and pleasure of young Lennox and the Onondaga to be present at the councils, and though they said nothing to their elders unless asked for an opinion, they always listened with eagerness to everything. Now Willet, Rogers and Daganoweda drew together, and Black Rifle and Haace, their dark eyes gleaming, made report to them.

"A strong force, at least one hundred and fifty men, lies about five miles to the north, on the shore of the lake," said Black Rifle. "About twenty Frenchmen are with it, and it is commanded by St. Luc. I saw him from the bushes. He has with him the Canadian, Dubois. De Courcelles and Jumonville are there also. At least a hundred warriors and Frenchmen are on the lake, in canoes and long boats. I saw Tandakora too."

"A formidable force," said Willet. "Do you wish to turn back, Daganoweda?"

The eyes of the Mohawk chieftain glittered and he seemed to swell both in size and stature.

"We are a hundred," he replied proudly. "What does it matter how many they are? I am astonished that the Great Bear should ask me such a question."

Willet laughed softly.

"I asked it," he said, "because I knew what the answer would be. None other could come from a Mohawk chieftain."

Again the eyes of Daganoweda glittered, but this time with pride.

"Shall we advance and attack St. Luc's force tonight?" said Willet, turning to Rogers.

"I think it would be best," replied the Mountain Wolf. "A surprise is possible tonight only. Tomorrow his scouts are sure to find that we are near. What say you, Daganoweda?"

"Tonight," replied the Mohawk chief, sententiously.

There was no further discussion, and the whole force, throwing out skirmishers, moved cautiously northward through the great, green wilderness. It was a fair night for a march, not enough moonlight to disclose them at a distance, and yet enough to show the way. Robert kept close to Tayoga, who was just behind Willet, and they bore in toward the lake, until they were continually catching glimpses of its waters through the vast curtain of the forest.

Robert's brain once more formed pictures, swift, succeeding one another like changes of light, but in high colors. The great lake set in the mountains and glimmering under the moon had a wonderful effect upon his imagination. It became for the time the core of all the mighty struggle that was destined to rage so long in North America. The belief became a conviction that whoever possessed Andiatarocte and Oneadatote was destined to possess the continent.

The woods themselves, like the lake, were mystic and brooding. Their heavy foliage was ruffled by no wind, and no birds sang. The wild animals, knowing that man, fiercer than they, would soon join in mortal combat, had all fled away. Robert heard only the faint crush of moccasins as the hundred, white and red, sped onward.

An hour, and a dim light showed on a slope gentler than the rest, leading down to the lake. It was a spark so faint and vague that it might have passed to the ordinary eye as a firefly, but rangers and Mohawks knew well that it came from some portion of St. Luc's camp and that the enemy was close at hand. Then the band stopped and the three leaders talked together again for a few moments.

"I think," said Willet, "that the force on land is in touch with the one in the boats, though a close union has not been effected. In my opinion we must rush St. Luc."

"There is no other way," said Rogers.

"It is what I like best," said Daganoweda.

They promptly spread out, the entire hundred in a half circle, covering a length of several hundred yards, and the whole force advanced swiftly. Robert and Tayoga were in the center, and as they rushed forward with the others, their moccasined feet making scarcely any sound, Robert saw the fireflies in the forest increase, multiply and become fixed. If he had felt any doubt that the camp of St. Luc was just ahead it disappeared now. The brilliant French leader too, despite all his craft, and lore of the forest, was about to be surprised.

Then he heard the sharp reports of rifles both to right and left. The horns of the advancing crescent were coming into contact with St. Luc's sentinels. Then Daganoweda, knowing that the full alarm had been given, uttered a fierce and thrilling cry and all the Mohawks took it up. It was a tremendous shout, making the blood leap and inciting to battle.

Robert, by nature kindly and merciful, felt the love of combat rising in him, and when a bullet whistled past his ear a fury against the enemy began to burn in his veins. More bullets came pattering upon the leaves, and one found its target in a ranger who was struck through the heart. Other rangers and Mohawks received wounds, but under the compelling orders of their leaders they held their fire until they were near the camp, when nearly a hundred rifles spoke together in one fierce and tremendous report.

St. Luc's sentinels and skirmishers were driven back in a minute or two, many of them falling, but his main force lay along a low ridge, timbered well, and from its shelter his men, French and Indians, sent in a rapid fire. Although taken by surprise and suffering severely in the first rush, they were able to stem the onset of the rangers and Mohawks, and soon they were uttering fierce and defiant cries, while their bullets came in showers. The rangers and Mohawks also took to cover, and the battle of the night and the wilderness was on.

Robert pulled Tayoga down, and the two lay behind a fallen log, where they listened to the whining of an occasional bullet over their heads.

"We may win," said the Onondaga gravely, "but we will not win so easily. One cannot surprise Sharp Sword (St. Luc) wholly. You may attack when he is not expecting it, but even then he will make ready for you."

"That's true," said Robert, and he felt a curious and contradictory thrill of pleasure as he listened to Tayoga. "It's not possible to take the Chevalier in a trap."

"No, Dagaeoga, it is not. I wish, for the sake of our success, that some other than he was the leader of the enemy, but Manitou has willed that my wish should not come true. Do you not think the dark shadow passing just then on the ridge was Tandakora?"

"The size indicated to me the Ojibway, and I was about to seize my rifle and fire, but it's too far for a shot with any certainty. I think our men on the horns of the crescent are driving them in somewhat."

"The shifting of the firing would prove that it is so, Dagaeoga. Our sharpshooting is much better than theirs, and in time we will push them down to the lake. But look at Black Rifle! See how he craves the battle!"

The swart ranger, lying almost flat on the ground, was creeping forward, inch by inch, and as Robert glanced at him he fired, a savage in the opposing force uttering his death yell. The ranger uttered a shout of triumph, and, shifting his position, sought another shot, his dark body drawn among the leaves and grass like that of some fierce wild animal. He fired a second time, repeated his triumphant shout and then his sliding body passed out of sight among the bushes.

Both Rogers and Willet soon joined Robert and Tayoga behind the logs where they had a good position from which to direct the battle, but Daganoweda on the right, with all of his Mohawks, was pushing forward steadily and would soon be able to pour a flanking fire into St. Luc's little army. The forest resounded now with the sharp reports of the rifles and the shouts and yells of the combatants. Bullets cut leaves and twigs, but the rangers and the Mohawks were advancing.

"Do you know how many men we have lost, Rogers?" asked Willet.

"Three of the white men and four of the Mohawks have been slain, Dave, but we're winning a success, and it's not too high a price to pay in war. If Daganoweda can get far enough around on their left flank we'll drive 'em into the lake, sure. Ah, there go the rifles of the Mohawks and they're farther forward than ever. That Mohawk chief is a bold fighter, crafty and full of fire."

"None better than he. I think they're well around the flank, Rogers. Listen to their shouts. Now, we'll make a fresh rush of our own."

They sprang from the shelter of the log, and, leading their men, rushed in a hundred yards until they dropped down behind another one. Robert and Tayoga went with them, firing as they ran, borne on by the thrill of combat, but Robert felt relief nevertheless when he settled again in the shelter of the second log and for the time being was secure from bullets.

"I think," said Willet to Rogers, "that I'll go around toward the left, where the flanking force is composed mostly of rangers, and press in there with all our might. If the two horns of the crescent are able to enclose St. Luc, and you charge at the center, we should win the victory soon."

"It's the right idea, Dave," said Rogers. "When we hear your shots and a shout or two we'll drive our hardest."

"I'd like to take Tayoga and Robert with me."

"They're yours. They're good and brave lads, and I'll need 'em, but you'll need 'em too. How many more of the men here will you want?"

"About ten."

"Then take them too."

Willet, with Robert, Tayoga and the ten, began a cautious circuit in the darkness toward the western horn of the crescent, and for a few minutes left the battle in the distance. As they crept through the bushes, Robert heard the shouts and shots of both sides and saw the pink flashes of flame as the rifles were fired. In the darkness it seemed confused and vague, but he knew that it was guided by order and precision. Now and then a spent bullet pattered upon the leaves, and one touched him upon the wrist, stinging for a moment or two, but doing no harm.

But as they passed farther and farther to the west the noise of the battle behind them gradually sank, while that on the left horn of the crescent grew.

In a few more minutes they would be with the rangers who were pressing forward so strenuously at that point, and as Robert saw dusky figures rise from the bushes in front of them he believed they were already in touch. Instead a dozen rifles flashed in their faces. One of the rangers went down, shot through the head, dead before he touched the ground, three more sustained slight wounds, including Robert who was grazed on the shoulder, and all of them gave back in surprise and consternation. But Willet, shrewd veteran of the forest, recovered himself quickly.

"Down, men! Down and give it back to 'em!" he cried. "They've sent out a flanking force of their own! It was clever of St. Luc!"

All the rangers dropped on their faces instantly, but as they went down they gave back the fire of the flanking party. Robert caught a glimpse of De Courcelles, who evidently was leading it, and pulled trigger on him, but the Frenchman turned aside at that instant, and his bullet struck a St. Regis Indian who was just behind him. Now the return volley of the rangers was very deadly. Two Frenchmen were slain here and four warriors, and De Courcelles, who had not expected on his circling movement to meet with a new force, was compelled to give back. He and his warriors quickly disappeared in the forest, leaving their dead behind them, and Willet with his own little force moved on triumphantly, soon joining his strength to that of the rangers on the left.

The combined force hurled itself upon St. Luc's flank and crumpled it up, at the same time uttering triumphant shouts which were answered from the right and center, rangers and Mohawks on all fronts now pressing forward, and sending in their bullets from every covert. So fierce was their attack that they created the effect of double or triple their numbers, and St. Luc's French and Indians were driven down the slope to the edge of the lake, where the survivors were saved by the second band in the canoes and great boats.

The defeated men embarked quickly, but not so quickly that several more did not fall in the water. At this moment Robert saw St. Luc, and he never admired him more. He, too, was in forest green, but it was of the finest cloth, trimmed with green yet darker. A cap of silky fur was on his head, and his hair was clubbed in a queue behind. March and forest battle had not dimmed the cleanliness and neatness of his attire, and, even in defeat, he looked the gallant chevalier, without fear and without reproach.

St. Luc was in the act of stepping into one of the long boats when a ranger beside Robert raised his rifle and took aim squarely at the Frenchman's heart. It was not a long shot and the ranger would not have missed, but young Lennox at that moment stumbled and fell against him, causing the muzzle of his weapon to be deflected so much that his bullet struck the uncomplaining water. Robert's heart leaped up as he saw the chevalier spring into the boat, which the stalwart Indians paddled swiftly away.

The entire Indian fleet now drew together, and it was obviously making for one of the little islands, so numerous in Andiatarocte, where it would be safe until the English and Americans built or brought boats of their own and disputed the rulership of the lake. But the rangers and the Mohawks, eager to push the victory, rushed down to the water's edge and sent after the flying fleet bullets which merely dropped vainly in the water. Then they ceased, and, standing there, uttered long thrilling shouts of triumph.

Robert had never beheld a more ferocious scene but he felt in it, too, a sort of fierce and shuddering attraction. His veins were still warm with the fire of battle, and his head throbbed wildly. Everything took on strange and fantastic shapes, and colors became glaring and violent. The moonlight, pouring down on the lake, made it a vast sea of crumbling silver, the mountains on the farther shores rose to twice or thrice their height, and the forests on the slopes and crests were an immense and unbroken curtain, black against the sky.

Five or six hundred yards away hovered the Indian fleet, the canoes and boats dark splotches upon the silver surface of the water. The island upon which they intended to land was just beyond them, but knowing that they were out of rifle range they had paused to look at the victorious force, or as much of it as showed itself, and to send back the defiant yells of a defeated, but undaunted band.

Robert clearly saw St. Luc again, standing up in his boat, and apparently giving orders to the fleet, using his small sword, as a conductor wields a baton, though the moonlight seemed to flash in fire along the blade as he pointed it here and there. He beheld something fierce and unconquerable in the man's attitude and manner. He even imagined that he could see his face, and he knew that the eye was calm, despite defeat and loss. St Luc, driven from the field, would be none the less dangerous than if he had been victor upon it.

The whole Indian fleet formed in a half circle and the Chevalier ceased to wave orders with his sword. Then he drew himself up, stood rigidly erect, despite his unstable footing, faced the land, and, using the sword once more, gave a soldier's salute to the foe. The act was so gallant, so redolent of knightly romance that despite themselves the rangers burst into a mighty cheer, and the Mohawks, having the Indian heart that always honored a brave foe, uttered a long and thrilling whoop of approval.

Robert, carried away by an impulse, sprang upon a rock and whirled his rifle around his head in an answering salute. St. Luc evidently saw, and evidently, too, he recognized Robert, as he lifted his sword in rejoinder. Then the Indians, bent to their paddles, and the fleet, hanging together, swept around the island and out of sight. But they knew that the French and Indian force landed there, as fires soon blazed upon its heavily-wooded crest, and they saw dusky figures passing and repassing before the flames.

"The victory has been given to us tonight," said Tayoga gravely to Robert, "but Manitou has not allowed us to complete it. Few triumph over St. Luc, and, though his manner may have been gay and careless, his heart burns to win back what he has lost."

"I take it you're right, Tayoga," said Robert. "His is a soul that will not rest under defeat, and I fancy St. Luc on the island is a great danger. He can get at us and we can't get at him."

"It is true, Dagaeoga. If we strike we must strike quickly and then be off. This, for the time being, is the enemy's country, yet I think our leaders will not be willing to withdraw. Daganoweda, I know, will want to push the battle and to attack on the island."

The Onondaga's surmise was correct. The triumph of the rangers and the Mohawks, although not complete, was large, as at least one-third of St. Luc's force was slain, and the three leaders alike were eager to make it yet larger, having in mind that in some way they could yet reach the French and Indian force on the island. So they built their own fires on the slope and the Mohawks began to sing songs of triumph, knowing that they would infuriate the foe, and perhaps tempt him to some deed of rashness.

"Did you see anything of Tandakora?" asked Robert of Tayoga. "I know it's no crime to wish that he fell."

"No, it's no crime, Dagaeoga," replied the Onondaga soberly, "and my wish is the same as yours, but this time we cannot have it. I saw him in one of the boats as they passed around the island."

The two then sat by one of the fires and ate venison, thankful that they had escaped with only slight wounds, and as there was no immediate call for their services they wrapped themselves in their blankets, by and by, and went to sleep. When Robert awoke, the morning was about half gone and the day was bright and beautiful beyond compare.

Although the hostile forces still confronted each other there was no other evidence of war, and Robert's first feelings were less for man and more for the magnificence of nature. He had never seen Andiatarocte, the matchless gem of the mountains, more imposing and beautiful. Its waters, rippling gently under the wind, stretched far away, silver or gold, as the sunlight fell. The trees and undergrowth on the islands showed deepest green, and the waving leaves shifted and changed in color with the changing sky. Far over all was a deep velvet blue arch, tinged along the edges with red or gold.

Keenly sensitive to nature, it was a full minute before young Lennox came back to earth, and the struggles of men. Then he found Tayoga looking at him curiously.

"It is good!" said the Onondaga, flinging out his hand. "In the white man's Bible it is said that Manitou created the world in six days and rested on the seventh, but in the unwritten book of the Hodenosaunee it is said that he created Andiatarocte and Oneadatote, and then reposed a bit, and enjoyed his work before he went on with his task."

"I can well believe you, Tayoga. If I had created a lake like George and another like Champlain I should have stopped work, and gloried quite a while over my achievement. Has the enemy made any movement while we slept?"

"None, so far as our people can tell. They have brought part of their fleet around to the side of the island facing us. I count six large boats and twenty canoes there. I also see five fires, and I have no doubt that many of the warriors are sleeping before them. Despite losses, his force is still larger than ours, but I do not think St. Luc, brave as he is, would come back to the mainland and risk a battle with us."

"Then we must get at him somehow, Tayoga. We must make our blow so heavy that it will check Dieskau for a while and give Colonel Johnson's army time to march."

"Even so, Dagaeoga. Look at the Mountain Wolf. He has a pair of field glasses and he is studying the island."

Rogers stood on a knoll, and he was making diligent use of his glasses, excellent for the time. He took them from his eyes presently, and walked down to Robert and Tayoga.

"Would you care to have a look?" he said to Robert.

"Thank you, I'd like it very much," replied young Lennox eagerly.

71

The powerful lenses at once brought the island very near, and trees and bushes became detached from the general mass, until he saw between them the French and Indian camp. As Tayoga had asserted, many of the warriors were asleep on the grass. When nothing was to be done, the Indian could do it with a perfection seldom attained by anybody else. Tandakora was sitting on a fallen log, looking at the mainland. As usual, he was bare to the waist, and painted frightfully. Not far away a Frenchman was sleeping on a cloak, and Robert was quite sure that it was De Courcelles. St. Luc himself was visible toward the center of the island. He, too, stood upon a knoll, and he, too, had glasses with which he was studying his foe.

"The command of the water," said Rogers, "is heavily against us. If we had only been quick enough to build big boats of our own, the tale to be told would have been very different."

"And if by any means," said Willet, "we contrive to drive them from the island, they can easily retreat in their fleet to another, and they could repeat the process indefinitely. George has many islands."

"Then why not capture their fleet?" said Robert in a moment of inspiration.

Rogers and Willet looked at each other.

"It's queer we didn't think of that before," said the hunter.

"'Twill be an attempt heavy with danger," said Rogers.

"So it will, my friend, but have we shirked dangers? Don't we live and sleep with danger?"

"I was merely stating the price, Dave. I was making no excuse for shirking."

"I know it, old friend. Whoever heard of Robert Rogers shunning danger? We'll have a talk with Daganoweda, and you, Robert, since you suggested the plan, and you, Tayoga, since you've a head full of wisdom, shall be present at the conference."

The Mohawk chieftain came, and, when the scheme was laid before him, he was full of eagerness for it.

"Every one of my warriors will be glad to go," he said, "and I, as becomes my place, will lead them. It will be a rare deed, and the news of it will be heard with wonder and admiration in all our castles."

He spoke in the language of the Ganeagaono, which all the others understood perfectly, and the two white leaders knew they could rely upon the courage and enthusiasm of the Mohawks.

"It depends upon the sun whether we shall succeed tonight or not," said Tayoga, glancing up at the heavens, "and at present he gives no promise of favoring us. The sun, as you know, Dagaeoga, is with us the Sun God, also, whom we call Areskoui, or now and then Aieroski, and who is sometimes almost the same as Manitou."

"I know," said Robert, who had an intimate acquaintance with the complex Pantheon of the Hodenosaunee, which was yet not so complex after all, and which also had in its way the elements of the Christian religion in all their beauty and majesty.

Tayoga gazed out upon Andiatarocte.

Robert's eyes followed the Onondaga's.

"It's true," he said, "that the Sun God, your Areskoui, and mine, too, for that matter, makes no promise to us. The warriors of the Hodenosaunee have looked upon Andiatarocte for many centuries, but doubtless there has never been a day before when any one of them saw it more beautiful and more gleaming than it is now."

"Yes, Dagaeoga, the waters slide and ripple before the wind, and they are blue and green, and silver and gold, and all the shades between, as the sunlight shifts and falls, but it is many hours until night and Areskoui may be of another mind by then."

"I know it, Tayoga. I remember the two storms on Champlain, and I don't forget how quickly they can come on either lake. I'm not praying for any storm, but I do want a dark and cloudy night."

"Dagaeoga should not be too particular," said Tayoga, his eyes twinkling. "He has told Areskoui exactly what kind of a night he wishes, but I think he will have to take just the kind of a night that Areskoui may send."

"I don't dispute it, Tayoga, but when you're praying to the Sun God it's as well to pray for everything you want."

"We'll watch Areskoui with more than common interest today, you and I, Dagaeoga, but the warriors of the Ganeagaono, even as the Hurons, the Abenakis and the Ojibways, will go to sleep. Behold, Daganoweda even now lies down upon his blanket!"

The Mohawk chief, as if sure that nothing more of importance was going to happen that day, spread his fine green blanket upon some leaves, and then settling himself in an easy posture upon it, fell asleep, while many of his warriors, and some of the rangers too, imitated his example. But Robert and Tayoga had slept enough, and, though they moved about but little, they were all eyes and ears.

Scouts had been sent far up and down the shores of the lake, and they reported that no other band was near, chance leaving the issue wholly to the two forces that now faced each other. Yet the morning, while remaining of undimmed beauty, had all the appearance of ease, even of laziness. Several of the rangers went down to the edge of the lake, and, removing their clothing, bathed in the cool waters. Then they lay on the slope until their bodies dried, dressed themselves, and waited patiently for the night.

The French and Indians, seeing them engaged in a pleasant task, found it well to do likewise. The waters close to the island were filled with Frenchmen, Canadians and Indians, wading, swimming and splashing water, the effect in the distance being that of boys on a picnic and enjoying it to the utmost.

Robert took a little swim himself, though he kept close to the shore, and felt much refreshed by it. When he had been dried by the sun and was bade in his clothes, he stretched himself luxuriously near the rangers on the slope, taking an occasional glance at the sun from under his sheltering hand.

"There is a little mist in the southwest," he said, after a long time, to Tayoga. "Do you think it possible that Areskoui will change his mind and cease to flood the world with beams?"

"I see the vapor," replied Tayoga, looking keenly. "It is just a wisp, no larger than a feather from the wing of an eagle, but it seems to grow. Areskoui changes his mind as he pleases. Who are we to question the purposes of the Sun God? Yet I take it, Dagaeoga, that the chance of a night favorable to our purpose has increased."

"I begin to think, Tayoga, that Areskoui does, in truth, favor us, through no merit of ours, but perhaps because of a lack of merit in Tandakora and De Courcelles. Yet, as I live, you're right when you say the cloud of mist or vapor is growing. Far in the southwest, so it seems to me, the air becomes dim. I know it, because I can't see the forests there as distinctly as I did a half hour ago, and I hold that the change in Areskoui's heart is propitious to our plan."

"A long speech, but your tongue always moves easily, Dagaeoga, and what you say is true. The mist increases fast, and before he goes down on the other side of the world the

Sun God will be veiled in it. Then the night will come full of clouds, and dark. Look at Andiatarocte, and you will see that it is so."

The far shores of the lake were almost lost in the vapors, only spots of forest green appearing now and then, a veil of silver being over the eastern waters. The island on which St. Luc lay encamped was growing indistinct, and the fires there shone through a white mist.

Tayoga stood up and gazed intently at the sun, before which a veil had been drawn, permitting his eyes to dwell on its splendors, now coming in a softened and subdued light.

"All the omens are favorable," he said. "The heart of Areskoui has softened toward us, knowing that we are about to go on a great and perilous venture. Tonight Tododaho on his star will also look down kindly on us. He will be beyond the curtain of the clouds, and we will not see him, but I know that it will be so, because I feel in my heart that it must be so. You and I, Dagaeoga, are only two, and among the many on this earth two can count for little, but the air is full of spirits, and it may be that they have heard our prayers. With the unseen powers the prayers of the humble and the lowly avail as much as those of the great and mighty."

His eyes bore the rapt and distant expression of the seer, as he continued to gaze steadily at the great silver robe that hung before the face of Areskoui's golden home. Splendid young warrior that he was, always valiant and skillful in battle, there was a spiritual quality in Tayoga that often showed. The Onondagas were the priestly nation of the Hodenosaunee and upon him had descended a mantle that was, in a way, the mantle of a prophet. Robert, so strongly permeated by Indian lore and faith, really believed, for a moment, that his comrade saw into the future.

But not the white youth and the red youth alone bore witness to the great change, the phenomenon even, that Areskoui was creating. Both Rogers and Willet had looked curiously at the sun, and then had looked again. Daganoweda, awaking, stood up and gazed in the intent and reverential manner that Tayoga had shown. The soul of the Mohawk chieftain was fierce. He existed for the chase and war, and had no love beyond them. There was nothing spiritual in his nature, but none the less he was imbued with the religion of his race, and believed that the whole world, the air, the forests, the mountains, and the lakes were peopled with spirits, good or bad. Now he saw one of the greatest of them all, Areskoui, the Sun God himself, in action and working a miracle.

The untamable soul of Daganoweda was filled with wonder and admiration. Not spiritual, he was nevertheless imaginative to a high degree. Through the silver veil which softened the light of the sun more and more, permitting his eyes to remain fixed upon it, he saw a mighty figure in the very center of that vast globe of light, a figure that grew and grew until he knew it was Areskoui, the Sun God himself.

A shiver swept over the powerful frame of Daganoweda. The Mohawk chieftain, whose nerves never quivered before the enemy, felt as a little child in the presence of the mighty Sun God. But his confidence returned. Although the figure of Areskoui continued to grow, his face became benevolent. He looked down from his hundred million miles in the void, beheld the tiny figure of Daganoweda standing upon the earth, and smiled. Daganoweda knew that it was so, because he saw the smile with his own eyes, and, however perilous the venture might be, he knew then it could not fail, because Areskoui himself had smiled upon it.

The great veil of mist deepened and thickened and was drawn slowly across all the heavens. Robert felt a strange thrill of awe. It was, in very truth, to him a phenomenon, more than an eclipse, not a mere passage of the moon before the sun for which science gave a natural account, but a sudden combination of light and air that had in it a tinge of the supernatural.

All the Mohawks were awake now, everybody was awake and everybody watched the sun, but perhaps it was Daganoweda who saw most. No tincture of the white man's religion had ever entered his mind to question any of his Iroquois beliefs. There was Areskoui, in the very center of the sun, mighty and shining beyond belief, and still smiling across his hundred million miles at the earth upon which Daganoweda stood. But, all the while he was drawing his silver robe, fold on fold, thicker and tighter about himself, and his figure grew dim.

One after another the distant islands in the lake sank out of sight, and the fires were merely a faint red glow on the one occupied by St. Luc. Over the waters the vapors swept in great billows and columns. Daganoweda drew a great breath. The sun itself was fading. Areskoui had shown his face long enough and now he meant to make the veil between himself and man impenetrable. He became a mere shadow, the mists and vapors rolled up wave on wave, and he was gone entirely. Then night came down over mountains, forest and Andiatarocte. The last fire on St Luc's island had been permitted to die out, and it, too, sank into the mists and vapors with the others, and was invisible to the watchers on the mainland slope.

But little could be seen of Andiatarocte itself, save occasional glimmers of silver under the floating clouds. Not a star was able to come out, and all the lake and country about it were wrapped in a heavy grayish mist which seemed to Robert to be surcharged with some kind of exciting solution. But the three leaders, Rogers, Willet and Daganoweda, gathered in a close council, did not yet give any order save that plenty of food be served to rangers and Mohawks alike.

Thus a long time was permitted to pass and the mists and vapors over Andiatarocte deepened steadily. No sound came from St. Luc's island, nor was any fire lighted there. For all the darkness showed, it had sunk from sight forever. It was an hour till midnight when the three leaders gave their orders and the chosen band began to prepare. Robert had begged to be of the perilous number. He could never endure it if Tayoga went and not he, and Willet, though reluctant, was compelled to consent. Willet himself was going also, and so was Daganoweda, of course, and Black Rifle, but Rogers was to remain behind, in command of the force on the slope.

Thirty rangers and thirty Mohawks, all powerful swimmers, were chosen, and every man stripped to the skin. Firearms, of necessity, were left behind with the clothes, but everyone buckled a belt around his bare body, and put in it his hatchet and hunting knife. The plan was to swim silently for the island and then trust to courage, skill and fortune. Buoyed up by the favor of Areskoui, who had worked a miracle for them, the sixty dropped into the water, and began their night of extreme hazard.

CHAPTER IX

ON ANDIATAROCTE

Robert, as was natural, swam by the side of Tayoga, his comrade in so many hardships and dangers, and, after the long period of tense and anxious waiting, he felt a certain relief that the start was made, even though it was a start into the very thick of peril.

Willet was on the right wing of the swimming column and Daganoweda was on the left, the white leader and the red understanding each other thoroughly, and ready to act in perfect unison. Beneath the hovering mists and above the surface of the water, the bronze faces of the Mohawks and the brown faces of the rangers showed, eager and fierce. There was not one among them whose heart did not leap, because he was chosen for such a task.

Robert felt at first a chill from the water, as Andiatarocte, set among its northern mountains, is usually cold, but after a few vigorous strokes the blood flowed warm in his veins again, and the singular exciting quality with which the mists and vapors seemed to be surcharged entered his mind also. The great pulse in his throat leaped, and the pulses in his temples beat hard. His sensitive and imaginative mind, that always went far ahead of the present, had foreseen all the dangers, and, physically at least, he had felt keen apprehension when he stepped into the lake. But now it was gone. Youth and the strong comrades around him gave imagination another slant, allowing it to paint wonderful deeds achieved, and victory made complete.

His eyes, which in his condition of superheated fancy enlarged or intensified everything manifold, saw a flash of light near him. It was merely Tayoga drawing his knife from his belt and putting the blade between his teeth, where the whitish mist that served for illumination had thrown back a reflection. He glanced farther down the swimming line and saw that many others had drawn their hunting knives and had clasped them between their teeth, where they would be ready for instant use. Mechanically he did likewise, and he felt something flow from the cold steel into his body, heating his blood and inciting him to battle. He knew at the time that it was only imagination, but the knowledge itself took nothing from the power of the sensation. He became every instant more eager for combat.

It seemed that Tayoga caught glimpses of his comrade's face and with his Onondaga insight read his mind.

"Dagaeoga, who wishes harm to nobody, now craves the battle, nevertheless," he said, taking the knife from between his teeth for a moment or two.

"I'm eager to be in it as soon as I can in order to have it over as soon as we can," said Robert, imitating him.

"You may think the answer wholly true, though it is only partly so. There come times when the most peaceful feel the incitement of war."

"I believe it's the strangeness of the night, the quality of the air we breathe and that singular veiling of the sun just when we wished it, and as if in answer to our prayers."

"That is one of the reasons, Dagaeoga. We cannot see Areskoui, because he is on the other side of the world now, but he turned his face toward us and bade us go and win. Nor can we see Tododaho on his star, because of the mighty veil that has been drawn between, but the great Onondaga chief who went away to eternal life more than four hundred centuries ago still watches over his own, and I know that his spirit is with us."

"Can you see the island yet, Tayoga? My eyes make out a shadow in the mist, but whether it's land, or merely a darker stream of vapor, I can't tell."

"I am not sure either, but I do not think it is land. The island is four hundred yards away, and the mist is so thick that neither the earth itself nor the trees and bushes would yet appear through it."

"You must be right, and we're swimming slowly, too, to avoid any splashing of the water that would alarm St. Luc's sentinels. At what point do you think we'll approach the island, Tayoga?"

"From the north, because if they are expecting us at all they will look for us from the west. See, Daganoweda already leads in the curve toward the north."

"It's so, Tayoga. I can barely make out his figure, but he has certainly changed our course. I don't know whether it's my fancy or not, but I seem to feel a change, too, in the quality of the air about us. A stream of new and stronger air is striking upon the right side of my face, that is, the side toward the south."

"It is reality and not your fancy, Dagaeoga. A wind has begun to blow out of the south and west. But it does not blow away the vapors. It merely sends the columns and waves of mist upon one another, fusing them together and then separating them again. It is the work of Areskoui. Though there is now a world between us and him he still watches over us and speeds us on to a great deed. So, Dagaeoga, the miracle of the sky is continued into the night, and for us. Areskoui will clothe us in a mighty blanket of mist and water and fire."

The Onondaga's face was again the rapt face of a seer, and his words were heavy with import like those of a prophet of old.

"Listen!" he said. "It is Areskoui himself who speaks!"

Robert shivered, but it was not from the cold of the water. It was because a mighty belief that Tayoga spoke the truth had entered his soul, and what the Onondaga believed he, too, believed with an equal faith.

"I hear," he replied.

A low sound, deep and full of menace, came out of the south, and rumbled over Andiatarocte and all the mountains about it. It was the voice of thunder, but Tayoga and Robert felt that its menace was not for them.

"One of the sudden storms of the lake comes," said the Onondaga. "The mists will be driven away now, but the clouds in their place will be yet darker, Areskoui still holds his shrouding blanket before us."

"But the lightning which will come soon, Tayoga, and which you meant, when you spoke of fire, will not that unveil us to the sentinels of St. Luc?"

"No, because only our heads are above the water and at a little distance they are blended with it. Yet the same flashes of fire will disclose to us their fleet and show us our way to it. Andiatarocte has already felt the wind in the south and is beginning to heave and surge."

Robert felt the lake lift him up on a wave and then drop him down into a hollow, but he was an expert swimmer, and he easily kept his head on the surface. The thunder rumbled again. There was no crash, it was more like a deep groan coming up out of the far south. The waters of Andiatarocte lifted themselves anew, and wave after wave pursued one another northward. A wind began to blow, straight and strong, but heavy floating clouds came in its train, and the darkness grew so intense that Robert could not see the face of Tayoga beside him.

Daganoweda called from the north end of the swimming line, and the word was passed from Mohawk and ranger until Willet at the south end replied. All were there. Not a man, white or red, had dropped out, and not one would.

"In a minute or two the lightning will show the way," said Tayoga.

As the last word left his lips a flaming sword blazed across the lake, and disclosed the island, wooded and black, not more than two hundred yards distant, and the dim shadows of canoes and boats huddled against the bank. Then it was gone and the blackness, thicker and heavier than ever, settled down over island, lake and mountain. But Robert, Tayoga and all the others had seen the prize they were seeking, and their course lay plain before them now.

Robert's emotion was so intense and his mind was concentrated so powerfully upon the object ahead that he was scarcely conscious of the fact that he was swimming. An expert in the water, he kept afloat without apparent effort, and the fact that he was one of fifty all doing the same thing gave him additional strength and skill. The lightning flashed

77

again, blue now, almost a bar of violet across the sky, tinting the waters of the lake with the same hue, and he caught another glimpse of the Indian fleet drawn up against the shore, and of the Indian sentinels, some sitting in the boats, and others standing on the land.

Then the wind strengthened, and he felt the rain upon his face. It was a curious result, but he sank a little deeper in the water to shelter himself from the storm. Light waves ran upon the surface of the lake, and his body lifted with them. The fleet could not be more than a hundred yards away now, and his heart began to throb hard with the thought of imminent action. Yet he knew that he was in a mystic and unreal world. His singular position, the night, the coming of the storm with its swift alternations of light and blackness, heated his blood and imagination until he saw many things that were not, and did not see some that were. He saw a triumph and the capture of the Indian fleet, and in his eager anticipation he failed to see the dangers just ahead.

The air grew much colder and the rain beat upon his face like hail. The thunder which had rumbled almost incessantly, like a mighty groaning, now ceased entirely, and the last flash of lightning burned across the lake. It showed the fleet of the foe not more than fifty yards away now, and, so far as Robert could tell, the Indian sentinels had yet taken no alarm. Three were crouched in the boats with their blankets drawn about their shoulders to protect them from the cold rain, and the four who had been standing on the land were huddled under the trees with their blankets wrapped about their bodies also.

"Do you think we'll really reach the fleet unobstructed?" whispered Robert to Tayoga.

"It does not seem possible," the Onondaga whispered back. "The favor of Areskoui is great to us, but the miracle he works in our behalf could hardly go so far. Now the word comes from both Daganoweda and the Great Bear, and we swim faster. The rain, too, grows and it drives in sheets, but it is well for us that it does so. Rifles and muskets cannot be used much in the storm, but our knives and tomahawks can. Perhaps this rain is only one more help that Areskoui has sent to us."

The swimming line was approaching fast, and a few more strokes would bring them to the canoes, when one of the warriors on the land suddenly came from the shelter of his tree, leaned forward a little and peered intently from under his shading hand. He had seen at last the dark heads on the dark water, and springing back he uttered a fierce whoop.

"Now we swim for our lives and victory!" said Tayoga.

Willet and Daganoweda, attempting no farther concealment, cried to their men to hurry. In a moment more the boarders were among the boats. Robert shut his eyes as the knives flashed in the dusk, and the dead bodies of the sentinels were thrown into the water. He seized the side of a long canoe, which he gladly found to be empty, pulled himself in, to discover Tayoga sitting just in front of him, paddle in hand also. All around him men, red and white, were laying hold of canoes and boats and at the edge of the water the sentinels were attacking.

On the island a terrific turmoil arose. Despite the rain a great fire flared up as the forces of St. Luc kindled some bonfire anew, and they heard him shouting in French and more than one Indian language to his men. They heard also heavy splashes, as the warriors leaped into the water to defend their fleet. A dark figure rose up by the side of the boat in which young Lennox and his comrade sat. The knife of Tayoga flashed and Robert involuntarily shut his eyes. When he opened them again the dark figure was gone, and the knife was back in the Onondaga's belt.

St. Luc, although surprised again, was rallying his men fast. The French were shouting their battle cries, the Indians were uttering the war whoop, as they poured down to the edge of the island, leaping into the lake to save their fleet. The water was filled with dusky forms, Mohawk and Huron met in the death grasp, and sometimes they found their fate beneath the waters, held tight in the arms of each other. Confused and terrible struggles for the boats ensued, and in the darkness and rain it was knife and hatchet and then paddles, which many snatched up and used as clubs.

Above the tumult Robert heard the trumpet tones of St. Luc cheering his men and directing them. Once he caught a glimpse of him standing up to his knees in the water, waving the small gold-hilted sword that he carried so often, and he might have brought him down with a bullet had he carried a rifle, but he would have had no thought of drawing trigger upon him. Then he was gone in the mist, and the gigantic painted figure of Tandakora appeared in his place for a moment. Then the mists closed in for a second time, and he saw through it only fleeting forms and flashes of fire, when rifles and muskets were fired by the enemy.

His feeling of unreality increased. The elements themselves had conspired to lend to everything a tinge weird and sinister to the last degree. There was a lull for a little in the wind and rain, but Andiatarocte was heaving, and great waves were chasing one another over the surface of the water, after threatening to overturn the canoes and boats for which both sides fought so fiercely. The thunder began to mutter again, furnishing a low and menacing under note like the growling of cannon in battle. Occasional streaks of lightning flashed anew across the lake, revealing the strained faces of the combatants and tinging the surface of the waters with red. Then both thunder and lightning ceased again, and wind and rain came with a renewed sweep and roar.

Robert and Tayoga still occupied their captured long boat alone, and they hovered near the edge of the battle, not ready to withdraw with the prize until their entire force, whether victor or vanquished, turned back from the island. Now and then Robert struck with his tomahawk at some foe who came swimming to the attack, but, as the violence of the storm grew, both he and Tayoga were compelled to take up their paddles, and use all their skill to keep the boat from being capsized. The shouting and the shots and the crash of the storm made a turmoil from which he could detach little, but he knew that the keen eyes of the Onondaga, dusk or no dusk, confusion or no confusion, would pierce to the heart of things.

"What do you see, Tayoga?" he exclaimed. "How goes the battle?"

"I cannot see as much as I wish, Dagaeoga, but it turns in our favor. I saw the Great Bear just then in a boat, and when the lightning flared last I saw Daganoweda in another. Beware, Dagaeoga! Beware!"

His shout of warning was just in time. A figure rose out of the water beside their boat, and aimed a frightful blow at him with a tomahawk. It was an impulse coming chiefly from the words of Tayoga, but Robert threw himself flat in the boat and the keen weapon whistled through the empty air. He sprang up almost instantly, and, not having time to draw either hatchet or knife, struck with his clenched fist at the dark face glaring over the side of the boat. It was a convulsive effort, and the fist was driven home with more than natural power. The figure disappeared like a stone dropped into the water.

Despite the dusk, Robert had seen the countenance, and he recognized the sinister features of the French spy whom they had tried to catch in Albany, the man whose name he had no doubt was Achille Garay. He had felt a fierce joy when his fist came into contact with his face, but he was quite sure the spy had not perished. Hardy men of the wilderness did not die from a blow with the naked hand. The water would revive him, and he would quickly come up again to fight elsewhere.

Tayoga leaned over suddenly and pulled in a dusky figure dripping with wounds, a Mohawk warrior, hurt badly and sure to have been lost without quick help. There was no time to bind up his hurts, as the combat was growing thicker and fiercer, and they drove their boat into the middle of it, striking out with hatchet and knife whenever an enemy came within reach.

A shrill whistle presently rose over all the noise of battle, and it seemed to have a meaning in it.

"What is it, Tayoga?" shouted Robert.

"It is the whistle of the Great Bear himself, and I have no doubt it is a signal to retire. Reason tells me, too, that it is so. We have captured as much of the enemy's fleet as we may at this time, and we must make off with it lest we be destroyed ourselves."

The whistle still rose shrill, penetrating and insistent, and at the other end of the line Daganoweda began to shout commands to the Ganeagaono. Robert and Tayoga paddled away from the island, and on either side of them they saw canoes and boats going in the same direction. Flashes of fire came from the land, where the French and Indians, raging up and down, sought to destroy those who had captured most of their fleet. But the darkness made their aim uncertain, almost worthless, and only two or three of the invaders were struck, none mortally. Twenty canoes and boats were captured, and the venture was a brilliant success. Areskoui had not worked his miracles in vain, and a triumphant shout, very bitter for the enemy, burst from rangers and Mohawks. Willet, alone in a captured canoe, paddled swiftly up and down the line, seeing like a good commander what the losses and gains might be, and also for personal reasons peering anxiously through the dusk for something that he hoped to see. Suddenly he uttered a low cry of pleasure.

"Ah, it is you, Robert!" he exclaimed. "And you, Tayoga! And both unhurt!"

"Yes, except for scratches," replied Robert. "I think that Tayoga's Areskoui was, in very truth, watching over us, and watching well. In the darkness and confusion all the bullets passed us by, but I was attacked at the boat's edge by a Frenchman, the one whom I saw in Albany, the one who I am quite sure is Achille Garay. Luck saved me."

"Some day we'll deal with that Achille Garay," said the hunter, "but now we must draw off in order, and see to our wounded."

He passed on in his canoe, and met Daganoweda in another. The young Mohawk chieftain was dripping from seven wounds, but they were all in the shoulders and forearms and were slight, and they were a source of pride to him rather than inconvenience.

"'Twas well done, Daganoweda," said Willet.

"It is a deed of which the Ganeagaono in their castles will hear with pride," said the Mohawk. "The fleet of Onontio and his warriors, or most of it, is ours, and we dispute with them the rulership of the lake."

"Great results, worthy of such a risk. I'm sorry we didn't take every boat and canoe, because then we might have cooped up St. Luc on his island, and have destroyed his entire force."

"It is given to no man, Great Bear, to achieve his whole wish. We have done as much as we hoped, and more than we expected."

"True, Daganoweda! True! What are your losses?"

"Nine of my men have been slain, but they fell as warriors of the Ganeagaono would wish to fall. Two more will die and others are hurt, but they need not be counted, since they will be in any other battle that may come. And what have you suffered, Great Bear?"

"Five of the rangers have gone into the hereafter, another will go, and as for the hurt, like your Mohawks they'll be good for the next fight, no matter how soon it comes. We'd better go along the line, Daganoweda, and caution them all to be steady. The wind and rain are driving hard and Andiatarocte is heaving mightily. We don't want to lose a man or a canoe."

"No, Great Bear, after taking the fleet in battle we must not give it up to the waters of the lake. See, the flare of a great fire on the mainland! The Mountain Wolf and the rest of the men await us with joy."

Then Daganoweda achieved a feat which Willet himself would have said a moment before was impossible. He stood suddenly upright in his rocking canoe, whirled his paddle around his head, and uttered a tremendous shout, long and thrilling, that pierced far above the roar of wind and rain. Then Mohawks and rangers took it up in a tremendous chorus, and the force of Rogers on land joined in, too, adding to the mighty volume. When it sank into the crash and thunder of the storm, a shrill whoop of defiance came from the island.

"Are they trying pursuit?" asked Robert.

"They would not dare," replied Tayoga. "They do not know, of course, that we have only the edges of our tomahawks and hunting knives with which to meet them, and even in the darkness they dread our rifles."

Robert glanced back, catching only the dark outline of the island through the rain and fog, and that, too, for but a moment, as then the unbroken dark closed in, and wind and rain roared in his ears. He realized for the first time, since their departure on the great adventure, that he was without clothes, and as the fierce tension of mind and body began to relax he felt cold. The rain was driving upon him in sheets and he began to paddle with renewed vigor in order to keep up his circulation.

"I'll welcome the fire, Tayoga," he said.

"And I, too," said the Onondaga in his precise fashion. "The collapse is coming after our mighty efforts of mind and body. We will not reach shore too soon. The Mountain Wolf and his men build the fire high, so high that it can defy the rain, because they know we will need it."

A shout welcomed them as they drew in to the mainland, and the spectacle of the huge fire, sputtering and blazing in the storm, was grateful to Robert. All the captured boats and canoes were drawn out of the water, well upon the shore, and then, imitating a favorite device of the Indians, they inverted the long boats, resting the ends on logs before the fires, and sat or stood under them, sheltered from the rain, while they warmed white or brown bodies in the heat of the flames.

"'Twas a great achievement, Dave," said Rogers to Willet, "and improves our position wonderfully, but 'twas one of the hardest things I've ever had to do to stand here, just waiting and listening to the roar of the battle."

"Tayoga says we were helped by Areskoui, and we must have been helped by some power greater than our own. We paid a price for our victory, though it wasn't too high, and tomorrow we'll see what St. Luc will do. 'Tis altogether possible that we may have a naval fight."

"It's so, Dave, but this is a fine deed you and Daganoweda and your men have done."

"Nothing more than you would have done, Rogers, if you had been in our place."

They spoke in ordinary tones, being men too much hardened to danger and mighty tasks to show emotion. Robert stood under the same inverted boat that sheltered them, and he heard their words in a kind of daze, his brain still benumbed after the long and terrible test. But it was a pleasant numbing, a provision of nature, a sort of rest that was akin to sleep.

The storm had not abated a particle. Wind and rain roared across Andiatarocte and along the slopes and over the mountains. The waters of the lake whenever they were disclosed were black and seething, and all the islands were invisible.

Robert looked mostly at the great fire that crackled and blazed so near. It was fed continually by Indians and rangers, who did not care for the rain, and it alone defied the storm. The sheets of rain, poured upon it, seemed to have no effect. The coals merely hissed as if it were oil instead of water, and the flames leaped higher, deep red at the heart and often blue at the edges.

Robert had never seen a more beautiful fire, a vast core of warmth and light that challenged alike darkness, wind and rain. There had been a time, so he had heard, in the remote, dim ages when man knew nothing of fire. It might have been true, but he did not see how man could have existed, and certainly no cheer ever came into his life. He turned himself around, as if he were broiling on a spit, and heated first one side and then the other, until the blood in his veins sparkled with new life and vigor. Then he dressed, still pervaded by that enormous feeling of comfort and content, and ate of the food that Rogers ordered to be served to the returned and refreshed men. He also resumed his rifle and pistol, but kept his seat under the inverted boat, where the rain could not reach him.

He would have slept, but the ground was too wet, and he waited with the others for the approach of day and the initiative of St. Luc. The rangers and Mohawks had made the first move, and it was now for the French leader to match it. Robert wondered what St. Luc would attempt, but that he would try something he never doubted for a moment.

A log was rolled beneath the long boat under which the leaders stood, and, spreading their blankets over it, they sat down on it. There was room at the end for Robert and Tayoga, too, and Robert found that his comfort increased greatly. He was in a kind of daze, that was very soothing, and yet he saw everything that went on around him. But he still looked mostly at the great fire which zealous hands fed and which stood up a pillar of light in the darkness and cold. He reflected dimly that it was a beautiful fire, a magnificent, a most magnificent fire. How the first man who saw the first fire must have rejoiced in it!

Toward morning the wind sank, and the sheets of rain grew thinner. Once or twice thunder moaned in the southwest, and there were occasional streaks of lightning, but they were faint, and merely disclosed fleeting strips of a black lake and a black forest.

"Before the sun rises the storm will be gone," said Tayoga. "The miracle that Areskoui worked in our behalf is finished, and the rest must be done by our own courage and skill. Who are we to ask more for ourselves than the Sun God has done?"

"We've been splendidly favored," said Robert, "and if he does not help us with another miracle he'll at least shine for us before long. After such a night as this, I'll be mighty glad to see the day, the green mountains, and the bright waters of Andiatarocte again."

"I feel the dawn already, Dagaeoga. The rain, as you see, has almost stopped, and the troubled wind will now be still. The storm will pass away, and it will leave not a mark, save a fallen tree here and there."

Tayoga's words came true. In a half hour both wind and rain died utterly, and they breathed an air clean and sweet, as if the world had been washed anew. A touch of silver appeared on the eastern mountains, and then up came the dawn, crisp and cool after the storm, and the world was more splendid and beautiful than ever. The green on slopes and ridges had been deepened and the lake was all silver in the morning light.

The islands stood up, sharp and clear, and there were the forces of St. Luc still on his island, and Rogers, through his powerful glasses, was able to make out the French leader himself walking about, while white men and Indians were lighting the fires on which they expected to cook their breakfasts.

Several boats and canoes were visible drawn upon the shore, showing that St. Luc had saved a portion of his fleet, and it appeared that he and his men did not fear another attack, or perhaps they wanted it. Meanwhile rangers and Mohawks prepared their own breakfasts and awaited with patience the word of their leaders. Apparently there was nothing but peace. It was a camping party on the island and another on the mainland, and the waters of the lake danced in the sunshine, reflecting one brilliant color after another.

"Reënforcements are coming for St. Luc," said Robert, who saw black specks on the lake to the eastward of the island. "I think that's a fleet of Indian canoes."

"It's what I expected," said Tayoga. "The French and their allies had complete control of Andiatarocte until we appeared, and it is likely, when the storm began to die, Sharp Sword sent for the aid that is now coming."

The canoes soon showed clear outlines in the intense sunlight, and, as well as Rogers could judge through his glasses, they brought about fifty men, ten of whom were Frenchmen. But there were no long boats, a fact at which they all rejoiced, as in a naval battle the canoes would be at a great disadvantage opposed to the heavier craft.

"When do you think it best to make the attack?" Willet asked the leader of the rangers.

"Within an hour," replied Rogers. "If we had been in condition we might have gone at them before their help came, but it was wise to let the men rest a little after last night's struggle."

"And it will be better for our purpose to beat two forces instead of one."

"So it will, and that's the right spirit, Dave. You can always be depended upon to take the cheerful view of things. It's good, old friend, for us to be together again, doing our best."

"So it is, and it's a time that demands one's best. The world's afire, and our part of it is burning with the rest. What do your glasses tell you now?"

"The reënforcements are landing on the island. St. Luc himself has gone forward to meet them. He's a fine leader. He impresses red men and white men alike, and he'll make the new force feel that it's the most important and timely in the world. Have you found anything in the woods, Black Rifle?"

"No," replied the swart forester, who had been circling about the camp. "Nobody is there. It's just ourselves and the fellows out there on the island."

"Do you see any more canoes, Rogers, coming to the help of St. Luc?" asked Willet.

The ranger searched long and carefully over the surface of the lake with his strong glasses and then replied:

"Not a canoe. If they have any more force afloat it's too far in the north to reach here in time. We've all of our immediate enemy before us, and we'll attack at once."

The boats and canoes were lifted into the water and the little force made ready for the naval battle.

CHAPTER X

THE NAVAL COMBAT

Robert and Tayoga went into a long boat with Willet, a boat that held eight men, all carrying paddles, while their rifles were laid on the bottom, ready to be substituted for the paddles when the time came. Daganoweda was in another of the large boats, and Rogers commanded a third, the whole fleet advancing slowly and in almost a straight line toward St. Luc's stronghold.

Doubtless many a combat between Indians had taken place on Andiatarocte in the forgotten ages, but Robert believed the coming encounter would be the first in which white men had a part, and, for the moment, he forgot his danger in the thrilling spectacle that opened before him.

St. Luc, when he saw the enemy approaching, quickly launched his own fleet, and filled it with men, although he kept it well in the lee of the land, and behind it posted a formidable row of marksmen, French, Canadians and Indians. Rogers, who had the general command, paddled his boat a little in front of the others and examined the defense cautiously through his glasses. Tayoga could see well enough with the naked eye.

"St. Luc is leaning on the stump of a wind-blown tree near the water," he said, "and he holds in his hand his small sword with which he will direct the battle. But there is a canoe almost at his feet, and if need be he will go into it. De Courcelles is in a large boat on the right, and Tandakora is in another on the left. On the land, standing behind St. Luc, is the Canadian, Dubois."

"A very good arrangement to meet us," said Willet. "St. Luc will stay on the island, but if he finds we're pressing him too hard, he'll have himself paddled squarely into the center of his fleet, and do or die. Now, it's a lucky thing for us that our rangers are such fine marksmen, and that they have the good, long-barreled rifles."

The boats containing the Mohawks were held back under the instructions of Rogers, despite the eagerness of Daganoweda, who, however, was compelled to yield to the knowledge that red men were never equal to the finest white sharpshooters, and it was important to use the advantage given to them by the long rifles. Willet's boat swung in by the side of that of Rogers, and several more boats and canoes, containing rangers, drew level with them. Rogers measured the distance anxiously.

"Do you think you can reach them with your rifle, Dave?" he asked.

"A few yards more and a bullet will count," replied the hunter.

"We'll go ahead, then, and tell me as soon as you think we're near enough. All our best riflemen are in front, and we should singe them a bit."

The boats glided slowly on, and, at the island, the enemy was attentive and waiting, with the advantage wholly on his side, had it not been for the rifles of great range, surpassing anything the French and Indians carried. St. Luc did not move from his position, and he was a heroic figure magnified in the dazzling sunlight.

Willet held up his hand.

"This will do," he said.

At a sign from Rogers the entire fleet stopped, and, at another sign from Willet, twenty rangers, picked marksmen, raised their rifles and fired. Several of the French and Indians fell, and their comrades gave forth a great shout of rage. Those in the canoes and boats fired, but all their bullets fell short, merely pattering in vain on the water. Daganoweda and his warriors, when they saw the result, uttered an exultant war whoop that came back in echoes from the mountains. Rogers himself rejoiced openly.

"That's the way to do it, Dave!" he cried. "Reload and give 'em another volley. Unless they come out and attack us we can decimate 'em."

Although it was hard to restrain the rangers, who wished to crowd closer, Rogers and Willet nevertheless were able to make them keep their distance, and they maintained a deadly fire that picked off warrior after warrior and that threatened the enemy with destruction. St. Luc's Indians uttered shouts of rage and fired many shots, all of which fell short. Then Robert saw St. Luc leave the stump and enter his waiting canoe.

"They'll come to meet us now," he said. "We've smoked 'em out."

"Truly they will," said Tayoga. "They must advance or die at the land's edge."

84

The portion of his fleet which St. Luc and his men had managed to save was almost as large as that of the Americans and Mohawks, and seeing that they must do it, they put out boldly from the land, St. Luc in the center in his canoe, paddled by a single Indian. As they approached, the rifles of Daganoweda's men came into action also, and St. Luc's force replied with a heavy fire. The naval battle was on, and it was fought with all the fury of a great encounter by fleets on the high seas. Robert saw St. Luc in his canoe, giving orders both with his voice and the waving of his sword, while the single Indian in the light craft paddled him to and fro as he wished, stoically careless of the bullets.

In the heat and fury of the combat the fleet of Rogers came under the fire of the French and Indians on the island, many being wounded and some slain. These reserves of St. Luc in their eagerness waded waist deep into the water, and pulled trigger as fast as they could load and reload.

A ranger in Willet's boat was killed and two more received hurts, but the hunter kept his little command in the very thick of the battle, and despite the great cloud of smoke that covered the fleets of both sides Robert soon saw that the rangers and Mohawks were winning. One of the larger boats belonging to St. Luc, riddled with bullets, went down, and the warriors who had been in it were forced to swim for their lives. Several canoes were rammed and shattered. Willet and Tayoga meanwhile were calmly picking their targets through the smoke, and when they fired they never missed.

The rangers, too, were showing their superiority as sharpshooters to the French and Indians, and were doing deadly execution with their long rifles. St. Luc, in spite of the great courage shown by his men, was compelled to sound the recall, and, hurriedly taking on board all the French and Indians who were on land, he fled eastward across the lake with the remnant of his force. Rogers pursued, but St. Luc was still able to send back such a deadly fire and his French and Indians worked so desperately with the paddles that they reached the eastern rim, abandoned the fragments of their fleet, climbed the lofty shore and disappeared in the forest, leaving Rogers, Willet, Daganoweda and their men in triumphant command of Andiatarocte, for a little while, at least.

But the victors bore many scars. More men had been lost, and their force suffered a sharp reduction in numbers. The three leaders, still in their boats, conferred. Daganoweda was in favor of landing and of pushing the pursuit to the utmost, even to the walls of Crown Point on Champlain, where the fugitives would probably go.

"There's much in favor of it," said Willet. "There's nothing like following a beaten enemy and destroying him, and there is also much to be said against it. We might run into an ambush and be destroyed ourselves. Although we've paid a price for it, we've a fine victory and we hold command of the lake for the time being. By pushing on we risk all we've won in order to obtain more."

But Daganoweda was still eager to advance, and urged it in a spirited Mohawk speech. Rogers himself favored it. The famous leader of rangers had a bold and adventurous mind. No risk was too great for him, and dangers, instead of repelling, invited him.

Robert, as became him, listened to them in silence. Prudence told him that they ought to stay on the lake, but his was the soul of youth, and the fiery eloquence of Daganoweda found an answer in his heart. It was decided at last to leave a small guard with the fleet, while rangers and Mohawks to the number of fifty should pursue toward Oneadatote. All three of the leaders, with Black Rifle, Tayoga and Robert, were to share in the pursuit, while a trusty man named White was left in command of the guard over the boats.

The fifty—the force had been so much reduced by the fighting that no more could be mustered—climbed the lofty shore, making their way up a ravine, thick with brush, until they came out on a crest more than a thousand feet above the lake. Nor did they forget, as they climbed, to exercise the utmost caution, looking everywhere for an ambush. They knew that St. Luc, while defeated, would never be dismayed, and it would be like him to turn on the rangers and Mohawks in the very moment of their victory and snatch it from them. But there was no sign of a foe's presence, although Daganoweda's men soon struck the trail of the fleeing enemy.

They paused at the summit a minute or two for breath, and Robert looked back with mixed emotions at Andiatarocte, a vast sheet of blue, then of green under the changing sky, the scene of a naval victory of which he had not dreamed a few days ago. But the lake bore no sign of strife now. The islands were all in peaceful green and the warlike boats were gone, save at the foot of the cliff they had just climbed. There they, too, looked peaceful enough, as if they were the boats of fishermen, and the guards, some of whom were aboard the fleet and some of whom lay at ease near the edge of the water, seemed to be men engaged in pursuits that had nothing to do with violence and war.

Tayoga's eyes followed Robert's.

"Andiatarocte is worth fighting for," he said. "It is well for us to be the rulers of it, even for a day. Where will you find a more splendid lake, a lake set deep in high green mountains, a lake whose waters may take on a dozen colors within a day, and every color beautiful?"

"I don't believe the world can show its superior, Tayoga," replied Robert, "and I, like you, am full of pride, because we are lords of it for a day. I hope the time will soon come when we shall be permanent rulers of both lakes, Andiatarocte and Oneadatote."

"We shall have to be mighty warriors before that hour arrives," said Tayoga, gravely. "Even if we gain Andiatarocte we have yet to secure a footing on the shores of Oneadatote. The French and their allies are not only in great force at Crown Point, but we hear that they mean to fortify also at the place called Ticonderoga by the Hodenosaunee and Carillon by the French."

The order to resume the march came, and they pressed forward on the trail through the deep woods. Usually at this time of the year it was hot in the forest, but after the great storm and rain of the night before a brisk, cool wind moved in waves among the trees, shaking the leaves and sending lingering raindrops down on the heads of the pursuers.

Black Rifle curved off to the right as a flanker against ambush, and two of Daganoweda's best scouts were sent to the left, while the main force went on directly, feeling now that the danger from a hidden force had been diminished greatly, their zeal increasing as the trail grew warmer. Daganoweda believed that they could overtake St. Luc in three or four hours, and he and his Mohawks, flushed with victory on the lake, were now all for speed, the rangers being scarcely less eager.

The country through which they were passing was wooded heavily, wild, picturesque and full of game. But it was well known to Mohawks and rangers, and the two lads had also been through it. They started up many deer that fled through the forest, and the small streams and ponds were covered with wild fowl.

"I don't wonder that the settlers fail to come in here on this strip of land between George and Champlain," said Robert to Tayoga. "It's a No Man's land, roamed over only by warriors, and even the most daring frontiersman must have some regard for the scalp on his head."

"I could wish it to be kept a No Man's land," said Tayoga earnestly.

"Maybe it will—for a long time, anyway. But, Tayoga, you're as good a trailer as Black Rifle or any Mohawk. Judging from the traces they leave, how many men would you say St. Luc now has with him?"

"As many as we have, or more, perhaps seventy, though their quality is not as good. The great footprint in the center of the trail is made by Tandakora. He, at least, has not fallen, and the prints that turn out are those of St. Luc, De Courcelles and doubtless of the officer Jumonville. The French leaders walked together, and here they stopped and talked a minute or two. St. Luc was troubled, and it was hard for him to make up his mind what to do."

"How do you know that, Tayoga?"

"Because, as he stood by the side of this bush, he broke three of its little stems between his thumb and forefinger. See, here are the stumps. A man like St. Luc would not have had a nervous hand if he had not been perplexed greatly."

"But how do you know it was St. Luc who stood by the bush, and not De Courcelles or Jumonville?"

"Because I have been trained from infancy, as an Onondaga and Iroquois, to notice everything. We have to see to live, and I observed long ago that the feet of St. Luc were smaller than those of De Courcelles or Jumonville. You will behold the larger imprints that turn out just here, and they face St. Luc, who stood by the bush. Once they not only thought of turning back to meet us, but actually prepared to do so."

"What proof have you?"

"O Dageaoga, you would not have asked me that question if you had used your eyes, and had thought a little. The print is so simple that a little child may read. The toes of their moccasins at a point just beyond the bush turn about, that is, back on the trail. And here the huge moccasins of Tandakora have taken two steps back. Perhaps they intended to meet us in full face or to lay an ambush, but at last they continued in their old course and increased their speed."

"How do you know they went faster, Tayoga?"

"O Dagaeoga, is your mind wandering today that your wits are so dull? See, how the distance between the imprints lengthens! When you run faster you leap farther. Everybody does."

"I apologize, Tayoga. It was a foolish question to be asked by one who has lived in the forest as long as I have. Why do you think they increased their speed, and how does St. Luc know that they are followed?"

"It may be that they know a good place of ambush farther ahead, and St. Luc is sure that he is pursued, because he knows the minds of Willet, Rogers and Daganoweda. He knows they are the kind of minds that always follow and push a victory to the utmost. Here the warriors knelt and drank. They had a right to be thirsty after such a battle and such a retreat."

He pointed to numerous imprints by the bank of a clear brook, and rangers and Mohawks, imitating the example of those whom they pursued, drank thirstily. Then they resumed the advance, and they soon saw that the steps of St. Luc's men were shortening.

"They are thinking again of battle or ambush," said Tayoga, "and when they think of it a second time they are likely to try it. It becomes us now to go most warily."

Daganoweda and Willet also had noticed St. Luc's change of pace, and stopping, they took counsel with themselves. About two miles ahead the country was exceedingly rough, cut by rocky ravines, and covered heavily with forest and thickets.

"If St. Luc elects to make a stand," said Willet, "that is the place he will choose. What say you, Daganoweda?"

"I think as the Great Bear thinks," replied the Mohawk chieftain.

"And you, Rogers?"

"Seems likely to me, too. At any rate, we must reckon on it."

"And so reckoning on it, we'd better stop and throw out more scouts."

Both Rogers and Daganoweda agreed, and flankers were sent off in each direction. Tayoga asked earnestly for this service, and Robert insisted on going with him. As the great skill of the Onondaga was known to the three leaders, he was obviously the proper selection for the errand, and it was fitting that Robert, his comrade in so many dangers and hardships, should accompany him. Daganoweda and Rogers said yes at once, and Willet was not able to say no. They were the best choice for such an errand, and although the hunter was reluctant for the youth, who was almost a son to him, to go on such a perilous duty, he knew that he must yield to the necessity.

The two lads went off to the left or northern flank, and in less than a minute the deep forest hid them completely from the main force. They were buried in the wilderness, and, for all the evidence that came to them, the band of rangers and Mohawks had ceased to exist.

They passed about a half mile to the north of the main force, and then they began to look everywhere for traces of trails, or evidence that an ambush was being prepared.

"Do you think St. Luc will make a new stand at the ridges?" asked Robert.

"All the chances favor it," replied the Onondaga. "We know that Sharp Sword, besides being a great leader, is full of pride. He will not like to go to Crown Point, and report that he has not only lost his fleet and the temporary command of Andiatarocte, but a large part of his force as well. If he can strike a heavy and deadly blow at his pursuers he will feel much better."

"Your reasoning seems good to me, and, therefore, it behooves us to be mighty careful. What do you take this imprint to be, Tayoga? Is it that of a human foot?"

"It is so very faint one can tell little of it. Your eye was keen, Dagaeoga, to have seen it at all, though I think the hoof of a buck and not the foot of a man trod here on the fallen leaves, but the tread was so light that it left only a partial impression."

"I can find no other trace like it farther on."

"No, the ground grows very hard and rocky, and it leaves no impression. We will advance for a little while toward the ridge, and then it will be well for us to lie down in some cover and watch, because I think St. Luc will send out skirmishers."

"And naturally he will send them to both right and left as we do."

"Of course, Dagaeoga."

"And then, if we keep moving on, we're sure to meet them?"

"It would appear so, Dagacoga."

"And for that reason, Tayoga, I'm in favor of the greatest care. I hope we'll come soon to a covert so deep and thick that when we hide in it we can't be seen five yards away."

"So do I, Dagaeoga. It is no shame to us to wish to save our lives. Lost, they would be of no use either to ourselves or to those whom we are here to serve. I think I see now the place that is waiting for us."

He pointed to a dense clump of scrub cedars growing on hard and rocky ground.

"I see," said Robert. "We can approach it without leaving any trail, and in that mass of green no foe will notice us unless his eyes are almost against us."

"Dagaeoga, at times, shows understanding and wisdom. The day may come when he will be a great scout and trailer—if he lives long enough."

"Go ahead, Tayoga, if it amuses you to make game of me. If humor can be produced at such a time I'm glad to be the occasion of it."

"It's best for us, Dagaeoga, to await all things with a light heart. Our fates are in the hands of Manitou."

88

"That's good philosophy, Tayoga, though I'm bound to say I can't look upon my life as a thing mapped out for me in every detail, though I live to be a hundred. Manitou knows what's going to happen, but I don't, and so my heart will jump anyhow when the danger comes. Now, you're sure we've left no trail among those rocks?"

"Not a trace, Dagaeoga. If Tododaho himself were to come back to earth he could not find our path."

"And you're sure that we're thoroughly hidden among these little cedars?"

"Quite sure of it. I doubt whether the bird singing over our heads sees us, and Manitou has given to the bird a very good eye that he may see his food, which is so small. It may be that the birds and animals which have given us warning of the enemy's approach before may do it again."

"At any rate, we can hope so. Are we as deserving now as we were then?"

"Yes, we can hope, Dagaeoga. Hope is never forbidden to anybody."

"I see that you're a philosopher, Tayoga."

"I try to be one," said the Onondaga, his eyes twinkling.

"Do you think that bird singing with so much power and beauty overhead sees us at last?"

"No, because he would certainly have stopped long enough to gratify his curiosity. Even a bird would want to know why strange creatures come into his thicket."

"Then as long as he sings I shall know that danger is not near. We have been watched over by birds before."

"Again you talk like a little child, Dagaeoga. I teach you the wisdom of the woods, and you forget. The bird may see a worm or a moth or something else that is good to eat, and then he will stop singing to dart for his food. A bird must eat, and his love of music often gives way to his love of food."

"You speak as if you were talking from a book."

"I learned your language mostly out of books, and so I speak as they are written. Ah, the song of the bird has stopped and he has gone away! But we do not know whether he has been alarmed by the coming of our enemy or has seen food that he pursues."

"It's food, Tayoga; I can hear him, faintly, singing in another tree, some distance to our right. Probably having captured the worm or the moth or whatever it was he was pursuing, and having devoured it, he is now patting his stomach in his pleasure and singing in his joy."

"And as a sentinel he is no longer of any use to us. Then we will watch for the little animals that run on the ground. They cannot fly over the heads of Ojibway and Caughnawaga warriors, and so, if our enemies come, they, too, are likely to come our way."

"Then I'll rest awhile, Tayoga, and it may be that I'll doze. If a rabbit runs in our direction wake me up."

"You may pretend to sleep, Dagaeoga, but you will not. You may close your eyes, but you cannot close your ears, nor can you still your nerves. One waits not with eyes and ears alone, but with all the fiber of the body."

"True, Tayoga. I was but jesting. I couldn't sleep if I tried. But I can rest."

He stretched himself in an easy position, a position, also, that allowed him to go into instant action if hostile warriors came, and he awaited the event with a calmness that surprised himself. Tayoga was crouched by his side, intent and also waiting.

A full half hour passed, and Robert heard nothing stirring in the undergrowth, save the wandering but gentle winds that rustled the leaves and whispered in the grass. Had he been left to himself he would have grown impatient, and he would have continued the scouting curve on which he had been sent. But he had supreme confidence in Tayoga. If the Onondaga said it was best for them to stay there in the bush, then it was best, and he would remain until his comrade gave the word to move on.

So sure was he of Tayoga that he did close his eyes for a while, although his ears and all the nerves of his body watched. But it was very peaceful and restful, and, while he lay in a half-dreamy state, he accumulated new strength for the crisis that might come.

"Any little animals running away yet, Tayoga?" he asked, partly in jest.

"No, Dagaeoga, but I am watching. Two rabbits not twenty feet from us are nibbling the leaves on a tiny weed, that is, they nibble part of the time, and part of the time they play."

"They don't sing like the bird, because they can't, but I take it from what you say they're just as happy."

"Happy and harmless, Dagaeoga. We Iroquois would not disturb them. We kill only to eat."

"Well, I've learned your way. You can't say, Tayoga, that I'm not, in spirit and soul at least, half an Iroquois, and spirit and soul mean more than body and manners or the tint of the skin."

"Dagaeoga has learned much. But then he has had the advantage of associating with one who could teach him much."

"Tayoga, if it were not for that odd little chord in your voice, I'd think you were conceited. But though you jest, it is true I've had a splendid chance to discover that the nations of the Hodenosaunee know some things better than we do, and do some things better than we do. I've found that the wisdom of the world isn't crystallized in any one race. How about the rabbits, Tayoga? Do they still eat and play, as if nobody anywhere near them was thinking of wounds and death?"

"The rabbits neither see nor hear anything strange, and the strange would be to them the dangerous. They nibble at the leaves a little, then play a little, then nibble again."

"I trust they'll keep up their combination of pleasure and sustenance some time, because it's very nice to lie here, rest one's overstrained system, and feel that one is watched over by a faithful friend, one who can do your work as well as his. You're not only a faithful friend, Tayoga, you're a most useful one also."

"Dagaeoga is lazy. He would not have as a friend one who is lazy like himself. He needs a comrade to take care of him. Perhaps it is better so. Dagaeoga is an orator; an orator has privileges, and one of his privileges is a claim to be watched over by others. One cannot speak forever and work, too."

Robert opened his eyes and smiled. The friendship between him and Tayoga, begun in school days, had been tested by countless hardships and dangers, and though each made the other an object of jest, it was as firm as that of Orestes and Pylades or that of Damon and Pythias.

"What are the rabbits doing now?" asked young Lennox, who had closed his eyes again.

"They eat less and play less," replied the Onondaga. "Ah, their attitude is that of suspicion! It may be that the enemy comes! Now they run away, and the enemy surely comes!"

Robert sat up, and laid his rifle across his knee. All appearance of laziness or relaxation disappeared instantly. He was attentive, alert, keyed to immediate action.

"Can you see anything, Tayoga?" he whispered.

"No, but I think I hear the sound of footsteps approaching. I am not yet sure, because the footfall, if footfall it be, is almost as light as the dropping of a feather."

Both remained absolutely still, not moving a leaf in their covert, and presently a huge and sinister figure walked into the open. It seemed to Robert that Tandakora was larger than ever, and that he was more evil-looking. His face was that of the warrior who would show no mercy, and his body, save for a waistcloth, was livid with all the hideous devices of war paint. Behind him came a Frenchman whom Robert promptly recognized as Achille Garay, and a half dozen warriors, all of whom turned questing eyes toward the earth.

"They look for a trail," whispered Tayoga. "It is well, Dagaeoga, that we took the precaution to walk on rocks when we came into this covert, or Tandakora, who is so eager for our blood, would find the traces."

"Tandakora costs me great pain," Robert whispered back. "It's my misfortune always to be seeing him just when I can't shoot at him. I'm tempted to try it, anyhow. That's a big, broad chest of his, and I couldn't find a finer target."

"No, Dagaeoga, on your life, no! Our scalps would be the price, and some day we shall take the life of Tandakora and yet keep our own. I know it, because Tododaho has whispered it to me in the half world that lies between waking and sleeping."

"You're right, of course, Tayoga, but it's a tremendous temptation."

The Onondaga put his hand on his lips to indicate that even a whisper now was dangerous, and the two sank once more into an utter silence. The chest of Tandakora still presented a great and painted target, and Robert's hand lay on the trigger, but his will kept him from pressing it. Yet he did not watch the Ojibway chief with more eagerness than he bestowed upon the Frenchman, Achille Garay.

Garay's face was far from prepossessing. In its way it was as evil as that of Tandakora. He had sought Robert's life more than once. In the naval battle he had seen the Frenchman pull trigger upon him. Why? Why had he singled him out from the others in the endeavor to make a victim of him? There must be some motive, much more powerful than that of natural hostility, and he believed now if they were discovered that not Tayoga but he would be the first object of Garay's attack.

But Tandakora and his men passed on, bearing to the right and from the main force. Robert and Tayoga saw their figures vanish among the bushes and heard the fall of their moccasins a little longer, and then the question of their own course presented itself to them. Should they go back to Rogers with a warning of the hostile flankers, or should they follow Tandakora and see what he meant? They decided finally in favor of the latter course, and passing quietly from their covert, began to trail those who were seeking to trail a foe. The traces led toward the west, and it was not hard to follow them, as Tandakora and his men had taken but little care, evidently not thinking any scouting rangers or Mohawks might be near.

Robert and Tayoga followed carefully for several hundred yards; then they were surprised to see the trail curve sharply about, and go back toward the main force.

"We must have passed them," said Robert, "although we were too far away to see each other."

"It would seem so," said the Onondaga. "Tandakora may have come to the conclusion that no enemy is on his extreme flank, and so has gone back to see if any has appeared nearer the center."

"Then we must follow him in his new course."

"If we do what we are sent to do we will follow."

"Lead on, Tayoga."

The Onondaga stooped that the underbrush might hide him, advanced over the trail, and Robert was close behind. The thickets were very still. All the small wild creatures, usually so numerous in them, had disappeared, and there was no wind. Tayoga saw that the imprints of the moccasins were growing firmer and clearer, and he knew that Tandakora and his men were but a short distance ahead. Then he stopped suddenly and he and Robert crouched low in the thicket.

They had heard the faint report of rifles directly in front, and they believed that Tandakora had come into contact with a party of rangers or Mohawks. As they listened, the sound of a second volley came, and then the echo of a faint war whoop. Tayoga rose a little higher, perhaps expecting to see something in the underbrush, and a rifle flashed less than forty yards away.

The Onondaga fell without a cry before the horrified eyes of his comrade, and then, as Robert heard a shout of triumph, he saw an Indian, horribly painted, rush forward to seize what he believed to be a Mohawk scalp.

Young Lennox, filled with grief and rage, stood straight up, and a stream of fire fairly poured from the muzzle of his rifle as his bullet met the exultant warrior squarely in the heart. The savage fell like a log, having no time to utter his death cry, and paying no further attention to him, feeling that he must be merely a stray warrior from the main band, Robert turned to his fallen comrade.

Tayoga was unconscious, and was bleeding profusely from a wound in the right shoulder. Robert seized his wrist and felt his pulse. He was not dead, because he detected a faint beat, but it was quite evident that the wound from a big musket bullet had come near to cutting the thread of life.

For a moment or two Lennox was in despair, while his heart continued to swell with grief and rage. It was unthinkable that the noblest young Onondaga of them all, one fit to be in his time the greatest of sachems, the very head and heart of the League, should be cut down by a mere skulker. And yet it had happened. Tayoga lay, still wholly unconscious, and the sounds of firing to the eastward were increasing. A battle had begun there. Perhaps the full forces of both sides were now in conflict.

The combat called to Robert, he knew that he might bear a great part in it, but he never hesitated. Such a thought as deserting his stricken comrade could not enter his mind. He listened a moment longer to the sounds of the conflict now growing more fierce, and then, fastening Tayoga's rifle on his back with his own, he lifted his wounded comrade in his arms and walked westward, away from the battle.

CHAPTER XI

THE COMRADES

Robert settled the inert form of the Onondaga against his left shoulder, and, being naturally very strong, with a strength greatly increased by a long life in the woods, he was able to carry the weight easily. He had no plan yet in his mind, merely a vague resolve to carry Tayoga outside the fighting zone and then do what he could to resuscitate him. It was an unfortunate chance that the hostile flankers had cut in between him and the main force of Rogers, but it could not be helped, and the farther he was from his own people the safer would he and Tayoga be.

Two hundred yards more and putting his comrade on the ground he cut away the deerskin, disclosing the wound. The bullet had gone almost through the shoulder, and as he felt of its path he knew with joy that it had touched no bone. Then, unless the loss of blood became great, it could not prove mortal. But the bullet was of heavy type, fired from the old smoothbore musket and the shock had been severe. Although it had not gone quite through the shoulder he could feel it near the surface, and he decided at once upon rude but effective surgery.

Laying Tayoga upon his face, he drew his keen hunting knife and cut boldly into the flesh of the shoulder until he reached the bullet. Then he pried it out with the point of the knife, and threw it away in the bushes. A rush of blood followed and Tayoga groaned, but Robert, rapidly cutting the Onondaga's deerskin tunic into suitable strips, bound tightly and with skill both the entrance and the exit of the wound. The flow of blood was stopped, and he breathed a fervent prayer of thankfulness to the white man's God and the red man's Manitou. Tayoga would live, and he knew that he had saved the life of his comrade, as that comrade had more than once saved his.

Yet both were still surrounded by appalling dangers. At any moment St. Luc's savages might burst through the woods and be upon them. As he finished tying the bandage and stood erect the flare of the fighting came from a point much nearer, though between them and the ranger band, forbidding any possible attempt to rejoin Rogers and Willet. Tayoga opened his eyes, though he saw darkly, through a veil, and said in feeble tones:

"They have closed again with the forces of St. Luc. You would be there, Dagaeoga, to help in the fighting. Go, I am useless. It is not a time to cumber yourself with me."

"If I lay there as you are, and you stood here as I am would you leave me?" asked Robert.

The Onondaga was silent.

"You know you wouldn't," continued Robert, "and you know I won't. Listen, the battle comes nearer. St. Luc must have received a reënforcement."

He leaned forward a little, cupping his ear with his right hand, and he heard distinctly all the sounds of a fierce and terrible conflict, rifle shots, yells of the savages, shouts of the rangers, and once or twice he thought he saw faintly the flashes of rifles as they were fired in the thickets.

"Go," said Tayoga again. "I can see that your spirit turns to the battle. They may not find me, and, perhaps in a day, I shall be able to walk and take care of myself."

Robert made no reply in words, but once more he lifted the Onondaga in his sinewy arms, settled his weight against his left shoulder and resumed his walk away from the battle. Tayoga did not speak, and Robert soon saw that he had relapsed again into unconsciousness. He went at least three hundred yards before resting, and all the while the battle called to him, the shots, the yells and the shouts still coming clearly through the thin mountain air.

He rested perhaps fifteen minutes, and he saw that, while Tayoga was unconscious, the flow of blood was still held in check by the bandages. Resuming his burden, he went on through the forest, a full quarter of a mile now, and the last sound of the battle sank into nothingness behind him. He was consumed with anxiety to know who had won, but there was not a sign to tell.

He came to a brook, and putting Tayoga down once more, he bathed his face freely, until the Onondaga opened his eyes and looked about, not with a veil before his eyes now, but clearly.

"Where are we, Dagaeoga?" he asked.

"I'd tell you if I could, but I can't," replied Robert, cheerfully, rejoiced at the sight of his comrade's returning strength.

"You have left the battle behind you?"

"Yes. I can state in general terms that we're somewhere between Andiatarocte and Oneadatote, which is quite enough for you to know at the present time. I'm the forest doctor, and as this is the first chance I've ever had to exert authority over you, I mean to make the most of it."

Tayoga smiled wanly.

"I see that you have bound up my wound," he said. "That was well. But since I cannot see the wound itself I do not know what kind of a bullet made it."

"It wasn't a bullet at all, Tayoga. It was a cannon ball, though it came out of a wide-mouthed musket, and I'm happy to tell you that it somehow got through your shoulder without touching bone."

"The bullet is out?"

"Yes, I cut it out with this good old hunting knife of mine."

Again Tayoga smiled wanly.

"You have done well, Dagaeoga," he said. "Did I not say to others in your defense that you had intelligence and, in time, might learn? You have saved my life, a poor thing perhaps, but the only life I have, and I thank you."

Robert laughed, and his laugh was full of heartiness. He saw the old Tayoga coming back.

"You'll be a new man tomorrow," he said. "With flesh and blood as healthy as yours a hole through your shoulder that I could put my fist in would soon heal."

"What does Dagaeoga purpose to do next?"

"You'll find out in good time. I'm master now, and I don't intend to tell my plans. If I did you'd be trying to change 'em. While I'm ruler I mean to be ruler."

"It is a haughty spirit you show. You take advantage of my being wounded."

"Of course I do. As I said, it's the only chance I've had. Stop that! Don't try to sit up! You're not strong enough yet. I'll carry you awhile."

Tayoga sank back, and, in a few more minutes, Robert picked him up and went on once more. But he noticed that the Onondaga did not now lie a dead weight upon his shoulder. Instead, there was in him again the vital quality that made him lighter and easier to carry. He knew that Tayoga would revive rapidly, but it would be days before he was fit to take care of himself. He must find not only a place of security, but one of shelter from the fierce midsummer storms that sometimes broke over those mountain slopes. Among the rocks and ravines and dense woods he might discover some such covert. Food was contained in his knapsack and the one still fastened to the back of Tayoga, food enough to last several days, and if the time should be longer his rifle must find more.

The way became rougher, the rocks growing more numerous, the slopes increasing in steepness, and the thickets becoming almost impenetrable.

"Put me down," said Tayoga. "We are safe from the enemy, for a while at least. All the warriors have been drawn by the battle, and, whether it goes on now or not, they have not yet had time to scatter and seek through the wilderness."

"I said I was going to be absolute master, but it looks, Tayoga, as if you meant to give advice anyhow. And as your advice seems good, and I confess I'm a trifle weary, I'll let you see if you can sit up a little on this heap of dead leaves, with your back against this old fallen trunk. Here we go! Gently now! Oh, you'll soon be a warrior again, if you follow my instructions!"

Tayoga heaved a little sigh of relief as he leaned back against the trunk. His eyes were growing clearer and Robert knew that the beat of his pulse was fuller. All the amazing vitality that came from a powerful constitution, hard training and clean living was showing itself. Already, and his wound scarcely two hours old, his strength was coming back.

"You look for a wigwam, Dagaeoga?" he said.

"Well, scarcely that," replied Robert. "I'm not expecting an inn in this wilderness, but I'm seeking some sort of shelter, preferably high up among the rocks, where we might find protection from storms."

"Two or three hundred yards farther on and we'll find it."

"Come, Tayoga, you're just guessing. You can't know such a thing."

"I am not guessing at all, Dagaeoga, and I do know. Your position as absolute ruler was brief. It expired between the first and second hour, and now you have an adviser who may become a director."

"Then proceed with your advice and direction. How do you know there is shelter only two or three hundred yards farther on?"

"I look ahead, and I see a narrow path leading up among the rocks. Such paths are countless in the wilderness, and many of them are untrodden, but the one before my eyes has sustained footsteps many times."

"Come down to earth, Tayoga, and tell me what you see."

"I see on the rocks on either side of this path long, coarse hairs. They were left by a wild animal going back and forth to its den. It was a large wild animal, else it would not have scraped against the rocks on either side. It was probably a bear, and if you will hand me the two or three twisted hairs in the crevice at your elbow I will tell you."

Robert brought them to him and Tayoga nodded assent.

"Aye, it was a bear," he said, "and a big one."

"But how do you know his den is only two or three hundred yards away?"

"That is a matter of looking as far as the eyes can reach. If you will only lift yours and gaze over the tops of those bushes you will see that the path ends against a high stone face or wall, too steep for climbing. So the den must be there, and let us hope, Dagaeoga, that it is large enough for us both. The bear is likely to be away, as this is summer. Now, lift me up. I have talked all the talk that is in me and as much as I have strength to utter."

Robert carried him again, and it was hard traveling up the steep and rocky path, but Tayoga's words were quickly proved to be true. In the crumbling face of the stone cliff they found not only an opening but several, the bear having preferred one of the smaller to the largest, which ran back eight or ten feet and which was roomy enough to house a dozen men. It bore no animal odor, and there was before it an abundance of dead leaves that could be taken in for shelter.

"Now Manitou is kind," said Tayoga, "or it may be that Areskoui and Tododaho are still keeping their personal watch over us. Lay me in the cave, Dagaeoga. Thou hast acquitted thyself as a true friend. No sachem of the Onondagas, however great, could have been greater in fidelity and courage."

Robert made two beds of leaves. On one he spread the blanket that was strapped to Tayoga's back. Then he built his own place and felt that they were sheltered and secure for the time, and in truth they were housed as well as millions of cave men for untold centuries had been. It was a good cave, sweet-smelling, with pure, clean air, and Robert saw that if it rained the water would not come in at the door, but would run past it down the slope, which in itself was one of the luckiest strokes of fortune.

Tayoga lay on his blanket on his bed of leaves, and, looking up at the rough and rocky roof, smiled. He had begged Robert to leave him and go to the battle, and he knew that if his comrade had gone, he, wounded as he was, would surely have perished. If a hostile

95

skirmisher did not find him, which was more than likely, he would have been overcome by the fever of his wound, and, lying unconscious while some rainstorm swept over him, his last chance would be gone. He could feel the fever creeping into his veins now, and he knew that they had found the refuge just in time. Yet he was grateful and cheerful, and in his heart he said silent thanks to Tododaho, Areskoui and Manitou. Then he called to Robert.

"See if you can find water," he said. "There should be more than one stream among these rocky hollows. Bring the water here in your cap and wash my wound."

Iroquois therapeutics were very simple, but wonderfully effective, and, as Robert had seen both Onondagas and Mohawks practice their healing art, he understood. He discovered a good stream not many yards away, and carefully removing Tayoga's bandages, and bringing his cap filled to the brim with water, he cleansed the wound thoroughly. Then the bandages were put on again firmly and securely. This in most cases constituted the whole of the Iroquois treatment, so far as the physical body was concerned. The wound must be kept absolutely clean and away from the air, nature doing the rest. Now and then the juices of powerful herbs were used, but they were not needed for one so young and so wholesome in blood as Tayoga.

When the operation was finished the Onondaga lay back on his bed and smiled once more at the rough and rocky roof.

"Again you show signs of intelligence, Dagaeoga," he said. "As you have learned to be a warrior, perhaps you can learn to be a medicine man also, not the medicine man who deals with spirits, but one who heals. Now, as you have done your part, I shall do mine."

"What do you mean, Tayoga?"

"I will resolve to be well. You know that among my people the healers held in highest honor are those who do not acknowledge the existence of any disease at all. The patient is sick because he has not willed that he should be well. So the medicine man exerts a will for him and by reciting to himself prayers or charms drives away the complaint which the sick man fancies that he has. Now, I do not accept all their belief. A bullet has gone through my shoulder, and I know it. Nothing can alter the fact. Yet I do know that the will has great control over the nerves, which direct the body, and I shall strengthen my will as much as I can, and make it order my body to get well."

Robert knew that what he said was true. Already the Iroquois were, and long had been, practicing what came to be known much later among the white people as Christian Science.

"Try to sleep, Tayoga," he said. "I know the power of your will. If you order yourself to sleep, sleep you will. I have your rifle and mine, and if the enemy should come I think I can hold 'em off."

"They will not come," said Tayoga, "at least, not today nor in the night that will follow. They are so busy with the Great Bear and the Mountain Wolf and Daganoweda that they will not have time to hunt among the hills for the two who have sought refuge here. What of the skies, Dagaeoga? What do they promise?"

Robert, standing in the entrance, took a long look at the heavens.

"Rain," he replied at last; "I can see clouds gathering in the west, and a storm is likely to come with the night. I think I hear distant thunder, but it is so low I'm not sure."

"Areskoui is good to us once more. The kindness of his heart is never exhausted. Truly, O Dagaeoga, he has been a shield between us and our enemies. Now the rain will come, it will pour hard, it will sweep along the slopes, and wash away any faint trace of a trail that we may have left, thus hiding our flight from the eyes of wandering warriors."

"All that's true, and now that you've explained it to your satisfaction, you obey me, exercise your will and go to sleep. I've recovered my rulership, and I mean to exercise it to the full for the little time that it may last."

Tayoga obeyed, composing himself in the easiest attitude on his blanket and bed of leaves, and he exerted his will to the utmost. He wished sleep, and sleep must come, yet he knew that the fever was still rising in his veins. The shock and loss of blood from the great musket ball could not be dismissed by a mere effort of the mind, but the mind nevertheless could fight against their effects and neutralize them.

As the fever rose steadily he exerted his will with increasing power. He said to himself again and again how fortunate he was to be watched over by such a brave and loyal friend, and to have a safe and dry refuge, when other warriors of his nation, wounded, had lain in the forest to die of exhaustion or to be devoured by wild beasts. He knew from the feel of the air that a storm was coming, and again he was thankful to his patron saint, Tododaho, and also to Areskoui, and to Manitou, greatest of all, because a bed and a roof had been found for him in this, the hour of his greatest need.

The mounting fever in his veins seemed to make his senses more vivid and acute for the time. Although Robert could not yet hear in reality the rumbling thunder far down in the southwest, the menace came very plainly to the ears of Tayoga, but it was no menace to him. Instead, the rumble was the voice of a friend, telling him that the deluge was at hand to wash away all traces of their flight and to force their enemies into shelter, while his fever burned itself out.

Tayoga on his blanket, with the thick couch of dry leaves beneath, could still see the figure of Robert, rifle across his knees, crouched at the doorway, a black silhouette against the fading sky. The Onondaga knew that he would watch until the storm came in full flood, and nothing would escape his keen eyes and ears. Dagaeoga was a worthy pupil of Willet, known to the Hodenosaunee as the Great Bear, a man of surpassing skill.

Tayoga also heard the rushing of the rain, far off, coming, perhaps, from Andiatarocte, and presently he saw the flashes of lightning, every one a vast red blaze to his feverish eyes. It was only by the light of these saber strokes across the sky that he could now see Robert, as the dark had come, soon to be followed by floods of rain. Then he closed his eyes, and calling incessantly for sleep, refused to open them again. Sleep came by and by, though it was Tarenyawagon, the sender of dreams, who presided over it, because as he slept, and his fever grew higher, visions, many and fantastic, flitted through his disordered brain.

Robert watched until long after the rain had been pouring in sheets, and it was pitchy dark in the cave. Then he felt of Tayoga's forehead and his pulse, and observed the fever, though without alarm. Tayoga's wound was clean and his blood absolutely pure. The fever was due and it would run its course. He could do nothing more for his comrade at present, and lying down on his own spread of leaves, he soon fell asleep.

Robert's slumber was not sound. Although the Onondaga might be watched over by Tododaho, Areskoui and even Manitou himself, he had felt the weight of responsibility. The gods protected those who protected themselves, and, even while he slept, the thought was nestling somewhere in his brain and awoke him now and then. Upon every such occasion he sat up and looked out at the entrance of the cave, to see, as he had hoped, only the darkness and black sheets of driving rain, and also upon every occasion devout thanks rose up in his throat. Tayoga had not prayed to his patron saint and to the great Areskoui and Manitou in vain, else in all that wilderness, given over to night and storm, they would not have found so good a refuge and shelter.

Tayoga's fever increased, and when morning came, with the rain still falling, though not in such a deluge as by night, it seemed to Robert, who had seen many gunshot wounds, that it was about at the zenith. The Onondaga came out of his sleep, but he was delirious for a little while, Robert sitting by him, covering him with his blanket and seeing that his hurt was kept away from the air.

The rain ceased by and by, but heavy fogs and vapors floated over the mountains, so dense that Robert could not see more than fifteen or twenty feet beyond the mouth of the cave, in front of which a stream of water from the rain a foot deep was flowing. He was thankful. He knew that fog and flood together would hide them in absolute security for another day and night at least.

He ate a little venison and regretted that he did not have a small skillet in which he could make soup for Tayoga later on, but since he did not have it he resolved to pound venison into shreds between stones, when the time came. Examining Tayoga again, he found, to his great joy, that the fever was decreasing, and he washed the wound anew. Then he sat by him a long time while the morning passed. Tayoga, who had been muttering in his fever, sank into silence, and about noon, opening his eyes, he said in a weak voice:

"How long have we been here, Dagaeoga?"

"About half of the second day is now gone," replied Robert, "and your fever has gone with it. You're as limp as a towel, but you're started fairly on the road to recovery."

"I know it," said Tayoga gratefully, "and I am thankful to Tododaho, to Areskoui, to Manitou, greatest of all, and to you, Dagaeoga, without whom the great spirits of earth and air would have let me perish."

"You don't owe me anything, Tayoga. It's what one comrade has a right to expect of another. Did you exert your will, as you said, when you were delirious, and help along nature with your cure?"

"I did, Dagaeoga. Before I lapsed into the unconsciousness of which you speak, I resolved that today, when my fever should have passed, my soul should lift me up. I concentrated my mind upon it, I attuned every nerve to that end, and while I could not prevent the fever and the weakness, yet the resolution to get well fast helps me to do so. By so much does my mind rule over my body."

"I've no doubt you're right about it. Courage and optimism can lift us up a lot, as I've seen often for myself, and you're certainly out of danger now, Tayoga. All you have to do is to lie quiet, if the French and Indians will let us. In a week you'll be able to travel and fight, and in a few weeks you'll never know that a musket ball passed through your shoulder. When do you think you can eat? I'll pound some of the venison very fine."

"Not before night, and then but little. That little, though, I should have. Tomorrow I will eat much more, and a few days later it will be all Dagaeoga can do to find enough food for me. Be sure that you wait on me well. It is the first rest that I have had in a long time, and it is my purpose to enjoy it. If I should be fretful, humor me; if I should be hungry, feed me; if I should be sleepy, let me sleep, and see that I am not disturbed while I do sleep; if my bed is hard, make me a better, and through it all, O Dagaeoga, be thou the finest medicine man that ever breathed in these woods."

"Come, now, Tayoga, you lay too great a burden upon me. I'm not all the excellencies melted into one, and I've never pretended to be. But I can see that you're getting well, because the spirit of rulership is upon you as strong as ever, and, since you're so much improved, I may take it into my mind to obey your commands, though only when I feel like it."

The two lads looked at each other and laughed, and there was immense relief in Robert's laugh. Only now did he admit to himself that he had been terribly alarmed about Tayoga, and he recognized the enormous relief he felt when the Onondaga had passed his crisis.

98

"In truth, you pick up fast, Tayoga," he said whimsically. "Suppose we go forth now and hunt the enemy. We might finish up what Rogers, Willet and Daganoweda have left of St. Luc's force."

"I would go," replied Tayoga in the same tone, "but Tododaho and Areskoui have told me to bide here awhile. Only a fear that my disobedience might cause me to lose their favor keeps me in the cave. But I wish you to bear in mind, Dagaeoga, that I still exert my will as the medicine men of my nation bid the sick and the hurt to do, and that I feel the fevered blood cooling in my veins, strength flowing back into my weak muscles, and my nerves, that were all so loose and unattuned, becoming steady."

"I'll admit that your will may help, Tayoga, but it's chiefly the long sleep you've had, the good home you enjoy, and the superb care of Dr. Robert Lennox of Albany, New York, and the Vale of Onondaga. On the whole, weighing the question carefully, I should say that the ministrations of Dr. Lennox constitute at least eighty per cent of the whole."

"You are still the great talker, Dagaeoga, that you were when you defeated St. Luc in the test of words in the Vale of Onondaga, and it is well. The world needs good talkers, those who can make speech flow in a golden stream, else we should all grow dull and gloomy, though I will say for you, O Lennox, that you act as well as talk. If I did not, I, whose life you have saved and who have seen you great in battle, should have little gratitude and less perception."

"I've always told you, Tayoga, that when you speak English you speak out of a book, because you learned it out of a book and you take delight in long words. Now I think that 'gratitude' and 'perception' are enough for you and you can rest."

"I will rest, but it is not because you think my words are long and I am exhausted, Dagaeoga. It is because you wish to have all the time yourself for talking. You are cunning, but you need not be so now. I give my time to you."

Robert laughed. The old Tayoga with all his keenness and sense of humor was back again, and it was a sure sign that a rapid recovery had set in.

"Maybe you can go to sleep again," he said. "I think it was a stupor rather than sleep that you passed through last night, but now you ought to find sleep sweet, sound and healthy."

"You speak words of truth, O great white medicine man, and it being so my mind will make my body obey your instructions."

He turned a little on his side, away from his wounded shoulder, and either his will was very powerful or his body was willing, as he soon slept again, and now Tarenyawagon sent him no troubled and disordered dreams. Instead his breathing was deep and regular, and when Robert felt his pulse he found it was almost normal. The fever was gone and the bronze of Tayoga's face assumed a healthful tint.

Then Robert took a piece of venison, and pounded it well between two stones. He would have been glad to light a fire of dry leaves and sticks, that he might warm the meat, but he knew that it was yet too dangerous, and so strong was Tayoga's constitution that he might take the food cold, and yet find it nutritious.

It was late in the afternoon when the Onondaga awoke, yawned in human fashion, and raised himself a little on his unwounded shoulder.

"Here is your dinner, Tayoga," said Robert, presenting the shredded venison. "I'm sorry it's not better, but it's the best the lodge affords, and I, as chief medicine man and also as first assistant medicine man and second assistant medicine man, bid you eat and find no fault."

"I obey, O physician, wise and stern, despite your youth," said Tayoga.
"I am hungry, which is a most excellent sign, and I will say, too, that
I begin to feel like a warrior again."

He ate as much as Robert would let him have, and then, with a great sigh of content,
sank back on his bed of leaves.

"I can feel my wound healing," he said. "Already the clean flesh is spreading over the
hurt and the million tiny strands are knitting closely together. Some day it shall be said in
the Vale of Onondaga that the wound of Tayoga healed more quickly than the wound of
any other warrior of our nation."

"Good enough as a prophecy, but for the present we'll bathe and bind it anew. A little
good doctoring is a wonderful help to will and prediction."

Robert once more cleansed the hurt very thoroughly, and he was surprised to find its
extremely healthy condition. It had already begun to heal, a proof of amazing vitality on
the part of Tayoga, and unless the unforeseen occurred he would set a record in recovery.
Robert heaped the leaves under his head to form a pillow, and the young warrior's eyes
sparkled as he looked around at their snug abode.

"I can hear the water running by the mouth of the cave," he said. "It comes from last
night's rain and flood, but what of tonight, Dagaeoga? The skies and what they have to
say mean much to us."

"It will rain again. I've been looking out. All the west is heavy with clouds and the light
winds come, soaked with damp. I don't claim to be any prophet like you, Tayoga, because
I'm a modest man, I am, but the night will be wet and dark."

"Then we are still under the protection of Tododaho, of Areskoui and of Manitou,
greatest of all. Let the dark come quickly and the rain fall heavily, because they will be a
veil about us to hide us from Tandakora and his savages."

All that the Onondaga wished came to pass. The clouds, circling about the horizon,
soon spread to the zenith, and covered the heavens, hiding the moon and the last star. The
rain came, not in a flood, but in a cold and steady pour lasting all night. The night was not
only dark and wet outside, but it was very chill also, though in the cave the two young
warriors, the white and the red, were warm and dry on their blankets and beds of leaves.

Robert pounded more of the venison the next morning and gave Tayoga twice as much
as he had eaten the day before. The Onondaga clamored for an additional supply, but
Robert would not let him have it.

"Epicure! Gourmand! Gorger!" said young Lennox. "Would you do nothing but eat?
Do you think it your chief duty in this world to be a glutton?"

"No, Dagaeoga," replied Tayoga, "I am not a glutton, but I am yet hungry, and I warn
thee, O grudging medicine man, that I am growing strong fast. I feel upon my arm
muscles that were not there yesterday and tomorrow or the next day my strength will be
so great that I shall take from you all the food of us both and eat it."

"By that time we won't have any left, and I shall have to take measures to secure a new
supply. I must go forth in search of game."

"Not today, nor yet tomorrow. It is too dangerous. You must wait until the last moment.
It is barely possible that the Great Bear or Black Rifle may find us."

"I don't think so. We'll have to rely on ourselves. But at any rate,
I'll stay in the cave today, though I think the rain is about over.
Don't you see the sun shining in at the entrance? It's going to be a
fine day in the woods, Tayoga, but it won't be a fine day for us."

"That is true, Dagaeoga. It is hard to stay here in a hole in the rocks, when the sun is
shining and the earth is drying. The sun has brought back the green to the leaves and the

100

light now must be wonderful on Andiatarocte and Oneadatote. Their waters shift and change with all the colors of the rainbow. It fills me with longing when I think of these things. Go now, Dagaeoga, and find the Great Bear, the Mountain Wolf and Daganoweda. I am well past all danger from my wound, and I can take care of myself."

"Tayoga, you talk like a foolish child. If I hear any more such words I shall have to gag you, for two reasons, because they make a weariness in my ear, and because if anyone else were to hear you he would think you were weak of mind. It's your reputation for sanity that I'm thinking about most. You and I stay here together, and when we leave we leave together."

Tayoga said no more on the subject. He had known all the while that Robert would not leave him, but he had wished to give him the chance. He lay very quiet now for many hours, and Robert sitting at the door of the cave, with his rifle across his knees, was also quiet. While a great talker upon occasion, he had learned from the Iroquois the habit of silence, when silence was needed, and it required no effort from him.

Though he did not speak he saw much. The stream, caused by the flood, still flowed before the mouth of the cave, but it was diminishing steadily. By the time night came it would sink to a thin thread and vanish. The world itself, bathed and cleansed anew, was wonderfully sweet and fresh. The light wind brought the pleasant odors of flower and leaf and grass. Birds began to sing on the overhanging boughs, and a rabbit or two appeared in the valley. These unconscious sentinels made him feel quite sure that no savages were near.

Curiosity about the battle between the forces of St. Luc and those of the rangers and Mohawks, smothered hitherto by his anxiety and care for Tayoga, was now strong in his breast. It was barely possible that St. Luc had spread a successful ambush and that all of his friends had fallen. He shuddered at the thought, and then dismissed it as too unlikely. Tayoga fell asleep again, and when he awoke he was not only able to sit up, but to walk across the cave.

"Tomorrow," he said, "I shall be able to sit near the entrance and load and fire a rifle as well as ever. If an enemy should come I think I could hold the refuge alone."

"That being the case," said Robert, "and you being full of pride and haughtiness, I may let you have the chance. Not many shreds of our venison are left, and as I shall have in you a raging wolf to feed, I'll go forth and seek game. It seems to me I ought to find it soon. You don't think it's all been driven away by marching rangers and warriors, do you, Tayoga?"

"No, the rangers and warriors have been seeking one another, not the game, and perhaps the deer and the moose know it. Why does man think that Manitou watches over him alone? Perhaps He has told the big animals that they are safer when the men fight. On our way here I twice saw the tracks of a moose, and it may be your fortune to find one tomorrow, Dagaeoga."

"Not fortune, at all, Tayoga. If I bring down one it will be due to my surpassing skill in trailing and to my deadly sharpshooting, for which I am renowned the world over. Anyhow, I think we can sleep another night without a guard and then we'll see what tomorrow will bring forth."

CHAPTER XII

THE SINISTER SIEGE

Dawn came, very clear and beautiful, with the air crisp and cool. Robert divided the last of the venison between Tayoga and himself, and when he had eaten his portion he was still hungry. He was quite certain that the Onondaga also craved more, but a stoic like Tayoga would never admit it. His belief the day before that this was the time for him to go forth and hunt was confirmed. The game would be out, and so might be the savages, but he must take the chance.

Tayoga had kept his bow and quiver of arrows strapped to his back during their retreat, and now they lay on a shelf in the cave. Robert looked at them doubtfully and the eyes of the Onondaga followed him.

"Perhaps it would be best," he said.

"I can't bend the bow of Ulysses," said Robert, "but I may be able to send in a useful arrow or two nevertheless."

"You can try."

"But I don't want any shot to go amiss."

"Strap your rifle on your back, and take the bow and arrows also. If the arrows fail you, or rather if you should fail the arrows, which always go where they are sent, you can take the rifle, with which you are almost as good as the Great Bear himself. And if you should encounter hostile warriors prowling through the woods the rifle will be your best defense."

"I'll do as you advise, Tayoga, and do you keep a good watch at the entrance. You're feeling a lot stronger today, are you not?"

"So much so that I am almost tempted to take the bow and arrows myself, while I leave you on guard."

"Don't be too proud and boastful. Let's see you walk across the cave."

Tayoga rose from the bed of leaves, on which he had been sitting, and strode firmly back and forth two or three times. He was much thinner than he had been a week before, but his eyes were sparkling now and the bronze of his skin was clear and beautiful. All his nerves and muscles were under complete control.

"You're a great warrior again, Tayoga, thanks to my protecting care," said Robert, "but I don't think you're yet quite the equal of Tododaho and Hayowentha when they walked the earth, and, for that reason, I shall not let you go out hunting. Now, take your rifle, which I saved along with you, and sit on that ledge of stone, where you can see everything approaching the cave and not be seen yourself."

"I obey, O Dagaeoga. I obey you always when the words you speak are worth being obeyed. See, I take the seat you direct, and I hold my rifle ready."

"Very good. Be prepared to fire on an instant's notice, but be sure you don't fire at me when I come striding down the valley bearing on my shoulders a fat young deer that I have just killed."

"Have no fear, Dagaeoga. I shall be too glad to see you and the deer to fire."

With the rifle so adjusted across his back that, if need be, he could disengage it at once, the quiver fastened also and Tayoga's bow in his hand, Robert made ready.

"Now, Tayoga," he said, "exert that famous will of yours like a true medicine man of the Hodenosaunee. While I am absent, so direct me with the concentrated power of your mind that I shall soon find a fat young deer, and that my arrow shall not miss. I'll gratefully receive all the help you can give me in this way, though I won't neglect, if I see the deer, to take the best aim I can with bow and arrow."

"Do not scoff, O Dagaeoga. The lore and belief of my nation and of the whole Hodenosaunee are based upon the experience of many centuries. And do you not say in your religion that the prayer of the righteous availeth? Do you think your God, who is the same as my Manitou, intended that only the prayers of the white men should have weight, and that those of the red men should vanish into nothingness like a snowflake melting in the air? I may not be righteous,—who knows whether he is righteous or not?—but, at least, I shall pray in a righteous cause."

"I don't mock, Tayoga, and maybe the power of your wish, poured in a flood upon me, will help. Yes, I know it will, and I go now, sure that I will soon find what I seek."

He left the cave and passed up the valley, full of confidence. The earnestness of Tayoga had made a great impression upon him, clothing him about with an atmosphere that was surcharged with belief, and, as he breathed in this air, it made his veins fairly sparkle, not alone with hope, but with certainty.

He walked up a deep defile which gradually grew shallower, and then ascended rapidly. Finally he came out on a crest, crowned with splendid trees, and he drew a great breath of pleasure as he looked upon a vast green wilderness, deepened in color by the long and recent rains, and upon the far western horizon a dim but splendid band of silver which he knew was Andiatarocte. A lover of beauty, and with the soul of a poet, he could have stood, gazing a long time, but there was a sterner task forward than the contemplation of nature in the wild.

He must sink the poet in the hunter, and he began to look for tracks of game, which he felt sure would be plentiful in the forest, since men had long been hunting one another instead of the deer. He had an abundance of will of his own, but he felt also, despite a certain incredulity of the reason, that the concentrated will of his distant comrade was driving him on.

He walked about a mile, remaining well under cover, having a double object, to keep himself hidden from foes and also to find traces of game. His confidence that he would find it, and very quickly, was not abated, and, at the end of a mile, he saw a broad footprint on the turf that made him utter a low exclamation of delight. It was larger than that of a cow, and more pointed. He knew at once that it had been made by a moose, the great animal which was then still to be found in the forests of Northern New York.

The tracks led northward and he studied them with care. The wind had risen and was blowing toward him, which was favorable for his pursuit, as the sound of his own footsteps rustling the grass or breaking a little stick would not be likely to reach the ear of the moose. He was convinced, too, that the tracks were not much more than two hours old, and since the big animal was likely to be rambling along, nibbling at the twigs, the chance was in favor of the hunter overtaking him very soon.

It was easy to follow the trail, the hoof prints were so large, and he soon saw, too, the broken ends of twigs that had been nibbled by the moose, and also exposed places on the trunks of trees where the bark had been peeled off by the animal's teeth. He was sure that the game could not be much more than a mile ahead, and his soul was filled with the ardor of the chase. He was confident that he was pursuing a big bull, as the fact was indicated by the size of the prints, the length of the stride, and the height at which the moose had browsed on the twigs. There were other facts he had learned among the Iroquois, indicating to him it was a bull. While the tracks were pointed, they were less pointed than those the cow generally makes, and the twigs that had been nibbled were those of the fir, while the cow usually prefers the birch.

103

The tracks now seemed to Robert to grow much fresher. Tayoga, with his infallible eye and his wonderful gifts, both inherited and improved, would have known just how fresh they were, but Robert was compelled to confine his surmise to the region of the comparative. Nevertheless, he knew that he was gaining upon the moose and that was enough. But as it was evident by his frequent browsing that the animal was going slowly, he controlled his eagerness sufficiently to exercise great wariness on his own part. It might be that while he was hunting he could also become the hunted. It was not at all impossible that the warriors of Tandakora would fall upon his own track and follow.

He looked back apprehensively, and once he returned and retraced his steps for a little distance, but he could discern no evidence of an enemy and he resumed his pursuit of the moose, going faster now, and seeing twigs which apparently had been broken off only a few minutes before. Then, as he topped a little rise, he saw the animal itself, browsing lazily on the succulent bushes. It was a large moose, but to Robert, although an experienced hunter, it loomed up at the moment like an elephant. He had staked so much upon securing the game, and the issue was so important that his heart beat hard with excitement.

The wind was still in his favor, and, creeping as near as he dared, he fitted an arrow to Tayoga's bow and pulled the string. The arrow struck well in behind the shoulder and the moose leaped high. Another arrow sang from the bow and found its heart, after which it ran a few steps and fell. Robert's laborious task began, to remove at least a part of the skin, and then great portions of the meat, as much as he could carry, wrapped in the folds of the skin, portions from which he intended to make steaks.

He secured at least fifty pounds, and then he looked with regret at the great body. He was not one to slay animals for sport's sake, and he wished that the rangers and Mohawks might have the hundreds of pounds of good moose meat, but he knew it was not destined for them. As he drew away with his own burden his heirs to the rest were already showing signs of their presence. From the thick bushes about came the rustling of light feet, and now and then an eager and impatient snarl. Red eyes showed, and as he turned away the wolves of the hills made a wild rush for the fallen monarch. Robert, for some distance, heard them yapping and snarling over the feast, and, despite his own success in securing what he needed so badly, he felt remorse because he had been compelled to give so fine an animal over to the wolves.

His heart grew light again as he made his way back to the defile and the cave. He carried enough food to last Tayoga and himself many days, if necessity compelled them to remain long in the cave, but he did not forget in his triumph to take every precaution for the hiding of his trail, devoutly glad that it was hard ground, thick with stones, on which he could step from one to another.

Thus he returned, bearing his burden, and Tayoga, sitting near the entrance, rifle on knee, greeted him with becoming words as one whom Tododaho and Areskoui had guided to victory.

"It is well, Dagaeoga," he said. "I was wishing for you to find a moose and you found one. You were not compelled to use the rifle!"

"No, the bow served, but I had to shoot two arrows where you would have shot only one."

"It is no disgrace to you. The bow is not the white man's weapon, at least not on this continent. You withdrew the arrows, cleaned them and returned them to the quiver?"

"Yes. I didn't forget that. I know how precious arrows are, and now, Tayoga, since it's important for you to get back your strength faster than a wounded man ever got it back before, I think we'd better risk a fire, and broil some of these fat, juicy steaks."

"It is a danger, but we will do it. You gather the dead wood and we will build the fire beside the mouth of the cave. Both of us can cook."

It was an easy task for two such foresters to light a fire with flint and steel, and they soon had a big bed of coals. Then they broiled the steaks on the ends of sharpened sticks, passing them back and forth quickly, in order to retain the juices.

"Now, Tayoga," announced Robert, "I have a word or two to say to you."

"Then say them quickly and do not let your eloquence become a stream, because I am hungry and would eat, and where the moose steaks are plenty talk is needed but little."

"I merely wished to tell you that besides being our hunter, I'm also the family doctor. Hence I give you my instructions."

"What are they, O youth of many words?"

"You can eat just as much of the moose steak as you like, and the quicker you begin the better you will please me, because my manners won't allow me to start first. Fall on, Tayoga! Fall on!"

They ate hungrily and long. They would have been glad had they bread also, but they did not waste time in vain regrets. When they had finished and the measure of their happiness was full, they extinguished the coals carefully, hid their store of moose meat on a high ledge in the cave, and withdrew also to its shelter.

"How much stronger do you feel now, Tayoga?" asked Robert.

"In the language of your schools, my strength has increased at least fifty per cent in the last hour."

"I've the strength of two men myself now, and thinking it over, Tayoga, I've come to the conclusion that was the best moose I ever tasted. He was a big bull, and he may not have been young, but he furnished good steaks. I'm sorry he had to die, but he died in a good cause."

"Even so, Dagaeoga, and since we have eaten tremendously and have cooked much of the meat for further use, it would be best for us to put out the fire, and hide all trace of it, a task in which I am strong enough to help you."

They extinguished carefully every brand and coal, and even went so far as to take dead leaves from the cave and throw them over the remains of the fire in careless fashion as if they had been swept there by the wind.

"And now," said Robert, "if I had the power I would summon from the sky another mighty rain to hide all signs of our banquet and of the preparations for it. Suppose, Tayoga, you pray to Tododaho and Areskoui for it and also project your mind so forcibly in the direction of your wish that the wish will come true."

"It is well not to push one's favor too far," replied Tayoga gravely. "The heavens are too bright and shining now for rain. Moreover, if one should pray every day for help, Tododaho and Areskoui would grow tired of giving it. I think, however, that we have covered our traces well, and the chance of discovery here by our enemies is remote."

They put away the moose meat on a high ledge in the cave, and sat down again to wait. Tayoga's wound was healing rapidly. The miracle for which he had hoped was happening. His recovery was faster than that of any other injured warrior whom he had ever known. He could fairly feel the clean flesh knitting itself together in innumerable little fibers, and already he could move his left arm, and use the fingers of his left hand. Being a stoic, and hiding his feelings as he usually did, he said:

"I shall recover, I shall be wholly myself again in time for the great battle between the army of Waraiyageh and that of Dieskau."

"I think, too, that we'll be in it," said Robert confidently. "Armies move slowly and they won't come together for quite a while yet. Meantime, I'm wondering what became of the rangers and the Mohawks."

"We shall have to keep on wondering, but I am thinking it likely that they prevailed over the forces of St. Luc and have passed on toward Crown Point and Oneadatote. It may be that the present area of conflict has passed north and east of us and we have little to fear from our enemies."

"It sounds as if you were talking out of a book again, Tayoga, but I believe you're right."

"I think the only foes whom we may dread in the next night and day are four-footed."

"You mean the wolves?"

"Yes, Dagaeoga. When you left the body of the moose did they not appear?"

"They were fighting over it before I was out of sight. But they wouldn't dare to attack you and me."

"It is a strange thing, Dagaeoga, but whenever there is war in the woods among men the wolves grow numerous, powerful and bold. They know that when men turn their arms upon one another they are turned aside from the wolves. They hang upon the fringes of the bands and armies, and where the wounded are they learn to attack. I have noticed, too, since the great war began that we have here bigger and fiercer wolves than any we've ever known before, coming out of the vast wilderness of the far north."

"You mean the timber wolves, those monsters, five or six feet long, and almost as powerful and dangerous as a tiger or a lion?"

"So I do, Dagaeoga, and they will be abroad tonight, led by the body of your moose and the portion we have here. Tododaho, sitting on his star, has whispered to me that we are about to incur a great danger, one that we did not expect."

"You give me a creepy feeling, Tayoga. All this is weird and uncanny. We've nothing to fear from wolves."

"A thousand times we might have nothing to fear from them, but one time we will, and this is the time. In a voice that I did not hear, but which I felt, Tododaho told me so, and I know."

"Then all we have to do is to build a fire in front of the cave mouth and shut them off as thoroughly, as if we had raised a steel wall before us."

"The danger from a fire burning all night would be too great. While I do not think any warriors of the enemy are wandering in this immediate region, yet it is possible, and our bonfire would be a beacon to draw them."

"Then we'll have to meet 'em with bullets, but the reports of our rifles might also draw Tandakora's warriors."

"We will not use the rifles. We will sit at the entrance of the cave, and you shall fight them with my bow and arrows. If we are pressed too hard, we may resort to the rifles."

Tayoga's words were so earnest and sententious, his manner so much that of a prophet, that Robert, in spite of himself, believed in the great impending danger that would come in the dark, and the hair on the back of his neck lifted a little. Yet the day was still great and shining, the forest tinted gold with the flowing sunlight, and the pure fresh air blowing into the cave. There the two youths, the white and the red, took their seats at either side of the entrance. Tayoga held his rifle across his knees, but Robert put his and the quiver at his feet, while he held the bow and one arrow in his hands.

They talked a little from time to time and then relapsed into a long silence. Robert noticed that nothing living stirred in the defile. No more rabbits came out to play and no birds sang in the trees. He considered it a sign, nay more, an omen that Tayoga's prediction was coming true. The peril threatening them was great and imminent. His sense of the sinister and uncanny increased. A chill ran through his veins. The great shining day was going, and, although it was midsummer, a cold wind was herald of the coming twilight. He shivered again, and looked at the long shadows falling in the defile.

"Tayoga," he said, "that uncanny talk of yours has affected me, but I believe you've just made it all up. No wolves are coming to attack us."

"Dagaeoga does not believe anything of the kind. He believes, instead, what I have told him. His voice and his manner show it. He is sure the wolves are coming."

"You're right, Tayoga, I do believe it. There's every reason why I shouldn't, but, in very truth and fact, I do. Our fine day is going fast. Look how the twilight is growing on the mountains. From our nook here I can just see the rim of the sun, who is your God, Areskoui. Soon he will be gone entirely and then all the ridges will be lost in the dusk. I hope—and I'm not jesting either—that you've said your prayer to him."

"As I told you, Dagaeoga, one must not ask too many favors. But now the sun is wholly gone and the night will be dark. The wind rises and it moans like the soul of an evil warrior condemned to wander between heaven and earth. The night will be dark, and in two hours the wolves will be here."

Robert looked at him, but the face of the Onondaga was that of a seer, and once more the blood of the white youth ran chill in his veins. He was silent again, and now the minutes were leaden-footed, so slow, in truth, that it seemed an hour would never pass and the two hours Tayoga had predicted were an eternity. The afterglow disappeared and the darkness was deep in the defile. The trees above were fused into a black mass, and then, after an infinity of waiting, a faint note, sinister and full of menace, came out of the wilderness. Tayoga and Robert glanced at each other.

"It is as you predicted," said Robert.

"It is the howl of the great timber wolf from the far north who has made himself the leader of the band," said the Onondaga. "When he howls again he will be much nearer."

Robert waited for an almost breathless minute or two, and then came the malignant note, much nearer, as Tayoga had predicted, and directly after came other howls, faint but equally sinister.

"The great leader gives tongue a second time," said Tayoga, "and his pack imitate him, but their voices are not so loud, because their lungs are not so strong. They come straight toward us. Do you see, Dagaeoga, that your nerves are steady, your muscles strong and your eyes bright. I would that I could use the bow myself tonight, for the chance will be glorious, but Manitou has willed otherwise. It is for you, Dagaeoga, to handle my weapon as if you had been familiar with it all your life."

"I will do my best, Tayoga. No man can do more."

"Dagaeoga's best is very good indeed. Remember that if they undertake to rush us we will use our rifles, but they are to be held in reserve. Hark, the giant leader howls for the third time!"

The long, piercing note came now from a point not very distant. Heard in all the loneliness of the black forest it was inexpressively threatening and evil. Not until his own note died did the howl of his pack follow. All doubts that Robert may have felt fled at once. He believed everything that Tayoga had said, and he knew that the wolf-pack, reënforced by mighty timber wolves from the far north, was coming straight toward the cave for what was left of the moose meat and Tayoga and himself. His nerves shook for an instant, but the next moment he put them under command, and carefully tested the bowstring.

107

"It is good and strong," he said to Tayoga. "It will not be any fault of the bow and arrow if the work is not done well. The fault will be mine instead."

"You will not fail, Dagaeoga," said the Onondaga. "Your great imagination always excites you somewhat before the event, but when it comes you are calm and steady."

"I'll try to prove that you estimate me correctly."

As their eyes were used to the dusk they could see each other well, sitting on opposite sides of the cave mouth and sheltered by the projection of the rocks. The great wolf howled once more and the pack howled after him, but there followed an interval of silence that caused Robert to think they had, perhaps, turned aside. But Tayoga whispered presently:

"I see the leader on the opposite side of the defile among the short bushes. The pack is farther back. They know, of course, that we are here. The leader is, as we surmised, a huge timber wolf, come down from the far north. Do not shoot, Dagaeoga, until you get a good chance."

"Do you think I should wait for the leader himself?"

"No. Often the soul of a wicked warrior goes into the body of a wolf, and the wolf becomes wicked, and also full of craft. The leader may not come forward at first himself, but will send others to receive our blows."

There was no yapping and snarling from the wolves such as was usual, and such as Robert had often heard, but they had become a phantom pack, silent and ghost-like, creeping among the bushes, sinister and threatening beyond all reckoning. Robert began to feel that, in very truth, it was a phantom pack, and he wondered if his arrows, even if they struck full and true, would slay. Nature, in her chance moments, touches one among the millions with genius, and she had so tipped him with living fire. His vivid and powerful imagination often made him see things others could not see and caused him to clothe objects in colors invisible to common eyes.

Now the wolves, with their demon leader, were moving in silence among the bushes, and he felt that in truth he would soon be fighting with what Tayoga called evil spirits. For the moment, not the demon leader alone, but every wolf represented the soul of a wicked warrior, and they would approach with all the cunning that the warriors had known and practiced in their lives.

"Do you see the great beast now, Tayoga?" he whispered.

"No, he is behind a rock, but there is another slinking forward, drawing himself without noise over the ground. He must have been in life a savage from the far region, west of the Great Lakes, perhaps an eater of his own kind, as the wolf eats his."

"I see him, Tayoga, just there on the right where the darkness lies like a shroud. I see his jaws slavering too. He comes forward as a stalker, and I've no doubt the soul of a most utter savage is hidden in his body. He shall meet my arrow."

"Wait a little, Dagaeoga, until you can be sure of your shot. There is another creeping forward on the left in the same manner, and you'll want to send a second arrow quickly at him."

"I never saw a wolf-pack attack in this way before. They come like a band of warriors with scouts and skirmishers, and I can see that they have a force massed in the center for the main rush."

"In a few more seconds you can take the wolf on the right. Bury your arrow in his throat. It is as I said, Dagaeoga. Now that the moment has come your hand is steady, your nerves are firm, and even in the dusk I can see that your eyes are bright."

It was true. Robert's imagination had painted the danger in the most vivid colors, but now, that it was here, the beat of his pulse was as regular as the ticking of a clock. Yet the unreal and sinister atmosphere that clothed him about was not dispelled in the least, and he could not rid himself of the feeling that in fighting them he was fighting dead and gone warriors.

Nearer and nearer came the great wolf on his right, dragging his body over the ground for all the world like a creeping Indian. Robert's eyes, become uncommonly keen in the dusk, saw the long fangs, the slavering jaws and the red eyes, and he also saw the spot in the pulsing throat where he intended that the sharp point of his arrow should strike.

"Now!" whispered Tayoga.

Robert fitted the shaft to the string, and deftly throwing his weight into it bent the great bow. Then he loosed the arrow, and, singing through the air, it buried itself almost to the feather in the big beast's throat, just at the spot that he had chosen. The strangled howl of despair and death that followed was almost like that of a human being, but Robert did not stop to listen, as with all speed he fitted another arrow to the string and fired at the beast on the left, with equal success, piercing him in the heart.

"Well done, Dagaeoga," whispered Tayoga. "Two shots and two wolves slain. The skirmisher on the right and the skirmisher on the left both are gone. There will be a wait now while the living devour their dead comrades. Listen, you can hear them dragging the bodies into the bushes."

"After they have finished their cannibalism perhaps they will go away."

"No, it is a great pack, and they are very hungry. In ten or fifteen minutes they will be stalking us again. You must seek a shot at the giant leader, but it will be hard for you to get it because he will keep himself under cover, while he sends forth his warriors to meet your arrows. Ah, he is great and cunning! Now, I am more sure than ever that his body contains the soul of one of the most wicked of all warriors, perhaps that of a brother of Tandakora. Yes, it must be a brother, the blood of Tandakora."

"Then Tandakora's brother would better beware. My desire to slay him has increased, and if he's incautious and I get good aim I think I can place an arrow so deep in him that the Ojibway's wicked soul will have to seek another home."

"Hear them growling and snarling in the bushes. It is over their cannibalistic feast. Soon they will have finished and then they will come back to us."

The deadly stalking, more hideous than that carried on by men, because it was more unnatural, was resumed. Robert discharged a third arrow, but the fierce yelp following told him that he had inflicted only a wound. He glanced instinctively at the Onondaga, fearing a reproof, but Tayoga merely said:

"If one shoots many times one must miss sometimes."

A fourth shot touched nothing, but the Onondaga had no rebuke, a fifth shot killed a wolf, a sixth did likewise, and Robert's pride returned. The wolves drew off, to indulge in cannibalism again, and to consult with their leader, who carried the soul of a savage in his body.

Robert had sought in vain for a fair shot at the giant wolf. He had caught one or two glimpses of him, but they were too fleeting for the flight of an arrow, and, despite all reason and logic, he found himself accepting Tayoga's theory that he was, in reality, a lost brother of Tandakora, marshaling forward his forces, but keeping himself secure. After the snarling and yelping over the horrible repast, another silence followed in the bushes.

"Perhaps they've had enough and have gone away," said Robert, hazarding the hopeful guess a second time.

"No. They will make a new attack. They care nothing for those that have fallen. Watch well, Dagaeoga, and keep your arrows ready."

"I think I'll become a good bowman in time," said Robert lightly, to ease his feelings, "because I'm getting a lot of practice, and it seems that I'll have a lot more. Perhaps I need this rest, but, so far as my feelings are concerned, I wish the wolves would come on and make a final rush. Their silence and invisibility are pretty hard on the nerves."

He examined the bow carefully again, and put six arrows on the floor of the cave beside him, with the quiver just beyond them. Tayoga sat immovable, his rifle across his knees, ready in the last emergency to use the bullet. Thus more time passed in silence and without action.

It often seemed to Robert afterward that there was something unnatural about both time and place. The darkness came down thicker and heavier, and to his imaginative ear it had a faint sliding sound like the dropping of many veils. So highly charged had become his faculties that they were able to clothe the intangible and the invisible with bodily reality. He glanced across at his comrade, whom his accustomed eyes could see despite the blackness of the night. Tayoga was quite still. So far as Robert could tell he had not stirred by a hair's breadth in the last hour.

"Do you hear anything?" whispered the white youth.

"Nothing," replied the Onondaga. "Not even a dead leaf stirs before the wind. There is no wind to stir it. But I think the pack will be coming again very soon. They will not leave us until you shoot their demon leader."

"You mean Tandakora's brother! If I get a fair chance I'll certainly send my best arrow at him, and I'm only sorry that it's not Tandakora himself. You persist in your belief that the soul of a wicked warrior is in the body of the wolf?"

"Of course! As I have said, it is surely a brother of Tandakora, because Tandakora himself is alive, and, as it cannot be his own, it must be that of a monstrous one so much like his that it can be only a brother's. That is why the wolf leader is so large, so fierce and so cunning. I persist, too, in saying that all the wolves of this pack contain the souls of wicked warriors. It is natural that they should draw together and hunt together, and hunt men as they hunted them in life."

"I'm not disputing you, Tayoga. Both day and night have more things than I can ever hope to understand, but it seems to me that night has the more. I've been listening so hard, Tayoga, that I can't tell now where imagination ends and reality begins, but I think I hear a footfall, as soft as that of a leaf dropping to the ground, but a footfall just the same."

"I hear it too, Dagaeoga, and it is not the dropping of a leaf. It is a wolf creeping forward, seeking to stalk us. He is on the right, and there are others on both right and left. Now I know they are warriors, or have been, since they use the arts of warriors rather than those of wolves."

"But if they should get in here they would use the teeth and claws of wolves."

"Teeth and claws are no worse than the torch, the faggot and the stake, perhaps better. I hear two sliding wolves now, Dagaeoga, but I know that neither is the giant leader. As before, he keeps under cover, while he sends forward others to the attack."

"Which proves that Tandakora's brother is a real general. I think I can make out a dim outline now. It is that of the first wolf on the right, and he does slide forward as if he were a warrior and not a wolf. I think I'll give him an arrow."

"Wait until he comes a dozen feet nearer, Dagaeoga, and you can be quite sure. But when you do shoot snatch up another arrow quicker than you ever did before in your life, because the leader, thinking you are not ready, may jump from the shelter of the rocks to drive the rest of the pack in a rush upon us."

"You speak as if they were human beings, Tayoga."

"Such is my thought, Dagaeoga."

"Very well. I'll bear in mind what you say, and I'll pick an arrow for Tandakora's brother."

He chose a second arrow carefully and put it on the ledge beside him, where it required but one sweep of his hand to seize it and fit it to the string, when the first had been sent. He now distinctly saw the creeping wolf, and again fancy laid hold of him and played strange tricks with his eyes. The creeping figure changed. It was not that of a wolf, but a warrior, intent upon his life. A strange terror, the terror of the weird and unknown, seized him, but in an instant it passed, and he drew the bowstring. When he loosed it the arrow stood deep in the wolf's throat, but Robert did not see it. His eyes passed on like a flash of lightning to a gigantic form that upreared itself from the rocks, an enormous wolf with red eyes, glistening fangs and slavering jaws.

"Now!" shot forth Tayoga.

Robert had already fitted a second arrow to the string and the immense throat presented a target full and fair. Now, as always in the moment of imminent crisis, his nerves were steady, never had they been more steady, and his eyes pierced the darkness. Never before and never again did he bend so well the bow of Ulysses. The arrow, feathered and barbed, hummed through the air, going as straight and swift as a bullet to its mark, and then it pierced the throat of the wolf so deep that the barb stood out on one side and the feathers on the other.

The wolf uttered a horrible growling shriek that was almost human to Robert, leaped convulsively back and out of sight, but for a minute or two they heard him threshing among the rocks and bushes. The whole pack uttered a dismal howl. Their sliding sounds ceased, and the last dim figure vanished.

"I think it is all over with Tandakora's brother," said Robert.

Tayoga said nothing, and Robert glanced at him. Beads of perspiration stood on the brow of the Onondago, but his eyes glittered.

"You have shot well tonight, O Dagaeoga," he said. "Never did a man shoot better. Tonight you have been the greatest bowman in all the world. You have slain the demon wolf, the leader of the pack. Perhaps the wicked soul that inhabited his body has gone to inhabit the body of another evil brute, but we are delivered. They will not attack again."

"How do you know that, Tayoga?"

"Because Tododaho, Tododaho who protects us, is whispering it to me. I do not see him, but he is leaning down from his star, and his voice enters my ear. Our fight with the wolf pack and its terrible leader is finished. Steady, Dagaeoga! Steady! Make no excuses! The greatest of warriors, the hero of a hundred battles, might well sink for a few moments after such a combat!"

Robert had collapsed suddenly. The great imagination driving forward his will, and attuning him for such swift and tremendous action, failed, now that the crisis had passed, and he dropped back against the ledge, though his fingers still instinctively clutched the bow. Darkness was before his eyes, and he was weak and trembling, but he projected his will anew, and a little later sat upright, collected and firm. Nevertheless, it was Tayoga who now took supreme command.

"You have surely done enough for one night, Dagaeoga," he said. "Tododaho himself, after doing so much, would have rested. Lie down now on your blanket and I will watch for the remainder of the darkness. It is true my left arm is lame and of no use for the present, but nothing will come."

"I'll do as you tell me, Tayoga," said Robert, "but first I give you back your bow and arrows. They've served us well, though I little thought I'd ever have to do work as a bowman."

He was glad enough to stretch himself on the blanket and leaves, as he realized that despite his will he had become weak. Presently he sank into a deep slumber. When he awoke the sun was shining in the mouth of the cave and Tayoga was offering him some of the tenderest of the moose steak.

"Eat, Dagaeoga," he said. "Though a warrior of the clan of the Bear, of the nation Onondaga of the great League of the Hodenosaunee, I am proud to serve the king of bowmen."

"Cease your jesting at my expense, Tayoga."

"It is not wholly a jest, but eat."

"I will. Have you seen what is outside?"

"Not yet. We will take our breakfast together, and then we will go forth to see what we may see."

They ate heartily, and then with rifles cocked passed into the defile, where they found only the bones of wolves, picked clean by the others. But the skeleton of the huge leader was gone, although the arrow that had slain him was lying among the rocks.

"The living must have dragged away his bones. A curious thing to do," said Robert.

Tayoga was silent.

CHAPTER XIII

TANDAKORA'S GRASP

They spent two more days in the cave, and Tayoga's marvelous cure proceeded with the same marvelous rapidity. Robert repeatedly bathed the wound for him, and then redressed it, so the air could not get to it. The Onondaga was soon able to flex the fingers well and then to use the arm a little.

"It is sure now," he said joyfully, "that Waraiyageh and Dieskau cannot meet before I am able to do battle."

"Anyhow, they wouldn't think of fighting until you came, Tayoga," said Robert.

Their spirits were very high. They felt that they had been released from great danger, some of which they could not fathom, and they would soon leave the hollow. Action would bring relief, and they anticipated eagerly what the world outside might disclose to them. Robert collected all the arrows he had shot in the fight with the wolf pack, cleaned them and restored them to the quiver. They also put a plentiful supply of the moose meat in their packs, and then he said:

"Which way, Tayoga?"

"There is but one way."

"You mean we should press on toward Crown Point, and find out what has become of our comrades?"

"That is it. We must know how ended their battle with St. Luc."

"Which entails a search through the forest. That's just what I wanted, but I didn't know how you felt about it with your lame shoulder."

"Tomorrow or next day I shall be able to use the shoulder if we have to fight, but we may not meet any of the French or their allied warriors. I have no wish at all to turn back."

"Then forward it is, Tayoga, and I propose that we go toward the spot where we left them in conflict. Such eyes as yours may yet find there signs that you can read. Then we'll know how to proceed."

"Well spoken, Dagaeoga. Come, we'll go through the forest as fast as we may."

The cave had been a most welcome place. It had served in turn as a home, a hospital and a fort, and, in every capacity, it had served well, but both Robert and Tayoga were intensely glad to be out again in the open world, where the winds were blowing, where vast masses of green rested and pleased the eye, and where the rustling of leaves and the singing of birds soothed the ear.

"It's a wonderful, a noble wilderness!" said Robert. "I'm glad I'm here, even if there are Frenchmen and Indians in it, seeking our lives. Why, Tayoga, I can feel myself growing in such an atmosphere! Tell me, am I not an inch taller than I was when I left that hollow in the rocks?"

"You do look taller," said the Onondaga, "but maybe it's because you stand erect now. Dagaeoga, since the wolves have been defeated, has become proud and haughty again."

"At any rate, your wonderful cure is still going on at wonderful speed. You use your left arm pretty freely and you seem to have back nearly all your old strength."

"Yes, Tododaho still watches over me. He is far better to me than I deserve."

They pushed on at good speed, returning on the path they had taken, when Tayoga received his wound, and though they slept one night on the way, to give Tayoga's wound a further chance, they came in time to the place where the rangers and the Mohawks had met St. Luc's force in combat. The heavy rains long since had wiped out all traces of footsteps there, but Robert hoped that the keen eyes of the Onondaga would find other signs to indicate which way the battle had gone. Tayoga looked a long time before he said anything.

"The battle was very fierce," he said at last. "Our main force lay along here among these bushes."

"How do you know, Tayoga?" asked Robert.

"It is very simple. For a long distance the bushes are shattered and broken. It was rifle balls and musket balls that did it. Indians are not usually good marksmen, and they shot high, cutting off twigs above the heads of the Mohawks and rangers."

"Suppose we look at the opposing ridge and line of bushes where St. Luc's warriors must have stationed themselves."

They crossed the intervening space of sixty or seventy yards and found that the bushes there had not been cut up so much.

"The rangers and Mohawks are the better marksmen," said Tayoga. "They aimed lower and probably hit the target much oftener. At least they did not cut off so many twigs."

He walked back into the open space between the two positions, his eye having been caught by something dark lying in a slight depression of the earth. It was part of the brushy tail of a raccoon, such as the borderers wore in their caps.

"Our men charged," said the Onondaga.

"Why do you say so?" asked Robert.

"Because of the raccoon tail. It was shot from the cap of one of the charging men. The French and the Indians do not wear such a decoration. See where the bullet severed it. I think St. Luc's men must have broken and run before the charge, and we will look for evidence of it."

They advanced in the direction of Champlain, and, two or three hundred yards farther on, Tayoga picked up a portion of an Indian headdress, much bedraggled.

"Their flight was headlong," he said, "or the warrior would not have lost the frame and feathers that he valued so much. It fell then, before the storm, as the muddy and broken condition of the feathers shows that it was lying on the ground when the great rain came."

"And here," said Robert, "is where a bullet went into the trunk of this big oak."

"Which shows that the rangers and Mohawks were still pursuing closely. It is possible that the French and Indians tried to make a brief stand at this place. Let us see if we can find the track of other bullets."

They discovered the paths of two more in tree trunks and saw the boughs of several shattered bushes, all leading in a line toward Crown Point.

"They were not able to stand long," said Tayoga. "Our men rushed them again. Ah, this shows that they must have been in a panic for a few moments."

He picked an Indian blanket, soiled and worn, from a gulley.

"See the mud upon it," he said. "It, too, fell before the rain, because when the flood came a stream ran in the gulley, a stream that has left the blanket in this state. The warrior must have been in tremendous haste to have lost his blanket. We know now that they were routed, and that the victory was ours. But it is likely that our leaders continued the pursuit toward Oneadatote and up to the walls of Crown Point itself. And if your wish be the same as mine, Dagaeoga, we will follow on."

"You know, Tayoga, that I wouldn't think of anything else."

"But the dangers grow thick as we approach Crown Point."

"Not any thicker for me than for you."

"To that I can make no reply. Dagaeoga is always ready with words."

"But while I want to go on, I'm not in favor of taking any needless risks. I like to keep my scalp on top of my head, the place where it belongs, and so I bid you, Tayoga, use those keen eyes and ears of yours to the utmost."

Tayoga laughed.

"Dagaeoga is learning wisdom," he said. "A great warrior does not throw his life away. He will not walk blind through the forest. I will do all I can with my ears and so will you."

"I mean to do so. Do you see that silver flash through the tangle of foliage? Don't you think it comes from the waters of Champlain?"

"It cannot be doubted. Once more we see the great lake, and Crown Point itself is not so many miles away. It is in my mind that Black Rifle, Great Bear, Mountain Wolf, Daganoweda and our men have been scouting about it."

"And we might meet 'em coming back. I've had that thought too."

They walked on toward Champlain, through a forest apparently without sign of danger, and Tayoga, hearing a slight noise in a thicket, turned off to the right to see if a deer were browsing there. He found nothing, but as the sound came again from a point farther on, he continued his search, leaving his comrade out of sight behind him. The thickets were very dense and suddenly the warning of Tododaho came.

He sprang back as quick as lightning, and doubtless he would have escaped had it not been for his wounded shoulder. He hurled off the first warrior who threw himself upon him, slipped from the grasp of a second, but was unable to move when the mighty Tandakora and another seized him by the shoulders.

114

But in the moment of dire peril he remembered his comrade and uttered a long and thrilling cry of warning, which the huge hand of Tandakora could not shut off in time. Then, knowing he was trapped and would only injure his shoulder by further struggles, he ceased to resist, submitting passively to the binding of his arms behind him.

He saw that Tandakora had seven or eight warriors with him, and a half dozen more were bounding out on the trail after Robert. He heard a shot and then another, but he did not hear any yell of triumph, and he drew a long breath of relief. His warning cry had been uttered in time. Dagaeoga would know that it was folly, for him also to fall into the hands of Tandakora, and he would flee at his greatest speed.

So he stood erect with his wrists bound behind him, his face calm and immovable. It did not become an Onondaga taken prisoner to show emotion, or, in fact, feeling of any kind before his captors, but his heart was full of anxiety as he waited with those who held him. A quarter of an hour they stood thus, and then the pursuing warriors, recognizing the vain nature of their quest, began to return. Tandakora did not upbraid them, because he was in high good humor.

"Though the white youth, Lennox, has escaped," he said in Iroquois, "we have done well. We have here Tayoga, of the clan of the Bear, of the nation Onondaga, of the League of the Hodenosaunee, one of our deadliest enemies. It is more than I had hoped, because, though so young, he is a great warrior, skillful and brave, and we shall soon see how he can bear the live coals upon his breast."

Still Tayoga did not move, nor did he visibly shudder at the threat, which he knew Tandakora meant to keep. The Ojibway had never appeared more repellent, as he exulted over his prisoner. He seemed larger than ever, and his naked body was covered with painted and hideous devices.

"And so I have you at last, Tayoga," he said. "Your life shall be short, but your death shall be long, and you shall have full chance to prove how much an Onondaga can bear."

"Whether it be much or little," said Tayoga, "it will be more than any Ojibway can endure."

The black eyes of Tandakora flashed angrily, and he struck Tayoga heavily in the face with his open palm. The Onondaga staggered, but recovered himself, and gazed steadily into the eyes of the Ojibway.

"You have struck a bound captive, O Tandakora," he said. "It is contrary to the customs of your nation and of mine, and for it I shall have your life. It is now written that you shall fall by my hand."

His calm tones, and the fearless gaze with which he met that of Tandakora, gave him all the aspect of a prophet. The huge Ojibway flinched for a moment, and then he laughed.

"If it is written that I am to die by your hand it is written falsely," he said, "because before another sun has set all chance for it will be gone."

"I have said that you will die by my hand, and I say it again. It is written," repeated Tayoga firmly.

Though he showed no emotion there was much mortification in the soul of the young Onondaga. He had practically walked into the hands of Tandakora, and he felt that, for the present, at least, there was a stain upon his skill as a forest runner. The blow of Tandakora had left its mark, too, upon his mind. He had imbibed a part of the Christian doctrine of forgiveness, but it could not apply to so deadly and evil an enemy as the Ojibway. To such an insult offered to a helpless prisoner the reply could be made only with weapons.

115

Although Tododaho from his star, invisible by day, whispered to him to be of good heart, Tayoga was torn by conflicting beliefs. He was going to escape, and yet escape seemed impossible. The last of the warriors who had gone on the trail of young Lennox had come in, and he was surrounded now by more than a dozen stalwart men. The promise of Tododaho grew weak. Although his figure remained firm and upright and his look was calm and brave he saw no possibility of escape. He thought of Daganoweda, of the Mohawks and the rangers, but the presence of Tandakora and his men indicated that they had gone back toward the army of Waraiyageh, and were perhaps with him now.

He thought of St. Luc, but he did not know whether the gallant Chevalier was alive or dead. But if he should come he would certainly keep Tandakora from burning him at the stake. Tayoga did not fear death, and he knew that he could withstand torture. No torture could last forever, and when his soul passed he would merely go to the great shining star on which Tododaho lived, and do to perfection, forever and without satiety, the things that he loved in life here.

But Tayoga did not want to die. As far as life here was concerned he was merely at the beginning of the chapter. So many things were begun and nothing was finished. Nor did he want to die at the hands of Tandakora, and allow his enemy to have a triumph that would always be sweet to the soul of the fierce Ojibway. He saw many reasons why he did not wish yet to go to Tododaho's great and shining star, despite the perfection of an eternal existence there, and, casting away the doubts that had assailed him, he hoped resolutely.

Tandakora had been regarding him with grim satisfaction. It may be that he read some of the thoughts passing in the mind of the Onondaga, as he said:

"You look for your white friends, Tayoga, but you do not see them. Nor will they come. Do you want to know why?"

"Why, Tandakora?"

"Because they are dead. In the battle back there, toward Andiatarocte, Daganoweda, the Mohawk, was slain. His scalp is hanging in the belt of a Pottawattomie who is now with Dieskau. Black Rifle will roam the forest no more. He was killed by my own men, and the wolves have eaten his body. The hunter Willet was taken alive, but he perished at the stake. He was a very strong man, and he burned nearly a whole day before the spirit left him. The ranger, Rogers, whom you called the Mountain Wolf, was killed in the combat, and the wolves have eaten his body, too."

"Now, I know, O Tandakora," said the Onondaga, "that you are a liar, as well as a savage and a murderer. Great Bear lives, Daganoweda lives, and the Mountain Wolf and Black Rifle live, too. St. Luc was defeated in the battle, and he has gone to join Dieskau at Crown Point, else he would be here. I see into your black heart, Tandakora, and I see there nothing but lies."

The eyes of the huge savage once more shot dark fire, and he lifted his hand, but once again he controlled himself, though the taunts of Tayoga had gone in deep and they stung like barbs. Then, feeling that the talk was not in his favor, but that the situation was all to his liking, he turned away and gave orders to his warriors. They formed instantly in single file, Tayoga near the center, Tandakora just behind him, and marched swiftly toward the north.

The Onondaga knew that their course would not bring them to Crown Point, which now lay more toward the east. Nor was it likely that they would go there. Dieskau and the French officers would scarcely allow him to be burned in their camp, and Tandakora would keep away from it until his hideous work was done.

Now Tayoga, despite his cynicism and apparent indifference, was all watchfulness. He knew that, for the present, any attempt to escape was hopeless, but he wished to observe the country through which he was passing, and see everything pertaining to it as far as the eye could reach. It was always well to know where one was, and he had been taught from infancy to observe everything, the practice being one of the important conditions of life in the wilderness.

The soul of Tandakora, who walked just behind him, was full of savage joy. It was true that Lennox had escaped, but Tayoga was an important capture. He was of a powerful family of the Onondagas, whom the Ojibway hated. Despite his youth, his fame as a warrior was already great, and in destroying him Tandakora would strike both at the Hodenosaunee and the white people who were his friends. Truly, it had been the Ojibway's lucky day.

As they went on, Tandakora's belief that it was his day of days became a conviction. Perhaps they would yet find Lennox, who had taken to such swift flight, and before the sun set they could burn the two friends together. His black heart was full of joy as he laughed in silence and to himself. In the forest to his right a bird sang, a sweet, piercing note, and he thought the shoulders of the captive in front of him quivered for a single instant. And well they might quiver! It was a splendid world to leave amid fire and pain, and the sweet, piercing note of the bird would remind Tayoga of all that he was going to lose.

There was no pity in the heart of Tandakora. He was a savage and he could never be anything but a savage. He might admire the fortitude with which Tayoga would endure the torture, but he would have no thought of remitting it on that account. The bird sang again, or another like it, because it was exactly the same sweet, piercing note, but now Tandakora did not see the shoulders of the Onondaga quiver. Doubtless after the first stab of pain that the bird had brought him he had steeled himself to its renewal.

Tandakora would soon see how the Onondaga could stand the fire. The test should be thorough and complete The Ojibway chieftain was a master artist upon such occasions, and, as he continued the march, he thought of many pleasant little ways in which he could try the steel of Tayoga's nature. The captive certainly had shown no signs of shrinking so far, and Tandakora was glad of it. The stronger the resistance the longer and the more interesting would be the test.

The Ojibway had in mind a certain little valley a few miles farther to the north, a secluded place where a leader of men like himself could do as he pleased without fear of interruption. Already he was exulting over the details, and to him, breathing the essence of triumph, the wilderness was as beautiful as it had ever been to Robert and Tayoga, though perhaps in a way that was peculiarly his own. Unlike Tayoga, he had heard little of the outside world, and he cared nothing at all for it. His thoughts never went beyond the forest, and the customs of savage ancestors were his. What he intended to do they had often done, and the tribes thought it right and proper.

"In half an hour, Tayoga, we will be at the place appointed," he said.

No answer.

"You said I would die at your hand, but there is only a half hour left in which to make good the prophecy."

Still no answer.

"Tododaho, the patron saint of the Onondagas, is hidden on his star, which is now on the other side of the world, and he cannot help you."

And still no answer.

"Does not fear strike into your heart, Tayoga? The flames that will burn you are soon to be lighted. You are young, but a boy, you are not a seasoned warrior, and you will not be able to bear it."

117

Tayoga laughed aloud, a laugh full and hearty. "I have heard frogs croak in the muddy edge of a pond," he said. "I could not tell what they meant, but there was as much sense in their voices as in yours, Tandakora."

"At last you have found your tongue, youth of the Onondagas. You have heard the frogs croak, but your voice at the stake will sound like theirs."

"The flames shall not be lighted around me, Tandakora."

"How do you know?"

"Tododaho has whispered in my ear the promise that he will save me. Twice has he whispered it to me as we marched."

"Tododaho in life was no warrior of the Ojibways," said Tandakora, "and since he has passed away he is no god of ours. His whispers, if he has whispered at all to you, are false. There is less than half an hour in which you can be saved, and Manitou himself would need all that time."

Tayoga gave him a scornful look. Tandakora was talking sacrilege, but he had no right to expect anything else from a savage Ojibway. He refused to reply. They came presently to the little valley that Tandakora had in mind, an open place, with a tree in the center, and much dead wood scattered about. Tayoga knew instinctively that this was their destination, and his heart would have sunk within him had it not been for the whispers of Tododaho that he had heard on the march. The Ojibway gave the word and the file of warriors stopped. The hills enclosing the valley were much higher on the right than elsewhere, and touching Tayoga on the arm, he said:

"Walk with me to the crest there."

Tayoga, without a word, walked with him, while the other warriors stood watching, musket or rifle in hand.

The Onondaga, wrists bound behind him, knew that he did not have the slightest chance of escape, even if he made a sudden dash into the woods. He would be shot down before he went a dozen steps, and his pride and will restrained the body that was eager for the trial.

They reached the crest, and Tayoga saw then that the hill itself rose from a high plateau. When he gazed toward the east he saw a vast expanse of green wilderness, beyond it a ribbon of silver, and beyond the silver high green mountains, outlined sharply against a sky of clear blue.

"Oneadatote," said Tandakora.

"Yes, it is the great lake," said Tayoga.

"And if you will turn and look in the other direction you will see where Andiatarocte lies," said Tandakora. "There are greater lakes to the west, some so vast that they are as big as the white man's ocean, but there is none more beautiful than these. Think, Tayoga, that when you stand here upon this hill you have Oneadotote on one side of you and Andiatarocte on the other, and all the country between is splendid, every inch of it. Look! Look your fill, Tayoga! I have brought you here that you might see, that this might be your last sight before you go to your Tododaho on his star."

The Onondaga knew that the Ojibway was taunting him, that the torture had begun, that Tandakora intended to contrast the magnificent world from which he intended to send him with the black death that awaited him so soon. But the dauntless youth appeared not to know.

"The lakes I have seen many times," he said. "They are, as you truly call them, grand and beautiful, and they are the rightful property of the Hodenosaunee, the great League to which my nation belongs. I shall come to see them many more times all through my life, and when I am an old, old man of ninety summers and winters I shall lay myself down on a high shore of Andiatarocte, and close my eyes while Tododaho bears my spirit away to his star."

It is possible that Tandakora's eyes expressed a fleeting admiration. Savage and treacherous as he was, he respected courage, and the Onondaga had not shown the slightest trace of fear. Instead, he spoke calmly of a long life to come, as if the shadow of death were not hovering near at that moment.

"Look again," he said. "Look around all the circle of the world as far as your eyes can reach. It may help you a half hour from now, when you are in the flames, to remember the cool, green forest. And I tell you, too, Tayoga, that your white friend Lennox, the one whom you call Dagaeoga, shall soon follow you into the other world and by the same flaming path. When you are but ashes, which will be by the setting of the sun, my warriors will take up his trail, and he cannot escape us."

"Dagaeoga will live long, even as I do," said Tayoga calmly. "His summers and winters will be ninety each, even as mine. Tododaho has whispered that to me also, and the whispers of Tododaho are never false."

Tandakora turned back toward the valley, motioning to his captive to descend, and Tayoga obeyed without resistance. The glen was secluded, just suited to his purpose, which required time, and he did not wish the Frenchman, St. Luc, to come upon him suddenly, and interfere with the pleasure that he anticipated.

He was quite sure that the forest was empty of everything save themselves, though he heard again and for the third time the note of the bird, piercing and sweet, trilling among the bushes.

The warriors, knowing what was to be done, were doing it already, having piled many pieces of dead wood around the trunk of the lone tree in the center of the opening. Two had cut shavings with their hunting knives, and one stood ready with flint and steel.

"Do you not tremble, Tayoga?" asked the Ojibway. "Many an old and seasoned warrior has not been able to endure the fire without a groan."

"You shall not hear any groan from me," replied Tayoga, "because I shall not stand among the flames."

"There is no way to escape them. Even now the pile is built, and the warrior is ready with flint and steel to make the sparks."

High, thrillingly sweet, came the voice of the bird in the bushes, and Tayoga suddenly leaped with all his might against the great chest of Tandakora. Vast as was the strength of the Ojibway he was thrown from his feet by the violent and unexpected impact, and as he fell Tayoga, leaping lightly away, ran like a deer through the bushes.

The warriors in the valley uttered a shout, but the reply was a shattering volley, before which half of them fell. Tandakora understood at once. If he had the mind and heart of a savage he had also all the craft and cunning of one whose life was incessantly in danger. Instead of springing up, he rolled from the crest of the hill, then, rising to a stooping position, darted away at incredible speed through the forest.

Rangers and Mohawks, Robert, Daganoweda, Willet, Black Rifle and Rogers at their head, burst into the glen and the Mohawks began the pursuit of Tandakora's surviving warriors, who had followed their leader in his flight. But Robert turned back to meet Tayoga and cut the thongs from his wrists.

"I thank you, Dagaeoga," said the Onondaga. "You came in time."

"Yes, they were making ready. A half hour more and we should have been too late. But you knew that we were coming, Tayoga?"

"Yes. I heard the bird sing thrice, but I knew the bird was in the throat of the Great Bear. I will say this, though, to you, Dagaeoga, that I have heard many birds sing and sing sweetly, but never any so sweetly as the one that sang thrice in the throat of the Great Bear."

"It is not hard for me to believe you," said Robert, smiling, "and I can tell you in turn, Tayoga, that your patron saint, Tododaho, must in very truth have watched over you, because when I heard your warning cry and took to flight, hoping for a chance later on to rescue you, I ran within two hours straight into the camp of the rangers and the Mohawks. You can easily surmise how glad I was to see them, and how quickly we followed Tandakora."

"And we'd have attacked sooner," said Willet, "but we could not get up all our force in time. We've annihilated this band, but I'm sure we did not get Tandakora. He fled like the wind, and we'll have to settle accounts with him some other day."

"It was not possible for Tandakora to fall before your arms today," said Tayoga.

"Why not?" asked Willet, curiously.

"It is reserved for him to die by my hand, though the time is yet far off. I know it, because Tododaho whispered it to me more than once today. Let him go now, but his hour will surely come."

"You may be right, Tayoga. I'm not one to question your prophecies, but it's not wise for us to continue the pursuit of him, as we've other things to do. We destroyed the forces of St. Luc in the battle, but he escaped with some of his men to Crown Point, and there are still Indian warriors in the forest, though we mean to continue skirmishing and scouting up to the walls of Crown Point, or until we meet Dieskau's army on the march."

Words of approval came from the fierce Daganoweda, who stood by, listening. The young Mohawk chieftain, in the midst of a great and terrible war, was living the life he loved. The Keepers of the Eastern Gate were taking revenge for Quebec, their lost Stadacona, and he and his warriors could boast already of more than one victory. Around him, too, stood the white allies whom he respected and admired most, Black Rifle, Willet, Rogers and Dagaeoga, the youth of golden speech. Willet, looking at him, read his mind.

"What do you say, Daganoweda?" he asked. "Now that Tayoga and Dagaeoga have been recovered, shall we go back and join the army of Waraiyageh, or shall we knock on the walls of Crown Point?"

"The time to turn back has not yet come," replied the Mohawk. "We must know all about the army of Dieskau before we return to Waraiyageh."

Willet laughed.

"I knew that would be your reply," he said. "I merely asked in order to hear you speak the words. As I've said already, it's in my mind to go on toward Crown Point, and I know Rogers feels that way too. But I think we'd first better rest and refresh ourselves a bit. Although Tayoga won't admit it, food and an hour or two of ease here in the very valley where they meant to burn him alive, will do him a power of good."

After throwing out competent sentinels, they lighted a fire by the very tree to which Tandakora meant to bind Tayoga for the flames, and broiled venison over the coals. They also had bread and samp, which were most welcome, and the whole force ate with great zest. The warriors, in their flight, had dropped Tayoga's bow and quiver of arrows, and their recovery gave him keen delight, though he said little as he strapped them over his shoulder.

They spent two hours in the valley, and for the Onondaga the air was full of the good spirits that watched over him. The dramatic and extraordinary change, occurring in a few minutes, made an ineffaceable impression upon a mind that saw meaning in everything.

Here was the glen in which he had been held by Tandakora and his most deadly enemies, and there was the lone tree against which they had already heaped the fuel for burning him alive. Such a sudden and marvelous change could not have come if he were not in the special favor of both Tododaho and Areskoui. Secure in his belief that he was protected by the mighty on their stars, he awaited the future with supreme confidence.

CHAPTER XIV

SHARP SWORD

The rangers and Mohawks had suffered a further thinning in the last conflict with St. Luc, but they were still a formidable body, not so much through numbers as through skill, experience, courage and quality of leadership. There was not one among them who was not eager to advance toward Crown Point and hazard every peril. But they were too wise in wilderness ways not to have a long and anxious council before they started, as there was nothing to be gained and much to be lost by throwing away lives in reckless attempts.

They decided at last on a wide curve to the west, in order that they might approach Crown Point from the north, where they would be least suspected, and they decided also that they would make most of the journey by night, when they would be better hidden from wandering warriors. So concluding, they remained in the glen much longer than they had intended, and the delay was welcome to Robert, whose nervous system needed much restoration, after the tremendous exertions, the hopes and fears of recent days.

But he was able to imitate the Onondaga calm. He spread his blanket on the turf, lay down upon it, and lowered his eyelids. He had no intention of going to sleep, but he put himself into that drowsy state of calm akin to the Hindoo's Nirvana. By an effort of the will he calmed every nerve and refused to think of the future. He merely breathed, and saw in a dim way the things about him, compelling his soul to stay a while in peace.

Most of the rangers and Mohawks were lying in the same stillness. Stern experience had taught them to take rest, and make the most of it when they could find it. Only the watchful sentinels at the rim of the valley and beyond stirred, and their moccasins made no sound as they slid among the bushes, looking and listening with all their eyes and ears for whatever might come.

The sun was sunk far in the western heavens, tinting with gold the surface of both lakes, for the rulership of which the nations fought, and outlining the mountains, crests and ridges, sharp and clear against a sky of amazing blue. Yet so vast was the wilderness and so little had it been touched by man, that the armies were completely hidden in it, and neither Dieskau nor Johnson yet knew what movement the other intended.

The east was already dim with the coming twilight when the three leaders stood up, and, as if by preconcerted signal, beckoned to their men. Scarcely a word was spoken, but everyone looked to his arms, the sentinels came in, and the whole force, now in double file, marched swiftly toward the north, but inclining also to the east. Robert and Tayoga were side by side.

"I owe thee many thanks, Dagaeoga," said the Onondaga.

"You owe me nothing," said Robert. "I but paid an installment on a debt."

Then they spoke no more for a long time, because there was nothing to say, and because the band was now moving so fast that all their breath was needed for muscular effort. The sun went down in a sea of golden clouds, then red fire burned for a little while at the rim of the world, and, when it was gone, a luminous twilight, which by and by faded into darkness, came in its place.

But the band in double file sped on through the dusk. Daganoweda, who knew the way, was at the head, and so skillful were they that no stick crackled and no leaf rustled as they passed. Mile after mile they flitted on, over hill and valley and through the deep woods. Far in the night they stopped to drink at a clear little brook that ran down to Lake Champlain, but no other halt was made until the dawn broke over a vast silver sheet of water, and high green mountains beyond.

"Oneadatote," said Tayoga.

"And a great lake it is," said Robert. "We had a naval encounter on it once, and now we've had a battle, too, on George."

"But the French and their allies hold all of Oneadatote, while we only dispute the possession of Andiatarocte. They will march against us from Crown Point on the shores of this lake."

"We'll take George from 'em, all of it, and then we'll come and drive 'em from Champlain, too."

The eyes of the Onondaga sparkled.

"Dagaeoga has a brave heart," he said, "and we will do all that he predicts, but, as I have said before, it will be a long and terrible war."

They descended to a point nearer the lake, but, still remaining hidden in the dense forest, ate their breakfast of venison, bread and samp, and drank again from a clear brook. They were now several miles north of Crown Point, and the leaders talked together again about the best manner of approach. They not only wished to see what the army of Dieskau was doing, but they thought it possible to strike some blow that would inflict severe loss, and delay his advance. Rogers used his glasses again, and was able to discern many Indian canoes on the lake, both north and south of the point where they lay, although they were mostly scattered, indicating no certain movement.

"Those canoes ought to be ours," he said. "'Tis a great pity that we've let the French take control of Champlain. It's easier to hold a thing in the beginning than it is, having let your enemy seize it without a fight, to win it back again."

"It's better to do that than to be rash," said Willet. "I was with Braddock when we marched headlong into the wilderness. If we had been slower then we'd have now a good army that we've lost. Still, it's hard to see the French take the lead from us. We dance to their tune."

"Dave," said Rogers, "I see a whole fleet of Indian canoes far down the lake below Crown Point. One can see many miles in such a clear air as this, and I'm sure they're canoes, though they look like black dots crawling on the water. Take the glasses and have a look."

Willet held the glasses to his eyes a long time, and when he took them down he said with confidence:

"They're canoes, a hundred of 'em at least, and while they hold complete command of the lake, it don't seem natural that so many of 'em should be in a fleet away down there below the French fort. It means something unusual. What do you think, Tayoga?"

"Perhaps Dieskau is already on the march," said the Onondaga. "The glories that St. Luc, Dumas, Ligneris and the others won at Duquesne will not let him sleep. He would surpass them. He would repeat on the shores of Andiatarocte what they did so triumphantly by the ford of the Monongahela."

"Thunderation!" exclaimed Rogers. "The boy may be right! They may be even now stealing a march on us! If our army down below should be wiped out as Braddock's was, then we might never recover!"

Robert, who could not keep from hearing all the talk, listened to it with dismay. He had visions of Johnson's army of untrained militia attacked suddenly by French veterans and a huge force of Indians. It would be like the spring of a monstrous beast out of the dark, and defeat, perhaps complete destruction for his own, would be the result. But his courage came back in an instant. The surprise could not be carried out so long as the band to which he belonged was in existence.

"I think," said Willet, "that we'd better go south along the shore of the lake, and approach as near to the fort as we dare. Then Daganoweda and a half dozen of his best warriors will scout under its very walls. Do you care for the task, Daganoweda?"

The eyes of the young Mohawk chieftain glittered. Willet had judged him aright. It would be no task for him, it would be instead a labor of pleasure. In fifteen minutes he was off with his warriors, disappearing like shadows in the undergrowth, and Robert knew that whatever report Daganoweda might bring back it would not only be true but full.

The main band followed, though far more slowly, keeping well back from the lake, that no Indian eye might catch their presence in the woods, but able, nevertheless, to observe for immense distances everything that passed on the vast silver sheet of water. Rogers observed once more the fleet of Indian canoes rowing southward, and he and Willet were firmer than ever in their belief that it indicated some measure of importance.

Their own march through the woods was peaceful. They frightened no game from their path, indicating that the entire region had been hunted over thoroughly by the great force that had lain at Crown Point, and, after a while, they passed a point parallel to the fort, though several miles to the westward. Willet, Tayoga and Robert looked for trails or traces of bands or hunters, but found none. Apparently the forest had been deserted by the enemy for some days, and their alarming belief was strengthened anew.

Four miles farther on they were to meet Daganoweda and his warriors, at a tiny silver pond among the hills, and now they hurried their march.

"I'm thinking," said Robert, "that Daganoweda will be there first, waiting with a tale to tell."

"All signs point to it," said Tayoga. "It is well that we came north on this scouting expedition, because we, too, may have something to say when we return to Waraiyageh."

"You know this pond at which we are to meet?"

"Yes, it is in the hills, and the forest is thick all about it. Often Onondaga and Mohawk have met there to take council, the one with the other."

In another hour they were at the pond, and they found the Mohawk chieftain and his men sitting at its edge.

"Well, Daganoweda," said Willet, "is it as we thought?" Daganoweda rose and waved his hand significantly toward the south.

"Dieskau with his army has gone to fall upon Waraiyageh," he said. "We went close up to the walls, and we even heard talk. The French and the warriors were eager to advance, and so were their leaders. It was said that St. Luc, whom we call Sharp Sword, urged them most, and the larger part of his great force soon started in canoes. A portion of it he left at Ticonderoga, and the rest is going on. They intend to take the fort called Lyman, that the English and Americans have built, and then to fall upon Waraiyageh."

"It is for us to reach Waraiyageh first," said Willet, quietly, "and we will. God knows there is great need of our doing it. If Johnson's army is swept away, then Albany will fall, the Hodenosaunee, under terrific pressure, might be induced to turn against us, and the Province of New York would be ravaged with fire and the scalping knife."

"But we will reach Waraiyageh and tell him," said Tayoga, firmly. "He will not be swept away. Albany will not fall, and nothing can induce the Hodenosaunee to join the French."

The eyes of the Great Bear glistened as he looked at the tall young warrior.

"That's brave talk, and it's true, too!" he exclaimed. "You shame us, Tayoga! If it's for us to save our army by carrying the news of Dieskau's sudden march, then we'll save it."

Daganoweda had told the exact truth. Dieskau had reached Crown Point with a force mighty then for the wilderness, and, after a short rest, he issued orders to his troops to be prepared for advance at a moment's notice. He especially directed the officers to keep themselves in light marching order, every one of them to take only a bearskin, a blanket, one extra pair of shoes, one extra shirt, and no luxuries at all.

His orders to the Indians showed a savagery which, unfortunately, was not peculiar then to him. In the heat of battle they were not to scalp those they slew, because time then was so valuable. While they were taking a scalp they could kill ten men. But when the enemy was routed completely they could go back on the field and scalp as they wished.

The Indian horde was commanded by Legardeur de St. Pierre, who had with him De Courcelles and Jumonville, and St. Luc with his faithful Dubois immediately organized a daring band of French Canadians and warriors to take the place of the one he had lost. So great was his reputation as a forest fighter, and so well deserved was it, that his fame suffered no diminution, because of his defeat by the rangers and Mohawks, and the young French officers were eager to serve under him.

It was this powerful army, ably led and flushed with the general triumph of the French arms, that Daganoweda and his warriors had seen advancing, though perhaps no one in all the force dreamed that he was advancing to a battle that in reality would prove one of the most decisive in the world's history, heavy with consequences to which time set scarcely any limit. Nor did Robert himself, vivid as was his imagination, foresee it. His thoughts and energies were bounded for the time, at least, by the present, and, with the others, he was eager to save Johnson's army, which now lay somewhere near Lake George, and which he was sure had been occupied in building forts, as Waraiyageh, having spent most of his life in the wilderness, knew that it was well when he had finished a march forward to make it secure before he undertook another.

The rangers and Mohawks now picked up the trail of Dieskau's army, which was moving forward with the utmost speed. Yet the obstinacy of his Indian allies compelled the German baron to abandon the first step in his plan. They would not attack Fort Lyman, as it was defended by artillery, of which the savages had a great dread, but they were willing to go on, and fall suddenly upon Johnson, who, they heard, though falsely, had no cannon. Dieskau and his French aides, compelled to hide any chagrin they may have felt, pushed on for Lake George with the pick of their army, consisting of the battalions of Languedoc, and La Reine, a strong Canadian force, and a much larger body of Indian warriors, among whom the redoubtable Tandakora, escaped from rangers and Mohawks, was predominant.

Willet, Rogers, Black Rifle, Daganoweda and their small but formidable band read the trail plainly, and they knew the greatness of the danger. Dieskau was not young, and he was a soldier of fortune, not belonging to the race that he led, but he was full of ardor, and the daring French partisans were urging him on. Robert felt certain that St. Luc himself was in the very van and that he would probably strike the first blow.

124

After they had made sure that Dieskau would not attack Fort Lyman, but was marching straight against Johnson, the little force turned aside, and prepared to make a circuit with all the speed it could command.

As Willet put it tersely:

"It's not enough for us to know what Dieskau means to do, but to keep him from doing it. It's muscle and lungs now that count."

So they deserved to the full the name of forest runners, speeding on their great curve, using the long, running walk with which both Indians and frontiersmen devoured space, and apparently never grew weary. In the night they passed Dieskau's army, and, from the crest of a lofty hill, saw his fires burning in a valley below. Tayoga and some of the Mohawks slipped down through the undergrowth and reported that the camp had been made with all due precaution—the French partisan leaders saw to that—with plenty of scouts about, and the whole force in swift, marching order. It would probably be up and away again before dawn, and if they were to pass it and reach Johnson in good time not a single moment could be wasted.

"Now I wonder," said Willet, "if they suspect the advance of this warning force. St. Luc, of course, knows that we were back there by Champlain, as we gave him the most complete proofs of it that human beings could give. So does Tandakora, and they may prevail upon Dieskau to throw out a swift band for the purpose of cutting us off. If so, St. Luc is sure to lead it. What do you say, Tayoga?"

"I think St. Luc will surely come," replied the Onondaga youth gravely. "We have been trailing the army of Dieskau, and tomorrow, after we have passed it, we shall be trailed in our turn. It does not need the whisper of Tododaho to tell me that St. Luc and Tandakora will lead the trailers, because, as we all know, they are most fitting to lead them."

"Then there's no sleep for us tonight," said Rogers; "we'll push on and not close our eyes again until we reach Colonel Johnson."

They traveled many miles before dawn, but with the rising of the sun they knew that they were followed, and perhaps flanked. The Mohawk scouts brought word of it. Daganoweda himself found hostile signs in the bushes, a bead or two and a strand of deerskin fringe caught on a bush.

"It's likely," said Willet, "that they were even more cautious than we reckoned. It may be that before Dieskau left his force at Ticonderoga he sent forward St. Luc with a swift band to intercept us and any others who might take a warning to Colonel Johnson."

"I agree with you," said Rogers. "St. Luc started before we did, and, all the time, has been ahead of us. So we have him in front, Dieskau behind, and it looks as if we'd have to fight our way through to our army. Oh, the Frenchmen are clever! Nobody can deny it, and they're always awake. What's your opinion, Daganoweda?"

"We shall have to fight," replied the Mohawk chieftain, although the prospect caused him no grief. "The traces that we have found prove Sharp Sword to be already across our path. We have yet no way to know the strength of his force, but, if a part of us get through, it will be enough."

Robert heard them talking, and while he was able once more to preserve outward calm, his heart, nevertheless, throbbed hard. More than any other present, with the possible exception of Tayoga, his imagination pictured what was to come, and before it was fought he saw the battle. They were to march, too, into an ambush, knowing it was there, but impossible to be avoided, because they must get through in some fashion or other. They were now approaching Andiatarocte again, and although the need of haste was still great they dropped perforce into a slow walk, and sent ahead more scouts and skirmishers.

Robert and Tayoga went forward on the right, and they caught through the bushes the gleam from the waters of a small stream that ran down to the lake. Going a little nearer, they saw that the farther bank was high and densely wooded, and then they drew back, knowing that it was a splendid place for an ambush, and believing that St. Luc was probably there. Tayoga lay almost flat, face downward, and stared intently at the high bank.

"I think, Dagaeoga," he said, "that so long as we keep close to the earth we may creep a little nearer, and perhaps our eyes, which are good, may be able to pick out the figures of our foes from the leaves and bushes in which they probably lie hidden."

They dragged themselves forward about fifty yards, taking particular care to make nothing in the thickets bend or wave in a manner for which the wind could not account. Robert stared a long time, but his eyes separated nothing from the mass of foliage.

"What do you see, Tayoga?" he whispered at last.

"No proof of the enemy yet, Dagaeoga. At least, no proof of which I am sure. Ah, but I do now! There was a flash in the bushes. It was a ray of sunlight penetrating the leaves and striking upon the polished metal of a gun barrel."

"It means that at least one Indian or Frenchman is there. Keep on looking and see if you don't see something more."

"I see a red feather. At this distance you might at first take it for a feather in the wing of a bird, but I know it is a feather in the scalplock of a warrior."

"And that makes two, at least. Look harder than ever, Tayoga, and tell me what more you see."

"Now I catch a glimpse of white cloth with a gleam of silver. The cloth is on the upper arm, and the silver is on the shoulder of an officer."

"A uniform and an epaulet. A French officer, of course."

"Of course, and I think it is Sharp Sword himself."

"Look once more, Tayoga, and maybe your eyes can pick out something else from the foliage."

"I see the back and painted shoulder of a warrior. It may be those of Tandakora, but I cannot be sure."

"You needn't be. You've seen quite enough to prove that the whole force of St. Luc is there in the bushes, awaiting us, and we must tell our leaders at once."

They crept back to the center, where Willet and Rogers lay, Daganoweda being on the flank, and told them what they had seen.

"It's good enough proof," said Rogers. "St. Luc with his whole force in the bushes means to hold the stream against us and keep us from taking a warning to Johnson, but the hardest way to do a thing isn't always the one you have to choose."

"I take it," said Willet, "that you mean to flank him out of his position."

"It was what I had in mind. What do you think, Dave?"

"The only possible method. Those Mohawks are wonders at such operations, and we'd better detail as many of the rangers as we can spare to join 'em, while a force here in the center makes a demonstration that will hold 'em to their place in the bushes. I'll take the picked men and join Daganoweda."

Rogers laughed.

"It's like you, Dave," he said, "to choose the most dangerous part, and leave me here just to make a noise."

"But the commander usually stays in the center, while his lieutenants lead on the wings."

"That's true. You have precedent with you, but it wouldn't have made any difference, anyhow."

"But when we fall on 'em you'll lead the center forward, and with such a man as St. Luc I fancy you'll have all the danger you crave."

Rogers laughed again.

"Go ahead, old fire-eater," he said. "It was always your way. I suppose you'll want to take Tayoga and Lennox with you."

"Oh, yes, I need 'em, and besides, I have to watch over 'em, in a way."

"And you watch over 'em by leading 'em into the very thickest of the battle. But danger has always been a lure for you, and I know you're the best man for the job."

Willet quickly picked twenty men, including Black Rifle and the two lads, and bore away with speed toward the flank where Daganoweda and the Mohawks already lay. As Robert left he heard the rifle shots with which the little force of Rogers was opening the battle, and he heard, too, the rifles and muskets of the French and Indians on the other side of the stream replying.

Fortunately, as the forest was very dense, and it was not possible for any of St. Luc's men to see the flanking movement, Willet and his rangers joined Daganoweda quickly and without hindrance, the eyes of the chieftain glittering when he saw the new force, and heard the plan to cross the stream far down and fall on St. Luc's flank.

"It is good," he said with satisfaction. "Sharp Sword has eyes to see much, but he cannot see everything."

"But one thing must be understood," said Willet, gravely. "If we see that we are getting the worst of the fight and our men are falling fast, the good runners must leave the conflict at once and make all speed for Waraiyageh. Tayoga, you are the fastest and surest of all, and you must leave first, and, Daganoweda, do you pick three of your swift young warriors for the same task."

"I have one request to make," said Tayoga.

"What is it?"

"When I leave let me take Dagaeoga with me. We are comrades who have shared many dangers, and he, too, is swift of foot and hardy. It may be that there will be danger also in the flight to Waraiyageh's camp. Then, if one should fall the other will go on."

"Well put, Tayoga. Robert, do you hear? If the tide seems to be turning against us join Tayoga in his flight toward Johnson."

Robert nodded, and the young warriors chosen by Daganoweda also indicated that they understood. Then the entire force began its silent march through the woods on their perilous encircling movement. They waded the river at a ford where the water did not rise above their knees, and entered the deep woods, gradually drawing back toward the point where St. Luc's force lay.

As they approached they began to hear the sounds of the little battle Rogers was waging with the French leader, a combat which was intended to keep the faculties and energies of the French and Indians busy, while the more powerful detachment under Willet and Daganoweda moved up for the main blow. Faint reports of rifle and musket shots came to them, and also the long whining yell of the Indians, so like, in the distance, to the cry of a wolf. Then, as they drew a little nearer they heard the shouts of the rangers, shouts of defiance or of triumph rattling continuously like a volley.

"That's a part of their duty," said Willet. "Rogers has only twenty men, but he means to make 'em appear a hundred."

"Sounds more like two hundred," said Robert. "It's the first time I ever heard one man shout as ten."

As they drew nearer the volume of the firing seemed to increase. Rogers was certainly carrying out his part of the work in the most admirable manner, his men firing with great rapidity and never ceasing their battle shouts. Even so shrewd a leader as St. Luc might well believe the entire force of rangers and Mohawks, instead of only twenty men, was in front of him. But Robert was quite sure from the amount of firing coming from the Frenchman's position that he was in formidable force, perhaps outnumbering his opponents two to one, and the fight, though with the advantage of a flank attack by Willet and Daganoweda, was sure to be doubtful. It seemed that Tayoga read his thought as he whispered:

"Once more, Dagaeoga, we may leave the combat together, when it is at its height. Remember the duty that has been laid upon us. If the battle appears doubtful we are to flee."

"A hard thing to do at such a time."

"But we have our orders from the Great Bear."

"I had no thought of disobeying. I know the importance of our getting through, if our force is defeated, or even held. Why couldn't our whole detachment have gone around St. Luc just as we've done, and have left him behind without a fight?"

"Because if the Mountain Wolf had not been left in his front, Sharp Sword would have discovered immediately the absence of us all and would have followed so fast that he would have forced us to battle on his terms, instead of our being able to force him on ours."

"I see, Tayoga. Look out!"

He seized the Onondaga suddenly and pulled him down. A rifle cracked in the bushes sixty or seventy yards in front of them, and a bullet whistled where the red youth's head had been. The shot came from an outlying sentinel of St. Luc's band, and knowing now that the time for a hidden advance had passed, Willet and all of his men charged with a mighty shout.

Their cheering also was a signal to the twenty men of Rogers on the other side of the river, and they, too, rushed forward. St. Luc was taken by surprise, but, as Robert had feared, his French and Indians outnumbered them two to one. They fell back a little, thus giving Rogers and his twenty a chance to cross the river, but they took up a new and strong position upon a well-wooded hill, and the battle at close range became fierce, sanguinary and doubtful.

Robert caught two glimpses of St. Luc directing his men with movements of his small sword, and once he saw another white man, who, he was sure was Dubois, although generally the enemy was invisible, keeping well under the shelter of tree and bush. But while human forms were hidden, the evidences of ferocious battle were numerous. The warriors on each side uttered fierce shouts, rifles and muskets crackled rapidly, now and then a stricken man uttered his death cry, and the depths of the forest were illuminated by the rapid jets of the firing.

The sudden and heavy attack upon his flank compelled St. Luc to take the defensive, and put him at a certain disadvantage, but he marshaled his superior numbers so well that the battle became doubtful, with every evidence that it would be drawn out to great length. Moreover, the chevalier had maneuvered so artfully that his whole force was now drawn directly across the path of the rangers and Mohawks, and the way to Johnson was closed, for the time, at least.

An hour, two hours, the battle swayed to and fro among the trees and bushes. Had their opponent been any other than St. Luc the three leaders, Willet, Rogers and Daganoweda, would have triumphed by that time, but French, Canadians and Indians alike drew courage from the dauntless Chevalier. More than once they would have abandoned the field, but he marshaled them anew, and always he did it in a manner so skillful that the loss was kept at the lowest possible figure.

The forest was filled with smoke, though the high sun shot it through with luminous rays. But no one looking upon the battle could have told which was the loser and which the winner. The losses on the two sides were about equal, and St. Luc, holding the hill, still lay across the path of rangers and Mohawks. Robert, who was crouched behind the trunk of a great oak, felt a light touch upon his arm, and, looking back, saw Tayoga.

"The time has come, Dagaeoga," said the Onondaga.

"What time?"

"The time for us to leave the battle and run as fast as we may to Waraiyageh."

"I had forgotten. The conflict here had gotten so much into my blood that I couldn't think of anything else. But, as I said it would be, it's hard to go."

"Go, Robert!" called Willet from a tree twenty feet away. "Curve around St. Luc. Do what Tayoga says—he can scent danger like an animal of the forest—and make all speed to Johnson. Maybe we'll join you in his camp later on."

"Good-by, Dave," said Robert, swallowing hard. He crept away with the Onondaga, not rising to his full height for a long time. Then the two stood for a few moments, listening to the sounds of the battle, which seemed to be increasing in violence. Far through the forest they faintly saw the drifting smoke and the sparks of fire from the rifles and muskets.

"Once more I say it's hard to leave our friends there," exclaimed Robert.

"But our path leads that way," said Tayoga, pointing southward.

They struck, without another word, into the long, loping run that the forest runners use with such effect, and sped southward. The sounds of the conflict soon died behind them, and they were in the stillness of the woods, where no enemy seemed near. But they did not decrease their pace, leaping the little brooks, wading the wider streams, and flitting like shades through forest and thicket. Twice they crossed Indian trails, but paid no heed to them. Once a warrior, perhaps a hunter, fired a long shot at them, but as his bullet missed they paid no attention to him, but, increasing their speed, fled southward at a pace no ordinary man could overtake.

"Now that we have left," said Robert, after a while, "I'm glad we did so. It will be a personal pleasure for us two to warn Johnson."

"We may carry the fate of a war with us, Dagaeoga. Think of that!"

"I've thought of it. But our friends behind us, engaged in the battle with St. Luc! What of them? Does Tododaho whisper to you anything about their fate?"

"They are great and skillful men, cunning and crafty in all the ways of the forest. They have escaped great dangers a thousand times before and Tododaho tells me they will escape the thousand and first. Be of good heart, Dagaeoga, and do not worry about them."

They dropped almost to a walk for a while, permitting their muscles to rest. Tayoga's wound had healed so fast, the miracle was so nearly complete, that it did not trouble him, and, after walking two hours, they struck into the long, easy run again. The miles dropped fast behind them, and now Johnson's camp was not far away. It was well for Tayoga and Robert that they were naturally so strong and that they had lived such healthy lives, as now they were able to go on all through the day, and the setting sun found them still traveling, the Onondaga leading with an eye as infallible for the way as that of a bird in the heavens. Some time after dark they stopped for a half hour and sat on fallen logs while they took fresh breath. Robert was apprehensive about Tayoga's wound and expressed his solicitude.

"There is no pain," replied the young warrior, "and there will be none. Tododaho and Areskoui gave me the miraculous cure for a purpose. It was that I might have the strength to be a messenger to Waraiyageh, because if he is crushed then the French and the Indians will strike at the Hodenosaunee, and they will ravage the Vale of Onondaga itself with fire and the tomahawk. Tododaho watches over his people."

"The stars have come out, Tayoga. Can you see the one on which Tododaho lives? And if so, what is he saying to you now?"

Tayoga looked up a long time. He had received the white man's culture, but the Indian soul was strong within him, nevertheless, and he was steeped, too, in Indian lore. All the legends of his race, all the Iroquois religion, came crowding upon him. A faint silvery vapor overspread the sky, the stars in myriads quivered and danced, and there in a remote corner of space was the great star on which Tododaho lived. It hung in the heavens a silver shield, small in the distance, but vast, Tayoga knew, beyond all conception. There were fine lines across its face, but they were only the snakes in Tododaho's hair.

Gradually the features and countenance of the great Onondaga emerged upon the star, and the blood of Tayoga ran in a chill torrent through his veins, though the chill was not the chill of fear. He was, in effect, meeting the mighty Onondaga of four hundred years ago, face to face. The forest around him glided away, Robert vanished, the solid earth melted from under his feet, and he was like a being who hung in the air suspended from nothing. He leaned his head forward a little in the attitude of one who listens, and he distinctly heard Tododaho say:

"Go on, Tayoga. As I have protected you so far on the way I shall protect you to the end. Four hundred years ago I left my people, but my watch over them is as vigilant now as it was when I was on earth. The nations of the Hodenosaunee shall not perish, and they shall remain great and mighty."

The voice ceased, the face of the mighty Onondaga disappeared, Tayoga was no longer suspended without a support in the air, the forest came back, and his good comrade, Robert Lennox, stood by his side, staring at him curiously.

"Have you been in a trance, Tayoga?" asked Robert.

"No, Dagaeoga, I have not, but I can answer your question. I not only heard Tododaho, but I saw him face to face. He spoke to me in a voice like the wind among the pines, and he said that he would watch over me the rest of the way, and that the Hodenosaunee should remain great and powerful. Come, Dagaeoga, all danger for us on this march has passed."

They rose, continued their flight without hindrance, and the next morning entered the camp of Johnson.

CHAPTER XV

THE LAKE BATTLE

Robert and Tayoga approached the American camp in the early dawn of a waning summer, and the air was crisp and cool. The Onondaga's shoulder, at last, had begun to feel the effects of his long flight, and he, as well as Robert, was growing weary. Hence it was with great delight that they caught the gleam of a uniform through a thicket, and knew they had come upon one of Johnson's patrols. It was with still greater delight as they advanced that they recognized young William Wilton of the Philadelphia troop, and a dozen men. Wilton looked wan and hollow-eyed, as if he had been watching all night, but his countenance was alert, and his figure erect nevertheless.

Hearing the steps of Tayoga and Robert in the bushes, he called sharply:

"Who's there?"

His men presented their arms, and he stepped forward, sword in hand. Robert threw up his own hands, and, emerging from the thicket, said in tones which he made purposely calm and even.

"Good morning, Will. It's happy I am to see you keeping such a good watch."

Then he dropped his hands and walked into the open, Tayoga following him. Wilton stared as if he had seen someone come back from another star.

"Lennox, is it really you?" he asked.

"Nobody else."

"You in the flesh and not a ghost?"

"In the flesh and no ghost."

"And is that Tayoga following you?"

"The Onondaga himself."

"And he is not any ghost, either?"

"No ghost, though Tandakora's men tried hard to make him one, and took a good start at it. But he's wholly in the flesh, too."

"Then shake. I was afraid, at first, to touch hands with a ghost, but, God bless you, Robert, it fills me with delight to see you again, and you, too, Tayoga, no less. We thought you both were dead, and Colden and Carson and Grosvenor and I and a lot of others have wasted a lot of good mourning on you."

Robert laughed, and it was probably a nervous laugh of relief at having arrived, through countless dangers, upon an errand of such huge importance.

"Both of you look worn out," said Wilton. "I dare say you've been up all night, walking through the interminable forest. Come, have a good, fat breakfast, then roll between the blankets and sleep all day long."

Robert laughed again. How little the young Quaker knew or suspected!

"We neither eat nor sleep yet, Will," he said. "Where is Colonel Johnson? You must take us to him at once!"

"The colonel himself, doubtless, has not had his breakfast. But why this feverish haste? You talk as if you and Tayoga carried the fate of a nation on your shoulders."

"That's just what we do carry. And, in truth, the fate of more than one, perhaps. Lead on, Will! Every second is precious!"

Wilton looked at him again, and, seeing the intense earnestness in the blue eyes of young Lennox, gave a command to his little troop, starting without another word across the clearing, Robert and Tayoga following close behind. The two lads were ragged, unkempt, and bore all the signs of war, but they were unconscious of their dilapidated appearance, although many of the young soldiers stared at them as they went by. They passed New England and New York troops cooking their breakfast, and on a low hill a number of Mohawks were still sleeping.

They approached the tent of Colonel Johnson and were fortunate enough to find him standing in the doorway, talking with Colonel Ephraim Williams and Colonel Whiting.

131

But he was so engrossed in the conversation that he did not see them until Wilton saluted and spoke.

"Messengers, sir!" he said.

Colonel Johnson looked up, and then he started.

"Robert and Tayoga!" he exclaimed. "I see by your faces that you have word of importance! What is it?"

"Dieskau's whole army is advancing," said Robert. "It long since left Crown Point, put a garrison in Ticonderoga, and is coming along Lake George to fall on you by surprise, and destroy you."

Waraiyageh's face paled a little, and then a spark leaped up in his eye.

"How do you know this?" he asked.

"I have seen it with my own eyes. I looked upon Dieskau's marching army, and so did Tayoga. St. Luc was thrown across our path to stop us, and we left Willet, Rogers and Daganoweda in battle with him, while we fled, according to instructions, to you."

"Then you have done well. Go now and seek rest and refreshment. You are good and brave lads. Our army will be made ready at once. We'll not wait for Dieskau. We'll go to meet him. What say you, Williams, and you, Whiting?".

"Forward, sir! The troops would welcome the order!" replied Colonel Williams, and Whiting nodded assent.

Johnson was now all activity and energy and so were his officers. He seemed not at all daunted by the news of Dieskau's rapid advance. Rather he welcomed it as an end to his army's doubts and delays, and as a strong incentive to the spirits of the men.

"Go, lads, and rest!" he repeated to Robert and Tayoga, and now that their supreme task was achieved they felt the need of obeying him. Both were sagging with weariness, and it was well for the Onondaga to look to his shoulder, which was still a little lame. As they saluted and left the tent a young Indian lad sprang toward them and greeted them eagerly. It was young Joseph Brant, the famous Thayendanega of later days, the brother of Molly Brant, Colonel William Johnson's Mohawk wife.

"Hail, Tayoga! Hail, Dagaeoga!" he exclaimed in the Mohawk tongue. "I knew that you were inside with Waraiyageh! You have brought great news, it is rumored already! It is no secret, is it?"

"We do have news, mighty news, and it is no secret," replied Robert. "It's news that will give you your opportunity of starting on the long path that leads to the making of a great chief. Dieskau has marched suddenly and is near. We're going to meet him."

The fierce young Mohawk uttered a shout of joy and rushed for his arms. Robert and Tayoga, after a brief breakfast, lay down on their blankets and, despite all the turmoil and bustle of preparation, fell asleep.

While the two successful but exhausted messengers slumbered, Colonel Johnson called a council of war, at which the chief militia officers and old Hendrik, the Mohawk sachem, were present. The white men favored the swift advance of a picked force to save Edward, one of the new forts erected to protect the frontier, from the hordes, and the dispatch of a second chosen force to guard Lyman, another fort, in the same manner. The wise old Mohawk alone opposed the plan, and his action was significant.

Hendrik picked up three sticks from the ground and held them before the eyes of the white men.

"Put these together," he said, "and you cannot break them. Take them one by one and you break them with ease."

But he could not convince the white leaders, and then, a man of great soul, he said that if his white comrades must go in the way they had chosen he would go with them. Calling about him the Mohawk warriors, two hundred in number, he stood upon a gun carriage and addressed them with all the spirit and eloquence of his race. Few of the Americans understood a word he said, but they knew from his voice that he was urging his men to deeds of valor.

Hendrik told the warriors that the French and their allies were at hand, and the forces of Waraiyageh were going out to meet them. Waraiyageh had always been their friend, and it became them now to fight by his side with all the courage the Ganeagaono had shown through unnumbered generations. A fierce shout came from the Mohawks, and, snatching their tomahawks from their belts, they waved them about their heads.

To the young Philadelphians and to Grosvenor, the Englishman, who stood by, it was a sight wild and picturesque beyond description. The Mohawks were in full war paint and wore little clothing. Their dark eyes flashed, as the eloquence of Hendrik made the intoxication of battle rise in their veins, and when two hundred tomahawks were swung aloft and whirled about the heads of their owners the sun flashed back from them in glittering rays. Now and then fierce shouts of approval burst forth, and when Hendrik finished and stepped down from the gun carriage, they were ready to start on a march, of which the wise old sachem had not approved.

The militia also were rapidly making ready, and Robert and Tayoga, awakened and refreshed, took their places with the little Philadelphia troop and the young Englishman, Grosvenor. Hendrik was too old and stout to march on foot, and he rode at the head of his warriors on a horse, lent him by Colonel Johnson, an unusual spectacle among the Iroquois, who knew little of horses, and cared less about them.

This was the main force, and the Philadelphia troop, with Robert, Tayoga and Grosvenor, was close behind the Iroquois as they plunged into the deep woods bordering the lake, a mass of tangled wilderness that might well house a thousand ambushes. Grosvenor glanced about him apprehensively.

"I don't like the looks of it," he said. "It reminds me too much of the forest into which we marched with Braddock, God rest his soul!"

"I wasn't there," said young Captain Colden, "but Heaven knows I've heard enough horrible tales about it, and I've seen enough of the French and Indians to know they're expert at deadly snares."

"But we fight cunning with cunning," said Robert, cheerfully. "Look at the Mohawks ahead. There are two hundred of 'em, and every one of 'em has a hundred eyes."

"And look at old Hendrik, trotting along in the very lead on his horse," said Wilton. "I'm a man of peace, a Quaker, as you know, but my Quakerish soul leaps to see that gallant Indian, old enough to be the grandfather of us all, showing the way."

"Bravery and self-sacrifice are quite common among Indians. You'll learn that," said Robert. "Now, watch with all your eyes, every man of you, and notice anything that stirs in the brush."

Despite himself, Robert's own mind turned back to Braddock also, and all the incidents of the forest march that had so terrible an ending. Johnson's army knew more of the wilderness than Braddock's, but the hostile force was also far superior to the one that had fought at Duquesne. The French were many times more numerous here than there, and, although he had spoken brave words, his heart sank. Like the old Mohawk chief, he knew the army should not have been divided.

The region was majestic and beautiful. Not far away lay the lake, Andiatarocte, glittering in the sun. Around them stretched the primeval forest, in which the green was touched with the brown of late summer. Above them towered the mountains. The wilderness, picturesque and grand, gave forth no sound, save that of their own marching. The regiments of Williams and Whiting followed the Mohawks, and the New England and New York men were confident.

Robert heard behind him the deep hum and murmur that an advancing army makes, the sound of men talking that no commands could suppress, the heavy tread of the regiments and the clank of metal. That wild region had seen many a battle, but never before had it been invaded by armies so great as those of Dieskau and Johnson, which were about to meet in deadly combat.

His apprehensions grew. The absence of sounds save those made by themselves, the lack of hostile presence, not even a single warrior or Frenchman being visible, filled him with foreboding. It was just this way, when he marched with Braddock, only the empty forest, and no sign of deadly danger.

"Tayoga! Tayoga!" he whispered anxiously. "I don't like it."

"Nor do I, Dagaeoga."

"Think you we are likely to march into an ambush again?"

"Tododaho on his star is silent. He whispers nothing to me, yet I believe the trap is set, just ahead, and we march straight into it."

"And it's to be another Duquesne?"

"I did not say so, Dagaeoga. The trap will shut upon us, but we may burst it. Behold the Mohawks, the valiant Ganeagaono! Behold all the brave white men who are used to the forest and its ways! It is a strong trap that can hold them, one stronger, I think, than any the sons of Onontio and their savage allies can build."

Robert's heart leaped up at the brave words of Tayoga.

"I think so, too," he said. "It may be an ambush, but if so we will break from it. Old Hendrik tried to stop 'em, to keep all our force together, but since he couldn't do it, he's riding at the very head of this column, a shining target for hidden rifles."

"Hendrik is a great sachem, and as he is now old and grown feeble of the body, though not of the mind, this may well be his last and most glorious day."

"I hope he won't fall."

"Perhaps he may wish it thus. There could be no more fitting death for a great sachem."

They ceased talking, but both continued to watch the forest on either side with trained eyes. There was no wind, though now and then Robert thought he saw a bough or a bush move, indicating the presence of a hidden foe. But he invariably knew the next instant that it was merely the product of an uncommonly vivid imagination, always kindling into a burning fire in moments of extreme danger. No, there was nothing in the woods, at least, nothing that he could see.

Ahead of him the band of Mohawks, old Hendrik on horseback at their head, marched steadily on, warily watching the woods and thickets for their enemies. They, at least, were in thorough keeping with the wildness of the scene, with their painted bodies, their fierce eyes and their glittering tomahawks. But around Robert and Tayoga were the young Philadelphians, trained, alert men now, and following them was the stream of New York and New England troops, strong, vigorous and alive with enthusiasm.

The wilderness grew wilder and more dense, the Mohawks entering a great gorge, forested heavily, down the center of which flowed a brook of black water. Thickets spread everywhere, and there were extensive outcroppings of rock. At one point rose precipices, with the stony slopes of French Mountain towering beyond. At another point rose West Mountain, though it was not so high, but at all points nature was wild and menacing.

134

The air seemed to Robert to grow darker, though he was not sure whether it was due to his imagination or to the closing in of the forests and mountains. At the same time a chill ran through his blood, a chill of alarm, and he knew instinctively that it was with good cause.

"Look at the great sachem!" suddenly exclaimed Tayoga.

Hendrik, loyal friend of the Americans and English, had reined in his horse, and his old eyes were peering into the thicket on his left, the mass of Mohawks behind him also stopping, because they knew their venerable leader would give no alarm in vain. Tayoga, Robert, Grosvenor and the Philadelphians stopped also, their eyes riveted on Hendrik. Robert's heart beat hard, and millions of motes danced in the air before his eyes.

The sachem suddenly threw up one hand in warning, and with the other pulled back his horse. The next instant a single rifle cracked in the thicket, but in a few seconds it was followed by the crashing fire of hundreds. Many of the Mohawks fell, a terrible lane was cut through the ranks of the Colonials, and the bullets whistled about the heads of the Philadelphia troop.

"The ambush!" cried Robert.

"The ambush!" echoed the Philadelphians.

Tayoga uttered a groan. His eyes had seen a sight they did not wish to see, however much he may have spoken of a glorious death for the old on the battlefield. Hendrik's horse had fallen beneath the leader, but the old chief leaped to his feet. Before he could turn a French soldier rushed up and killed him with a bayonet. Thus died a great and wise sachem, a devoted friend of the Americans, who had warned them in vain against marching into a trap, but who, nevertheless, in the very moment of his death, had saved them from going so completely into the trap that its last bar could close down.

A mighty wail arose from the Mohawks when they saw their venerated leader fall, but the wail merged into a fierce cry for vengeance, to which the ambushed French and Indians replied with shouts of exultation and increased their fire, every tree and bush and rock and log hiding a marksman.

"Give back!" shouted Tayoga to those around him. "Give back for your lives!"

The Mohawks and the frontiersmen alike saw they must slip from the trap, which they had half entered, if they were not to perish as Braddock's army had perished, and like good foresters they fell back without hesitation, pouring volley after volley into the woods and thickets where French and Indians still lay hidden. Yet the mortality among them was terrible. Colonel Williams noted a rising ground on their right, and led his men up the slope, but as they reached the summit he fell dead, shot through the brain. A new and terrible fire was poured upon his troops there from the bordering forest, and, unable to withstand it, they broke and began to retreat in confusion.

The young Philadelphians, with Robert, Tayoga and Grosvenor, rushed to their aid, and they were followed swiftly by the other regiment under Whiting. Yet it seemed that they would be cut to pieces when Robert suddenly heard a tremendous war cry from a voice he thought he knew, and looking back, he saw Daganoweda, the Mohawk, rushing into the battle.

The young chieftain looked a very god of war, his eyes glittering, the feathers in his headdress waving defiantly, the blade of his tomahawk flashing with light, when he swung it aloft. Now and then his lips opened as he let loose the tremendous war cry of the Ganeagaono. Close behind him crowded the warriors who had survived the combat with St. Luc, and there were Black Rifle, Willet, Rogers and the rangers, too, come just in time, with their stout hearts and strong arms to help stay the battle.

135

Robert himself uttered a shout of joy and the dark eyes of Tayoga glowed. But from the Mohawks of Hendrik came a mighty, thrilling cry when they saw the rush of their brethren under Daganoweda to their aid. Hendrik had fallen, and he had been a great and a wise sachem who would be missed long by his nation, but Daganoweda was left, a young chief, a very thunderbolt in battle, and the fire from his own ardent spirit was communicated to theirs. Willet, Black Rifle and the rangers were also pillars of strength, and the whole force, rallying, turned to meet the foe.

The French and Indians, sure now of a huge triumph, were rushing from their coverts to complete it, to drive the fugitives in panic and turmoil upon the main camp, where Johnson had remained for the present, and then to annihilate him and his force too. Above the almost continuous and appalling yells of the savages the French trumpets sang the song of victory, and the German baron who led them felt that he already clutched laurels as great as those belonging to the men who had defeated Braddock.

But the triumphant sweep of the Northern allies was suddenly met by a deadly fire from Mohawks, rangers and Colonials. Daganoweda and his men, tomahawk in hand, leaped upon the van of the French Indians and drove them back. The rangers and the frontiersmen, sheltering themselves behind logs and tree trunks, picked off the French regulars and the Canadians as they advanced. A bullet from the deadly barrel of Black Rifle slew Legardeur de St. Pierre, who led Dieskau's Indians, and whom they always trusted. The savage mass, wholly triumphant a minute ago, gave back, and the panic among the Mohawks and Colonials was stopped.

When St. Pierre fell Robert saw a gallant figure appear in his place, a figure taller and younger, none other than St. Luc himself, the Chevalier, arriving in time to help his own, just as Daganoweda, Willet and the others had come in time to aid theirs. The Chevalier was unhurt, and while one dauntless leader had fallen, another as brave and perhaps more skillful had taken his place. Robert saw him raise a whistle to his lips, and at its clear, piercing call, heard clearly above the crash of the battle, the Indians, turning, attacked anew and with yet greater impetuosity.

The smoke from so much firing was growing very thick, but through it the regulars of the regiments, Languedoc and La Reine, in their white uniforms, could be seen advancing, with the dark mass of the Canadians on one flank and the naked and painted Indians on the other, confident now that their check had been but momentary, and that the victory would yet be utter and complete.

Nevertheless, the Colonials and the Mohawks had rallied, order was restored, and while they were giving ground they were retreating in good formation, and with the rapid fire of their rifles were making the foe pay dearly for his advance.

Grosvenor had snatched up a rifle and ammunition from a fallen man, and was pulling trigger as fast as he could reload. His face was covered with smoke, perspiration and the stains of burned gunpowder, the whole forming a kind of brown mask, through which his eyes, nevertheless, gleamed with a dauntless light.

"It won't be Duquesne over again! It won't be! It won't be!" he repeated to all the world.

"But if you're not more careful you'll never know anything about it!" exclaimed Robert, as he grasped him suddenly by the coat and pulled him down behind a log, a half dozen musket balls whistling the next moment where his body had been. Grosvenor, in the moment of turmoil and excitement, did not forget to be grateful.

"Thanks, my dear fellow," he said to Robert. "I'll do as much for you some time."

Robert was about to reply, but a joyous shout from the rear stopped him. Over a hill behind them a strong body of provincials appeared coming to help. Waraiyageh in his camp had received news of ambush and battle, and knowing that his men must be in desperate case had hurried forward relief. Never was a force more welcome. Along the retreating line ran a welcoming shout, and all facing about as if by a single order, they gave the pursuing French and Indians a tremendous volley.

Robert saw regulars, Canadians and Indians drop as if smitten by a thunderbolt, and the whole pursuing army, reeling back, stopped. Then he heard the French trumpets again, and waiting behind the log, he saw that the hostile array was no longer advancing. The trumpets of Dieskau were sounding the recall, for the time, at least. Robert did not know until afterward that the Indian allies of the French had suffered so much that they were wavering, and not even the eloquence and example of St. Luc could persuade them, for the time being, to continue such a dangerous pursuit.

A few minutes of precious rest were allowed to the harried vanguard of Johnson, and now, holding their fire for a time when it would be needed more, the men continued to fall back toward the main camp, from which they had so recently come. The crash of rifles and muskets sank, but both sides were merely preparing for a new battle. Robert examined himself carefully, but found no trace of a wound.

"How is it with you, Tayoga?" he asked.

"Tododaho and Areskoui have protected me once more," replied the Onondaga. "The exertion has made my shoulder stiff and sore a little, but I have taken no fresh hurt."

"And you, Grosvenor?"

"My head is thumping at a terrible rate, but I feel that it will soon become quieter."

"Its ability to thump shows that you're full of life. How about your men, Captain Colden?"

"Four of my brave lads are sped. God rest their souls! They died in a good cause. Some of the others are wounded, but we won't count wounds now."

Robert was still able to see the indistinct figures of the French and Indians, through the clouds of smoke that hung between the two armies, but he saw also that they were not pursuing. At the distance he heard no sounds from them, and he presumed they were gathering up their dead and wounded, preparing for the new attack that would surely come.

"I was not in the first battle, but I will be in the second," a youthful voice said beside him, and he saw the Mohawk boy, Joseph Brant, his face glowing.

"We heard the firing," continued the boy, "and Colonel Johnson hurried forward a force, as you know. We are almost back at the camp now."

Robert had taken no notice of distance, but facing about, he saw the main camp not far away. Lucky it was for them that Waraiyageh and his officers were men of experience. They had sent enough men to help the vanguard break from the trap, but they had retained the majority, and had made them fortify with prodigious energy. A barricade of wagons, inverted boats, and trees hastily cut down had been built across the front. Three cannon were planted in the center, where it was expected the main Indian and French force would appear, and another was dragged to the crest of a hill to rake their flank.

The retreating force uttered a tremendous shout as they saw how their comrades had prepared for them, and then, in good order, sought the shelter of the barricade, where they were welcomed by those who had not yet been in battle.

"Get fresh breath while you may!" exclaimed Tayoga, as he threw himself down on the ground. "The delay will not be long. Sharp Sword will drive the warriors forward, and the regulars and Canadians will charge. It will be a great battle, and a desperate one, nor does Tododaho yet whisper to me which side will win."

Robert and his comrades breathed heavily for a while, until they felt new strength pouring back into their veins. Then they rose, looked to their arms and took their place in the line of battle. The trumpets of Dieskau were sounding again in the forest in front of them, and the new attack was at hand.

"Keep close, Grosvenor," said Robert. "They'll fire the first volley and we'll let it pass over our heads."

"I know the wisdom of what you say," replied the Englishman, "but it's hard to refrain from looking when you know a French army and a mass of howling savages are about to rush down upon you."

"But one must, if he intends to live and fight."

Clear and full sang the trumpets of Dieskau once more. Despite his advice to Grosvenor, Robert peeped over the log and saw the enemy gathering in the forest. The French regulars were in front, behind them the Canadians, and on the flanks hovered great masses of savages. Smoke floated over trees and bushes, and the forest was full of acrid odors. Far to the right he caught another glimpse of St. Luc in his splendid white and silver uniform, marshaling the Indians, a shining mark, but apparently untouched.

"The attack will be fierce," whispered Tayoga, who lay on his left. "They consider their check a matter of but a moment, and they think to sweep over us."

"But we have hundreds and hundreds of good rifles that say them nay. Is Tododaho still silent, Tayoga?"

The Onondaga looked up at the heavens, where the deep blue, beyond the smoke, was unstained. There was the corner, where the star, on which his patron saint lived, came out at night, but no light shone from the silky void and no whisper reached his ear. So he said in reply:

"The great Onondaga chieftain who went away four hundred years ago is silent today, and we must await the event."

"We won't have to wait long, because I hear a single trumpet now, and to me it sounds wonderfully like the call to charge."

The silver note thrilled through the woods, the French regulars and Canadians uttered a shout, which was followed instantly by the terrible yell of the Indians, and then the thickets crashed beneath the tread of the attacking army.

"Here they come!" shouted Grosvenor, and, laying his rifle across the log, he fired almost at random into the charging mass. Robert and Tayoga picked their targets, and their bullets sped true. All along the American line ran the fierce fire, the crest of the whole barricade blazing with red, while the artillery, which the savages always dreaded, opened on them with showers of grape.

The Indians, despite all the bravery and example of St. Luc, wavered, and, as their dead fell around them, they began to give forth laments, instead of triumphant yells. But the regulars in the center, led by Dieskau, came on as steadily as ever, and the little group behind the log, of which Tayoga and Robert were the leading spirits, turned their rifles upon them. Robert presently heard a youthful shout of exultation at the far end of the log, and he saw the boy, Joseph Brant, reloading the rifle which he had fired in his first battle. The French regulars suddenly stopped, and Grosvenor cried:

"It will be no Duquesne! No Duquesne again!"

The French were not withdrawing. Upon that field, as well as every other in North America, they showed that they were the bravest of the brave. Wheeling his regulars and Canadians to the right, Dieskau sought to crush there the three American regiments of Titcomb, Ruggles and Williams, and for an hour the battle at that point swayed to and fro, often almost hand to hand. Titcomb was slain and many of his officers fell, but when Dieskau himself came into view an American rifleman shot him through the leg. His adjutant, a gallant young officer named Montreuil, although wounded himself, rushed from cover, seized his wounded chief in his arms and bore him to the shelter of a tree.

But he was not safe long even there. While they were washing his wounds he was struck again by two bullets, in the knee and in the thigh. Two Canadians attempted to carry him to the rear. One was killed instantly, and Montreuil took his place, but Dieskau made them put him down and directed the adjutant to lead the French again in a desperate charge to regain a day that had started so brilliantly, and that now seemed to be wavering in the balance.

Colonel Johnson himself had been wounded severely, and had been compelled to retire to his tent, but the American colonels, at least those who survived, conducted the battle with skill and valor. The cannon, protected by the riflemen, still sent showers of grape shot among the French and Indians. The huge Tandakora with St. Luc tried to lead the savages anew upon the American lines, but the hearts of the red men failed them.

The French regulars, urged on by Montreuil, charged once more, and once more were driven back, and the Americans, rising from their logs and coverts, rushed forward in their turn. The regulars and Canadians were driven back in a rout, and Dieskau himself lying among the bushes was taken, being carried to the tent of Johnson, where the two wounded commanders, captor and captive, talked politely of many things.

The victory became more complete than the Americans had hoped. The Indians who had stayed far in the rear to scalp those fallen in the morning were attacked suddenly by a band of frontiersmen, coming to join Johnson's army, and, although they fought desperately and were superior in numbers, they were routed as Dieskau had been, the survivors fleeing into the forest.

Thus, late in the afternoon, closed the momentous battle of Lake George. The French and Indian power had received a terrible blow, the whole course of the war, which before had been only a triumphant march for the enemy, was changed, and men took heart anew as the news spread through all the British colonies.

When Dieskau's regulars, the Canadians and the Indians, broke in the great defeat, Robert, Tayoga, Willet, Grosvenor, the Philadelphia troop, Black Rifle and Daganoweda, all fierce with exultation, followed in pursuit. But the enemy melted away before them, and then, from the crest of a hill, Robert heard the distant note of a French song he knew:

Hier, sur le pont d'Avignon
J'ai oui chanter la belle
  Lon, la,
J'ai oui chanter la belle,
Elle chantait d'un ton si doux
  Comme une demoiselle
    Lon, la,
  Comme une demoiselle.

"At least he has escaped," said Robert.

"The bullet that kills him is not molded and never will be," said Tayoga.

"How do you know?" asked Willet, startled.

"Because Tododaho has whispered it to me. I heard his voice in the breath of the wind as we pursued through the forest."

Robert caught a glimpse of St. Luc, in his uniform of white and silver, still apparently unstained, erect and defiant. Then he disappeared and they heard only the singing of the wind among the leaves.

139

Printed in the USA
CPSIA information can be obtained
at www.ICGtesting.com
CBHW072153181124
17629CB00032B/790

9 781515 108078